MAGNETIC MEDIC
A COCKY HERO CLUB NOVEL

BY ALEXA PADGETT

Magnetic Medic is Book 1 in a series inspired by Vi Keeland and Penelope Ward's *British Bedmate*. It is published as part of the Cocky Hero Club world, a series of original works, written by various authors, and inspired by Keeland and Ward's *New York Times* bestselling series.

To find out more about all the Cocky Hero Club World books and authors, visit: www.cockyheroclub.com

ISBN-978-1-945090-29-5

Editor: Deborah Nemeth
Proofreading by: Kathleen Page and Charity Chimni
Photo Credit: Volles
Cover by: Chris Philpot

A sexy, new brother's best friend romance from USA Today bestselling author Alexa Padgett.

He's my brother's childhood friend. I'm pregnant with another man's baby. What a time to fall in love…

Coming home seemed like a good idea at the time. My ex-fiancé split, I was almost done with my master's degree, and I was already working at the family architecture firm. When I move in next door to pediatrician Ryder Mackay, I'm not expecting the connection—or the passion in his eyes that I feel deep in my soul. He's the best doctor for my baby, but he's *not* the guy I need.

Still, the way Ryder looks snuggling my puppy—and my infant daughter—to his rock-hard chest makes me wish this sexy, smart, compassionate man was *mine*.

Maybe, it's pregnancy hormones. Or…maybe *this* magnetic pull is **_forever_**.

For Judy.

Your L&D knowledge proved invaluable. Plus, you're one of the best people I know.

Chapter One
Aidy

I stood in my new condo, my first home and my present to myself this holiday season. Placing my hands on my ever-expanding bump, I took in the sparkling white appliances and mellow oak floors that created a seamless transition from dining, living, and kitchen areas.

Satisfaction bubbled up as I took in my accomplishments… until that niggling pang of loss slammed into me. Jeff should be here. Rather, I should still be in Houston, as we'd planned. But my plans no longer included Jeff or Houston.

I focused on my home—*my own* home. I'd waited a couple of months to buy because this specific condo had two bedrooms and it was the last to be completed, so no more workers would be traipsing through the building—a security consideration necessary for a young, single woman.

Nico, my oldest brother, set down a box and glanced around the room. "You're hustling on emptying those boxes," he said.

"I have to," I replied. "You carry them up so fast."

"I'm up five boxes on you, Nico," Knox, my middle brother, taunted. "You're getting soft, old man."

I smiled at Nico's scowl as he slid out of my door. Those two had always been competitive. I hoisted the box onto the kitchen counter, ignoring Knox's protests, and began unpacking it.

"Don't you have more to bring in?" I asked. "I'm almost done in here, so I'm unpacking faster than you're hauling, old man." I winked at Knox's frown. Those two were so easy to rile up. My brothers were tall and broad, but Nico's hair was the color of an acorn instead of Knox's honey-blond. They both had piercing eyes, though in different shades of gray, and long lashes from our mother.

Nico ran in with two boxes, which he set down, then dashed back outside. I laughed even as I cut through the tape and started pulling out my bakeware.

Fine. I was just as competitive as my brothers.

Knox set another box on the floor near the dishwasher, which I began to load with the bread pans I'd pulled out from the box Nico had brought up.

I might be back in the frozen tundra of Providence the week after Christmas, and I might be pregnant and alone, but I *would* finish my master's degree, and I would definitely make something more of myself than the single mother cliche Jeff seemed to think I'd become.

I was more than he gave me credit for, and I was *so* not going to be a cliché. I might have moved back to my home town but I'd jumped back into my research on eco-friendly interior architectural elements last month and had stacks of research for my thesis. Once my brothers left, I'd pull it out and start writing.

"We'll get the last of your stuff on this trip," Nico said.

Nico had always been my champion, and since my parents died, my father figure. Seven years my senior, he'd been forced to grow up too soon and continued to act like a stuffy middle-aged man instead of a cool business owner of thirty-one. Of course, since he'd had to slide into the parent role, he was not the first person I'd wanted to tell that I'd just found out I was pregnant and that Jeff left me—all in the same day. And he wasn't, but none of my friends in Houston had any experience with my current situation. In fact, they'd all been more freaked out than I was.

I'd broken down the next day and called Nico, hoping he'd be the brother I needed—not the one I'd left behind with a huge sigh of relief when I drove to Houston to attend Rice University. Nico had been silent for a couple of breaths before he asked me what I wanted to do.

I'd opened my mouth, but no words came out.

"Come home," he'd said. "You can work for Wright and Associates."

"W-what?"

"Come home, and you'll work with us. Just like I'd always planned. Like Dad wanted. We need another full-time architect, especially with your eye for the interior. Eco-design is a growing field. You're an asset, Aidy. Plus, you're technically a partner already."

Technically. Because our dad left the firm to all of us, equally.

Nico had rattled off a sum that was substantially higher than my current salary, one that would let me buy my own place and pay for childcare.

"And you can stay with me and I'll help you find a place to live."

"You're sure?"

The silence was long, but eventually, he said, "Yes."

So, I packed up my bags and drove out of Houston's muggy

heat and headed back north—back to the brother I'd been more than glad to leave six years ago.

My brothers dropped the last of my boxes inside my new digs.

"You win," I said with a sigh. "I couldn't get all the boxes in here unpacked as fast as you could carry them."

Knox gave me a side hug. "Well, you were destined to lose since we had to bring them in for you to unpack."

I smiled. Knox might be the most competitive, but he also had a big, soft heart, and I loved him for that.

"I think you'll like it here, and you're growing your net worth," Nico said. He settled on my sofa and threw his arm across the back, looking around with satisfaction. "You were smart to take advantage of the opportunity."

Yep. Old man banker talk right there. Nico needed a life.

My smile widened as I pulled muffin tins from the box. I'd dealt with all the paperwork from the bank and mortgage company myself. I'm sure Nico would have helped, but I needed to prove I could handle my finances. And I did it. At twenty-four, I owned my own place and was a partner in a well-known architectural firm.

Granted, buying a condo was beneficial for all of us. I'd lived in Nico's guest room for the past few months, which threw our typical ignore-each-other coping mechanisms into disarray. I might have asked Knox instead, but he'd been a grumbly mess since the Melinda Incident, and I decided to take my chances with Nico.

My oldest brother put up with my books scattered around his pristine bungalow, and he'd been correct that I should wait for a space that I loved, even as he frowned at my personal items littering his living room. Once again, I smiled at my new living space—that pride of homeownership bubbling up through my tummy.

The sensation spread through my midsection again. Not happiness. My daughter. I'd found out last week at my checkup that I was having a girl.

I gasped, tears springing to my eyes. Both my brothers jumped off the couch, faces tight in concern.

"It's fine," I murmured, blinking back the wetness as I smiled. I touched my tummy. "She's moving. I hadn't really felt it before."

"I hope she takes after her Uncle Knox and loves to ice skate," Knox said.

"If you take her to the rink, she probably will," I said.

"Like Dad did with me. I'm going to turn her into the hockey-lover you never were," Knox said.

He grinned wider. He moved to the fridge and pulled out a beer I'd stored in there when I'd arrived this morning, raising another to Nico, who nodded.

I closed the overflowing dishwasher and set it to start, thankful most of my dishes: glasses, mugs, and silverware would soon be clean and stored in the appropriate cabinets and drawers.

Knox tugged at a chunk of my hair that had escaped my ponytail, his easy-going smile masking the pain that always bubbled up when we discussed our parents.

"You found a cool place."

"I like it. I'm glad it was within my budget."

"We'll have to pay you more once you finish up that thesis." Knox glanced down at my belly, his brows tight in the start of a scowl.

"*If* I finish my thesis," I said. Because I hadn't managed to do so last semester, as I'd hoped. Nico freaked out when I told him I wanted to take a leave of absence, flat-out refusing to let me work at the family firm—and get the internship credits I needed to complete my degree—if I didn't promise I'd finish my thesis course.

He'd been right to push me, but that last email from my advisor still sent shame coursing through me. I refused to meet Knox's eyes because I didn't want him to know my advisor called me out on my lackluster performance since September. His comments were deserved since I'd spent my first few weeks barely able to file documents without sniffling.

But this was the *new* Aidy. I was strong, capable. No longer a weepy disaster who let a man's rejection keep me from achieving my goals. And I planned to prove I could ace my thesis, starting tonight. As soon as my brothers left.

"I ordered pizza as a thank you," I said. "But then I'm kicking you out. I want to work on my thesis."

"I could eat," Knox said, making us all laugh.

"You can always eat, Mr. Former Cornell Hockey Star," I said.

When the knock on my door came, I elbowed both my brothers back, refusing to let them pay for the pizza. I opened the door with a triumphant laugh.

The pizza delivery kid was flustered by my belly. "Can you carry these?" he asked.

He held the four boxes of pizza away from me.

"I'm pregnant not an invalid," I said, with a smile. I mean, he was a teenager, barely old enough to drive, and I guessed I should be glad he was looking out for me. But that didn't mean I couldn't give him some gentle advisement on independent women.

"And last time I checked, pizza wasn't as heavy as my purse or my briefcase that I manage to carry all by myself each day."

"Right," the kid stuttered, his cheeks flushing.

I kept my smile in place to take the sting out of my words. I heard a snort as I grabbed the boxes from the delivery guy and handed him the cash. He ambled off, giving me a clearer view of a man stopped at the door across the hall.

The guy turned to smirk at me. His nose and chin reminded me of the Spanish-Moroccan model, Abdel Abdelkader, the *Men's Health* model who'd created a juicing empire. I had bookmarked that issue. For the article on juicing, of course.

After I managed to move past that chiseled jaw, his eyes snagged my attention. They weren't gray and they weren't green, but a light, interesting combination of the two—like the underbelly of a new sage leaf. The color popped all the more against his tanned skin.

He smiled, those firm pink lips parting enough for me to catch the white teeth behind the fuller, lower, totally bitable one, and my gaze dropped to the dimple. Only one. On the left side, leaving a groove in his cheek. The faintest hint of dark scruff shadowed his mouth and chin, letting me know he'd shaved earlier but that he could grow that delicious scruff if he went away with a woman for the weekend.

"Aidy?" he asked.

"Yeah," I said, meeting Mr. Tall, Dark, and Oh-so-handsome's gaze. "Who are you…I know you, I think." I blinked again.

Those eyes. He looked familiar, and his smile seemed intimate, like I *should* know him, but I couldn't place him.

He tilted his head. "You do. I'm Ryder Mackay. I lived down the street from you..." he trailed off, his face freezing in a partial grimace. He cleared his throat. "That was a long time ago. I moved when you were in, like, kindergarten, maybe? You look the same." He smiled.

My breath caught in my throat. He was *better* looking than Abdel. Maybe a bit taller, definitely more chiseled...at least the parts I could see.

I wanted to tuck a thick strand of hair behind my ear but I was holding the pizza boxes. "Um. Thanks, I guess."

"Yeah, it was the hair that caught my attention," he said with a laugh.

I was a true strawberry blonde—emphasis on the strawberry. People tended to do double-takes when they saw me for the first time. For the most part, I enjoyed the attention. Nico complained I was both the moth and the flame.

"How are you?" Ryder asked. His gaze dropped to my tight T-shirt—tight because I hadn't bothered to buy maternity clothes. My boobs looked good in it, but it also showed off my bump, which was where Ryder's gaze slid. For some reason, I didn't like the brown-haired god staring at my obvious baby belly—and learning about my failed relationship.

But I didn't know him, so why should I care? Still, as I leaned against the doorframe, I settled the pizzas in front of my belly, blocking his view.

"I'm okay. So, you knew Nico or Knox?"

"Knox and I played in the tree fort your dad built. Or on the beach. Nico was too cool to hang out with Knox and me."

"Oh! You're the boy who moved to Boston," I said, remembering some long-ago conversations about Knox's bestie who'd gone to live with his aunt.

"And you're the little girl who loved to play with crabs," he said with a chuckle.

His smile widened. "I liked catching them with you. In fact, I was the one who taught you because Knox was always afraid they'd bite him."

We shared a smile. I felt a pang in my chest.

"I wish I could remember that," I said.

"Who are you talking to?" Nico opened the door wider.

"I was trying to invite—"

Nico followed my gaze and his eyes widened. "Ryder? Is that you?"

"Dude!" Knox called, his voice barreling into my ear. "Come in here. We need to catch up."

Nico took the boxes from me as Knox enveloped Ryder in a bear hug. I hovered in my doorway, unsure whether to follow or back up and give the guys time to reconnect.

"It's damn good to see you. It's been…"

Ryder's gaze touched on mine before he met my brother's. "Close to twenty years."

"Yeah. Man. Time flies. What have you been up to? I think I heard from someone in the old neighborhood that you went to medical school."

Ryder nodded. "I just finished my residency and took a position at a clinic nearby."

"Come inside Aidy's new place. You can tell us about your job and everything."

I wanted to throw up my hands in frustration. Sure, I planned to feed my brothers but then they were supposed to leave *immediately* after so I could get on with my thesis—not find a long lost friend and stay for hours catching up.

"What's your specialty?" Knox asked.

"Pediatrics," Ryder said.

"You're a pediatrician?" Nico asked. He raised his brows, his gaze boring into me. Yes, yes, I heard that this old chum was a baby doctor. I glanced at Ryder's hand, noting he wasn't wearing a ring.

Hot baby doc was single. I bet that made for lots of happy mommies.

"Excellent!" Knox said. "You hear that, Aidy? Ryder'll take care of your baby."

I smiled a little in their direction but didn't bother to reply. Ryder's eyes had widened, and he seemed a bit overwhelmed that Knox was planning out my life.

Welcome to the world of baby sister with two overprotective brothers, Ryder. The path is always bumpy.

"Hey," Knox said, noticing the consternation that had to be stamped on my face. I had a plan—feed them and get them out so I could realize the new Aidy's dream of a completed master's degree.

"Do you need to sit down?" Knox asked.

I shook my head. "I'm fine. Just need to pee."

Knox wrinkled his nose and disappeared into my kitchen. Oh,

god. I said that in front of Ryder. My gaze darted to his and his laughing eyes met mine.

Ryder leaned in closer as Knox made a disgusted sound. "I don't think you three have changed much in twenty years."

"I don't think we have either," I whispered back. "But, still, I shouldn't have said that in front of you." My cheeks flamed.

He chuckled. "I'm a doctor, Aidy, one who deals with babies. Pee is pretty much a constant in my life."

Knox called out, asking if Ryder wanted a beer. He raised his eyebrows to me, and I appreciated his silent question even as it annoyed me. Ryder seemed nice enough, and he was good looking, but I'd bought this place because I wanted to live alone.

I needed to prove that I could. And I would, just as I'd complete my thesis and get my degree.

When I returned to the living area, my brothers were already snarfing down food—without plates or napkins. I cringed at my brothers' boorishness and beelined to the kitchen for paper towels I'd already slid onto the under cabinet rod I'd attached earlier.

See? New Aidy was organized. Adult. Responsible.

All the words Nico would have *never* used to describe me even a couple of years ago.

"Where's your friend?" I asked. *Ryder.* Not like I'd forget his name. He was the most attractive guy I'd met in ages.

Nico chewed his bite before he answered. He even grabbed a napkin and wiped his fingers and lips.

"He had to go up to the hospital. Apparently, he's set up a baby-cuddler program for the ICU."

Ryder, the hot guy with the fabulous eyes, cuddled *babies*. Pretty much all my insides melted at the mental image.

"I got his card for you. And he's going to stop by tomorrow to make sure you're all set," Knox said.

"He doesn't need to do that," I murmured.

"He said he wanted to," Knox said, ripping me from my fantasy of Ryder, shirtless, a cherubic-faced girl resting against his powerful chest. At least, I assumed he was all sculpted muscle from my fleeting glance at his firm butt. And he snuggled babies.

Knox opened the box with the pesto chicken pizza that I loved and slid two slices onto a paper towel.

"Thanks," I said.

"Eat," he replied, tipping his head toward my plate and casting me a stern glare. "And I'm glad Ryder lives across the hall. Now I won't worry as much about you living alone. I always liked him."

I shot him a look. "You last saw him when he was, what? Nine?"

"Thirteen," Knox said. "His aunt and uncle brought him back one summer after he moved to Boston."

"He was a nice kid," Nico said. "Quiet. Didn't always agree with the crazy shit you wanted to get up to."

"Probably smart," Knox said.

I took a bite of my pizza, trying to quell the concern I felt at the idea of living across the hall from one of my brother's old friends—a spy across the hall.

"Did you know he lived here?" I asked Nico.

He shook his head, chewing his bite. Once he'd washed it down with most of the can of bubbly water he must have pulled out of my fridge, he said, "Can't say I'm sorry to know someone will be keeping an eye on you."

"What do you think I'm going to get up to?" I snapped. "I'm at the office for ten hours each day, and then I work on my thesis."

Nico settled his drink on the table with quiet care. "Well, then I guess us keeping you busy is a good thing." He dropped his gaze to my belly.

I stood up from my chair on shaking legs, my jaw tensed as anger coursed through me. "Oh, no, you don't. You don't get to make me feel bad about my choices in my own home. Time for you to go." I pointed to the door.

"What the hell?" Nico asked, his face scrunching in surprise.

I shook my head. "I get you're unhappy with me, and I know our relationship has been rocky for years, but there is no way—*no way*—you can judge me like that in *my* home." I shoved two of the pizza boxes in Nico's chest and marched over to the door. I stood there with it open, fuming. "That makes me feel…" My lip quivered. I swallowed. "You really hurt my feelings."

"Aidy…"

"Out," I snapped. I looked over at Knox. "Thank you for helping me move. You can take the rest. I shouldn't eat it anyway. There's a lot of sodium in pizza, which isn't great for my baby."

Knox gathered the boxes, his eyes dripping with an apology. He pressed a kiss to my cheek and nudged Nico out of my place. I locked the door with a flourish and sagged against the wall.

"Was that necessary?" Knox asked, his voice raised enough for me to hear through my door.

I couldn't hear Nico's response, but Knox's voice carried down the hall. "No wonder Aidy went to Rice instead of Rhode Island School of Design," Knox said. "You can be such a judgmental dick."

"I wasn't trying to be," Nico muttered.

"That's the problem. With Aidy, you just are, and it clearly upsets her," Knox said, surprising me as he came to my defense again.

I leaned my head against my locked front door and blinked back the tears Nico's thoughtless comment produced. I inhaled and stood up straight.

My brothers were gone, and I could now work on my thesis, as I'd wanted. Just *not* how I'd wanted to accomplish my goal.

Chapter Two
Ryder

The next evening, I raised my hand and knocked, creating a satisfying sharp rap-rap-rap on Aidy Wright's door. My hair was still damp from my shower at the gym, and I rotated my left shoulder, hoping the ache in my rotator cuff disappeared soon. The doctor's hockey team was scheduled to play a game against the Boys and Girls Club teens that weekend, and I wanted to play goalie. This was my first season with the Providence crew, but I'd enjoyed working with the kids—and playing hockey—since I started medical school. The league kept me in shape and helped me foster relationships with at-risk youth.

I waited, possibly twice as long as I would have for most people to answer the door, because she was pregnant. Aidy Wright, *pregnant*. I'd spent hours last night trying to wrap my head around that reality.

Well, that and the fact that she glowed with an internal radiance that had drawn me to her even as a kid. Aidy still seemed honest to a fault and was easy to fluster. And beautiful.

Not that I had any right noticing her attractiveness.

"Aidy?" I called.

I leaned more shoulder against the door frame.

Even as I'd talked to Knox last night, I'd found myself searching her face for the girl I'd once known, the sheltered younger sister of my best friend. I could've sworn something should have changed during the ensuing twenty years. Something huge. Well, in addition to being pregnant and seemingly single.

I'd understand if it had. I'd changed profoundly in that time, too. There were parts of my life I wouldn't admit to her, or her brothers...or even myself some days.

What surprised me was how familiar she appeared. The mischievous gleam in her bottle-green eyes and the strawberry blonde hair, the dusting of freckles over her nose—all those features reminded me of the young Aidy I remembered so fondly. Her chin was sharper, though, and her cheeks more defined. Her mouth seemed to have a stubbornness to it I didn't recall.

She'd been sassy and funny last night, and I'd looked forward to chatting with her again.

She was easy to talk to, her eyes still gleaming with the mischief I remembered from all those years before.

I pushed off the door frame and ambled toward my apartment.

The elevator pinged. I turned to see her exiting the car, excitement pooling in my belly. She juggled a couple sacks of groceries and her purse and briefcase.

I strode forward and relieved her of one of the bags.

"Thanks. Those were getting heavy."

I trailed a little behind her, enjoying the way her black skirt molded to her rounded ass. What was it my buddy and fellow physician Simon called this type of derriere? An apple bottom. I'd have to tell my work colleague and friend I'd found a lovely specimen.

He'd tell me none were as good as his fiancée's.

I'd have to disagree with him.

Aidy stopped, and I nearly stumbled. Maybe I shouldn't focus so hard on her ass.

"Your hair is the exact same color," I said, trying to cover up my awkwardness.

She glanced back over her shoulder and smiled. "Crazy, huh? I wanted it to darken to auburn, but no such luck."

"Why's that?" I asked. Still trying to recover my equilibrium. I was thirty years old, not fifteen, but something about Aidy made me feel as awkward and tongue-tied as I'd been during high school.

She shrugged as she pushed open her door. "Why do we want anything? Probably because we don't have it."

She dropped her keys into a bowl set on a table right beside the door and lowered her purse and briefcase onto the bench next to the table. I would never have guessed she moved in yesterday.

The little girl I remembered had been brash and impulsive. Messes careened in her wake. This woman might have the same hair and same big green eyes, but she'd matured…my gaze trailed across her back in a leisurely swipe. Yep. She was definitely *all* woman now.

She continued across her living room to the kitchen and set the bag on the counter. She reached back and took the sack from my arms, settling it next to the first. I mulled over her statement as she pulled out items.

"Want a drink?" she asked.

I frowned. "You think it's smart to invite a man you don't know into your place?"

She quirked an eyebrow. "My brother says you're a good guy."

I quashed the flicker of joy in my chest at those words. "Your brother doesn't know me anymore."

She stopped unpacking and tilted her head, studying me. "You're saying you're not a good man?" Her eyes sparkled. "Are you going to hurt me in some way, Ryder?"

I shook my head. "I'd never hurt you." The mere thought caused my stomach to curdle.

She smoothed back a stray tendril into her bun-thing on the back of her neck. "Then, I think it's safe to invite you to have a drink."

"Sure. Water would be great."

"Bubbly or still?"

"What is this—a restaurant?" I teased.

"Sparkling water seems to settle my stomach better than ginger or lemons. But I know it's not for everyone."

"I like sparkling water."

She turned around and grabbed a glass, then pulled a couple of cans from the fridge. I popped the top and let the water fizz into the glass while Aidy continued to unpack her groceries. She'd managed to cram a lot in those two sacks.

"You can tell Knox you did your check-in," she said.

"What?"

I spilled some water as I jerked the can. She grabbed a dishtowel and tossed it to me and I wiped up the mess. *Nice, Ryder. Really smooth.*

"Isn't that why you're here? To report back to Knox that I came straight home."

"I…no…I'm not going to tattle to your brother about your life, Aidy."

When she remained skeptical, I shoved my hands into my

pockets and rocked back on my heels, unsure how to proceed. If I were being honest, I enjoyed Aidy's company more than the idea of catching up on my patient notes or watching TV alone. I liked her soft push-back and her direct gaze. She reminded me some of Knox but nicer—and definitely better looking. She was…comforting. She reminded me of home. Of my mother. And I wanted more of Aidy, of that feeling.

"I'll get out of your way."

She sighed, her shoulders tugging forward. "That was rude of me—I'm still a bit upset with Nico for a comment he made yesterday. Stay, finish your drink. Tell me about Mondays at your clinic."

"If you're sure—"

"I am."

"Right. Well, Mondays are busy. We get a rush of sick kids first thing—because parents worried over the weekend."

"Makes sense. I hear you cuddle babies in your free time." She winked.

I chuckled. "I like kids. Always have." I shrugged. I'd liked playing with Aidy when she was little. I'd told my mom I considered it good practice for Molly.

My good mood dimmed as it always did when I thought of my baby sister.

"Hey, don't look so glum. I won't beg you to babysit. I just thought we could…hang out for a bit. I'm enjoying your company more than I expected, especially for Knox's spy."

I laughed. "Sorry. I was just thinking about something."

She leaned in, her eyes wide. "A deep, dark secret?" she whispered.

I smiled. "You look just like you did when I taught you how to catch a crab." I picked up my drink, took a big swallow.

She raised an eyebrow. "You're ignoring my deep dark secret comment, so that means you must have one. Is it deep or is it dark?"

More than one, and I definitely didn't want to share. "Don't we all have secrets?"

I swallowed. I shouldn't. I didn't want her asking more about what happened after I moved—was forced from my home and everything I knew and cared about.

"Would you like to stay for dinner?" she asked, tying on an apron. It was blue with white pinstripes and had pockets.

"No, I don't want to impose."

She popped the top on her drink and took a long swig from the can. I liked how unpretentious she was. How comfortable she looked in her work clothes with her hair pinned up and an apron covering her front. That brought my gaze down to her midsection. Her brothers were quick to spill her secrets.

Men could be such assholes.

"So, you live here alone?" I asked.

She bent down and pulled out a large enameled skillet. I remembered the set from her parents' kitchen.

"You can just ask me, you know," she said. She turned on the gas burner and drizzled some oil in the pan. She turned away and brought out a large stainless-steel pot that she began to fill with water.

"Ask you what?" I hedged.

She rolled her eyes as she carried the pot to the stove, turning on that burner. "Why I'm single and pregnant."

"Well, I wasn't sure you were."

"He left," she said, her lips turning down and her eyes dimming. She coated her chicken breasts in some seasoning.

"What do you mean, *left*?"

"The day I told him about the baby. He left me." She shrugged, but I saw her touch the ring finger on her left hand. I'd noted yesterday she wasn't wearing a ring—right after I realized she was pregnant.

Sure, I was an asshole for looking. Her words led me to worry that the guy she'd been with hurt her more than she'd let on. Sure, I'd planned to report back to Knox—he'd asked me to check in on Aidy, and my loyalty was to him, no matter how attractive I found her—probably *because* I found her desirable. That was wrong on so many levels as was my desire to spend more time with her.

I didn't push her to share more, though my curiosity ate at me. Her betrayal was more recent than mine, but those kinds of wounds could take decades to heal.

And with the single swipe of her thumb over her bare finger, protectiveness reared up. I wanted to hug her and make sure she knew she didn't deserve that level of hurt.

"You know what? That smells great. I'd love to stay."

Chapter Three
Aidy

I continued to whisk my sauce, unwilling to make a bigger deal about his staying. Ryder seemed a little shy and definitely off-kilter around me. While I'd been looking forward to a quiet evening alone, now that he was here, I wanted him to stay. I wanted to learn more about him, just as he seemed interested in me.

"I'm sorry that happened to you," Ryder said, his tone soft.

"Yeah, me, too. Well, sort of. I mean, if he couldn't handle the *idea* of fatherhood, how much worse would the situation get when he was actually a father?"

"Was he an architect, too?"

I shook my head. "Jeff's an aerial pilot with the forest service. That means he flies the planes that drop water or chemicals on large fires."

"Ah. We don't have many of those here, thankfully."

I flashed him a small grin. "Too right."

We were quiet, the sizzle of the vegetables in the pan a nice background to the silence. Finally, I blurted, "He was called out the day I told him about the baby, and, as far as I know, he still hasn't returned to the apartment we shared even though I told his sister when I moved out."

Jeff hopped from one fire to the next, offering to help in the huge Australian wildfires rather than return home to me. His sister sent me screenshots from a private group that showed just how Jeff was passing his time—and apparently he wasn't shy about public displays of affection with other women.

"That's…"

"Terrible." I sighed. "Clearly, I have terrible taste in men."

"Had."

My gaze flashed up to Ryder's. "What?"

"You had terrible taste in men, but you've learned from your mistakes."

I tilted my head and considered his statement. I smiled. "Right. I had terrible taste in my partner."

After a long moment in which I began to wonder if he felt the tingle of awareness that caused my heart to patter faster, he cleared his throat, looking at the pan.

"You sure I can't help with dinner?"

"Nope. I like to cook. But thanks for offering. My brothers wouldn't." I shot him an impish grin. "Just like I never offer to help clean up the messes I make in the kitchen."

He chuckled. "I see how you are. Lure us in with tasty treats then beat a hasty retreat when the real work comes."

"You know it," I said.

My smile returned. "Thanks for dropping the topic."

Laughter lightened Ryder's eyes and made some faint crinkles at the corner.

"I will, once you stop bringing it up."

I placed the chicken in the skillet where it sizzled merrily.

"Mmm," I said, meeting his gaze across the pan. "Doesn't that smell good."

This time, he threw his head back and laughed.

I continued to blend my sauce, grinning.

"You have a pretty smile," Ryder said.

I rolled my eyes. "That sounds like a pickup line. Like one someone would throw out in a bar."

He shook his head. "I was being sincere, but I work with a guy who drops those corny lines on all the women he meets."

"Oh? Let's hear one," I said.

He pondered me for a minute. "You're not a pickup-line woman, Aidy. You're too self-possessed, too confident to fall for those."

"Now I want to hear them even more," I said, grinning.

He cleared his throat. "I know a guy who says the best women have apple bottoms."

"Apple…what? Who has an apple bottom?"

He widened his eyes. "You, of course."

I giggled. "That's terrible." And super cute. *He* was cute. And he cuddled babies.

I threw the pasta in with the veggies, coating it, then added the chicken, needing something to do so I stopped staring at his chest and imagining my baby cuddled there.

"We're ready," I said. I heaped a plate of pasta, chicken, and veggies, and Ryder sniffed, making appreciative sounds as he headed toward the French farmhouse table I'd picked up at a flea market in Newport. At first, I'd worried it was too big for the space since it seated eight, but with the clean white lines of the kitchen, and my decision to use one couch and two armchairs around the low coffee table, I'd been able to use the large table as an anchor. It gleamed now that I'd sanded and waxed it.

I followed after him, a warm glow of happiness settling over me. Ryder waited to sit until I had.

"Dig in," I said, grabbing my fork. He bit into one of the tender pieces of asparagus, his eyes widening.

"What is this?" Ryder asked as soon as he swallowed.

I shrugged. "A lighter version of an Alfredo sauce." I frowned. "Can it be Alfredo without cheese in it?"

"Dunno. Still, it's great."

I smiled. "I'm glad you're enjoying it." I paused. "I'm glad you chose to stay."

My cheeks bloomed with color. Ryder cleared his throat, gaze dropping back to his plate. What was it about his slight discomfiture that made me want to sit in his lap and wrap my arms around him? And if I did so, would I be comforting him or would he be comforting me?

I took another bite, pondering the question to which I had no answer. Just that he affected me, and I…I *liked* it.

"So…ah…how long have you been working at the family firm?" He met my gaze, and I was struck again by the beauty of his eyes. The silvery-green popped against his tanned skin.

At my questioning look, he said, "Your brothers said you all worked there."

I nodded as I picked up my napkin. I dabbed at my mouth and set the square of cotton back in my lap.

"You're the only person I know who uses cloth napkins," Ryder said.

His gaze swept over my dining and living area.

"And this place is definitely a cohesively designed space. What would you call it?"

I darted him a glance. "My professors would say something like, 'a seemingly effortless and comfortable use of texture and furniture to create sophisticated feminine decor'." I wrinkled my nose. "Sounds stuffy and pretentious."

He settled back in his chair, his palms resting on his taut abdomen. While all the ladder back chairs were distressed, his was red. Mine was turquoise. I also had a yellow, green, blue, and purple one. Nico didn't like them, but I did. Plus, people could pick a color that suited their mood. Of course Ryder chose red—the bold color of power...or passion. Not that he'd been overly passionate. He'd been a gentleman. And I wasn't interested in passion or love. We'd just discussed my fiancé dumping my ass for hotter pastures...with willing wildlife. I sighed at my shitty metaphor, which seemed an extension of my shitty life choices.

I straightened my spine. That was the old Aidy's thinking. I was present, focused, organized, and ready to kick ass—at my job, at parenting. At life.

And this new Aidy was glad for a nice evening with a good looking guy. Of course, New Aidy wasn't interested in a relationship because men failed her. No, New Aidy understood her brothers put Ryder up to tonight, and she'd make sure Ryder told Nico and Knox she was sparkly and capable. New Aidy might even test drive Ryder...as a possible *pediatrician*.

There was nothing else—would be nothing else—between them. New Aidy didn't have an interest in jumping back into dating until she was positive she'd left her poor romantic choices far, far behind.

And she wasn't sure just yet. So, she'd follow her plan—complete her thesis, prepare for her daughter's arrival.

"This is way better than my place with its overstuffed leather sofas and a scarred coffee table I bummed off my aunt," Ryder said, bringing me back into the present. "I didn't bother with a dining table because I am rarely home for dinner."

He met my gaze, and I studied his, fascinated by the alternating flecks of green and gray that swirled around his pupils. *Remember the plan, Aidy. Be charming. Show your kickass adulting but do not get caught up in possible romance—you're not interested.*

"I'm an architect who specializes in eco-friendly interiors. This…" I waved my hand, "represents my taste but also my philosophy."

A slight confusion drifted over his face, but he nodded. "So, how long have you been back?"

"I moved back into Nico's place in September—the week after Labor Day."

"And Knox said something about a thesis?"

My brothers sure were chatty about my life with others. We'd need to discuss the idea of privacy.

"That's the last of my coursework for my master's degree," I said.

He glanced back at my midsection as if trying to calculate how far along I was. I dropped my hands over my belly in reflex. He raised his gaze to mine. Frustration seemed to mar his brow before he smoothed it out.

"I'm eighteen weeks pregnant."

His eyes widened, the green flaring brighter. "And you're

working full-time and planning to complete a thesis before the baby comes?"

"That way I'm fully certified as the firm's resident interior architect."

"I thought your degree was in design," he said.

I shook my head. "No, still architecture but I prefer to work in the interior whereas Nico, especially, likes to create the lines of the exterior. But, to me, a home is about comfort and that comes from what you put in it."

"I see."

I smirked. "I bet it's like me trying to understand medical jargon."

His face eased and he smiled. "Probably."

No one really understood my passion for interior spaces, but at least Nico and Knox respected my interest and talent, especially because it dovetailed well into their skill sets. "Clean living—healthy living—starts with a healthy home," I said.

Energy surged through me. I loved talking about this. "My father designed buildings and houses, but my mother instilled the importance of natural fibers and reusing or recycling materials. Remember our kitchen?"

He squinted, but then nodded. "I always thought those open shelves with your mom's dishes were really cool. So easy to grab a plate or a glass."

"Exactly," I said. My lips turned up as I remembered the comfort of her kitchen. "She asked my dad to reuse her old cabinets when they redid the space. But the cabinet doors weren't in great shape. Instead of tossing them into a landfill, she sanded them all down and then smoothed on an eco-friendly wood treatment. The rest of the house followed, over time. We had organic mattresses and bamboo sheets before they were really a known thing."

I sucked my lower lip into my mouth. "Sorry. I can rev up and get going on this topic."

He touched the edge of his glass, sliding his finger through the condensation. "You're passionate. That makes you spectacular at what you do."

He met my gaze, his face earnest. "I'm glad you found your passion."

Oh, no. *No.* New Aidy wasn't interested in men. Not even handsome ones who showed genuine interest in her. That meant tonight was to show Ryder, and by extension, her brothers that she was a capable professional. Time to refocus this conversation.

I chewed a bite.

"So, Mr. Pediatrician, you really would be able to help me with my daughter's medical needs?"

"You're having a girl?" he asked.

I smiled, and this one felt like it might split my face. "She's right on track. Dr. Yao says everything looks great."

"I know Dr. Yao. She refers many of her patients to us. We both have admitting privileges," he said.

"So, I should add you to my list of potential doctors to interview?" I asked. I meant it as a joke, but Ryder's gaze slid to my belly and back up to my face. The faint frown added to his conflicted look.

"I'd be honored to help out a Wright."

Ah. The family connection. Maybe he was surprised I was the

first of my siblings to have a child. He'd been too polite to say so, but I'd be a mom at twenty-five. That was young. New Aidy decided not to let Ryder's possible opinions worry her. After all, New Aidy's life choices were no one's business but her own.

"You're smart to interview multiple doctors. You want to be sure you trust that person with her well-being."

And I realized I was beginning to. During the time we'd spent together tonight, I'd had a meaningful conversation with Ryder, felt like we'd connected. He was a bit stiff, a little hard to get to know, but he obviously cared about the well-being of my child, and he seemed genuinely interested in my career, in me, as a person. That felt…freeing.

That I could trust a man who wasn't my brother was a huge step forward in healing my heart—and my confidence in myself. My baby deserved a tight-knit family who supported her. Maybe this move home, meeting Ryder, was supposed to happen. Maybe he was the right doctor for her—and a confidant for me. That was something I hadn't realized I'd needed so much, but this dinner reminded me that closeness wasn't to be feared.

I'd made a friend in Ryder, and I could develop other relationships with people who would care about both my baby and me. I deserved that.

I bit back a smile as I rose, picking up my plate.

Maybe I was *finally* on the right track.

Chapter Four
Aidy

I woke with a smile on my face for the first time in…I couldn't remember when I'd last awakened happy. Sure, it was still dark outside, and I had leg cramps, but none of that dampened my good mood—a first for me after months of consistent despondency.

Dinner last night with Ryder proved a revelation. He listened, considered what I said, and engaged me in a discussion about my green building passion. He'd showed me what I should be looking for in the people I wanted as friends. Sure, I had work colleagues, but, in those first weeks after my move, I'd needed to lick my wounds—and I'd been sure Jeff would call, begging my forgiveness. Making new connections, building relationships seemed pointless.

But now, I'd committed to building a life in Providence. That intimated a need for companionship, and Ryder was a great first candidate. When I'd started to clear the plates, he'd told me to sit and relax, and he cleaned the entire kitchen, which was a true and beautiful luxury. I was a messy cook, which I minded more now that I was also the kitchen cleaner.

While Ryder scrubbed, I ogled his forearms. Each time he flipped a dish to rinse, the muscles bunched and shifted. He was effortlessly sexy, and I appreciated his beauty.

That's what I planned to keep telling myself anyway, because I couldn't actually let my mind go there—where it wanted. He led the candidates as my daughter's pediatrician because I knew he would give my baby the best care possible, which made me calmer about the whole having-a-kid thing. Maybe, in time, Ryder would be a friend, but no way we'd be more than that.

Even if I were interested in dating, and even if I trusted myself to find the right guy this go-round, jumping into a relationship now wouldn't be smart.

Still, not thinking of him as a potential lover would be easy if he weren't so damned hot. And nice. And if his eyes stopped lingering on me like they could see every mussed and frazzled part of me and approved anyway.

When he left, my place expanded, leaving me adrift, so I'd brought my laptop to my bedroom. Settling back against the pillows, I shoved another under my computer and managed to complete an entire chapter of my thesis—the best one I'd written. I even outlined the next three thereafter, using my exuberance from the conversation with Ryder about interior space and its need to reflect a person's taste as well as the exterior environment to dictate my fingers. Drilling into my area of interest made this paper easier to write.

If I stuck to a strict schedule, I might manage to complete the first draft by the beginning of February. While it sucked that I had to pay for another semester of tuition, an early February turn-around would give my advisor time to read and make further suggestions prior to the end of the semester. The idea of actually completing my degree made my face split into a smile, which widened further when I found the sticky note on my door the next morning.

Thanks for dinner! It was so good I didn't mind cleaning your mess.
Ryder

I went back into my place and scribbled a reply.

You're welcome. And here I was hoping for another of your corny
pickup lines…

Don't be a stranger.

Aidy.

I stuck my note to his door and headed into the office. Nico
popped his head in, eyes wide when he found me standing at my
drafting table.

"You're here early."

"Baby wasn't interested in sleeping," I replied. I continued to
lean over my paper, straight-edge in hand. I completed the line
and inched back to study my rendering. Sure, I could do most of
this on the computer, and I would need to get the details into the
appropriate CAD software in order to show the client, but I preferred the pencil-and-paper method my dad used to use. Like my
love of interior that I'd inherited from my mom, my old-school
methods made me feel closer to my dad.

"I don't want you to tire yourself out," Nico said.

I turned to face him.

"I thought it was best that I was here—you know, staying out
of trouble."

His lips flattened. "I'm sorry, Aidy. I don't really think you're
trouble. Or in trouble."

I tilted my head. "I think you do," I said, slowly. "And I was a huge pain in high school, I know that, but I'm an adult, Nico. I've made choices I know you don't agree with or approve of—"

"I don't approve; you're right. And I don't think work is the appropriate place to discuss family issues."

I gritted my teeth. My brother was *such* an uptight man. I let my pencil slide to the tray at the bottom.

"You're right. I just want you to know that trusting Jeff was a mistake. Running away from the issues I didn't want to face prior to college was, too. I'm trying to rectify what I can."

He tapped the door, shifting his feet. "Could you get me those plans by noon?"

I sighed. Getting through to him was harder than I expected. "Sure."

Now that I had years between me and my angry, heartbroken responses to our parents' deaths, I could admit my reckless partying and clandestine sexual encounters were irresponsible. Worse, those decisions nearly cost me my future.

Nico had tried to rein me in, but I'd refused to take him seriously—until the day he dragged me from a party, kicking and screaming. It was still one of the most humiliating moments of my life. And it probably saved it as well. Or at least my opportunity to attend college and make something of myself. The girl my date went home with ended up pregnant and dropped out of school.

I shuddered to realize how close I'd come to that fate.

I frowned as I considered the problem from his viewpoint.

Nico and I had years of anger, hurt, and animosity to work through.

Part of that came to a head later that afternoon.

"You can't send Chloe those," I implored. "That's not the direction she wants to take."

"These are solid designs," he said, gesturing to the layouts on his computer screen.

"But it's not right for their target—"

"So what do *you* propose, Aidalynn? This hotel is a big deal for our firm, and we have to give them our best work."

"I agree. That's why I think you should consider—"

"You know what? I'll handle it. Clearly, you're not ready for this."

Not only did Nico use my full name—the one he knew I detested, no doubt in an effort to get me as ticked off as he was—he never even let me speak. At Nico's request the week before, I'd been the one to field calls from Chloe, the project lead for the Macintosh Hotels, and she and I had really clicked.

Between two working lunches and multiple phone calls, I now had a thick folder of The Mac's current and future business plans. Corporate's decision to go after the wealthy millennial market seemed rock solid and well thought out, which was why we'd talked at length about what, exactly, Millennial meant to Chloe and to The Mac.

Nico wanted to send some staid, lame-ass interiors to Chloe.

I slapped the renderings I'd done onto his desk. "You want to remove me from the meeting?" I gritted out. "What if I'm right? You could lose—"

"Go home, Aidy," Nico said, his voice cold. "I don't want you at this meeting."

I drew myself up. "Fine. But be sure to show her my not-ready drawings because *those* are exactly what she asked for."

I turned on my heel and walked out of the room. I made it back to my office, blinking back the tears I wouldn't let fall. I heard Chloe arrive but continued to pack up my bag. A few minutes later, Chloe waltzed into my office, a sheaf of papers in hand, Nico trailing behind her.

"I'm sorry you were called out and missed the beginning of our meeting, but I just had to tell you myself. These renderings of yours are splendid. Exactly the vibe we hoped for."

Chloe's British accent caused me to smile, and I refused to look at Nico as I answered. "I'm so glad you like them. Nico will be sure to incorporate any changes you need. Now, if you'll excuse me, I must be goi—"

"But I want to work with you," Chloe said, sinking into the chair in front of my desk.

I raised my gaze to Nico's, unsure how to handle this complication. His jaw ticked, annoyance spread across his features.

"I'm sure we can rearrange Aidy's schedule and make that happen," Nico said.

"Great. Because I wasn't asking." Chloe's tone remained polite, but steel entered her words. The implication was clear: either she got her way, or she walked.

Nico pressed his fingertips to the edge of my desk. "Thanks for taking this on," he said.

A spark of warmth that Chloe felt strongly enough about my work to insist I deal with her directly built in my chest even as I hoped I wasn't in over my head with this project.

Nico expected me to fail—that's why he'd pulled me from the meeting.

I straightened my spine as I settled back in my chair, pulling a pad and pen closer to take notes. I refused to consider the possibility of failure. New Aidy was in charge, and she would not let her brothers—or herself—down.

Chapter Five
Aidy

The next morning, I completed a set of site plans on a renovation for one of the admirals at the Naval Station, Newport. He'd decided to add a home theater and a gym. I grinned, enjoying my time with my straight edge and Sharpies as I completed the site settings. I planned to meet with him and his wife at two that afternoon. Knox suggested I run with this one, no doubt to test my readiness with The Mac Hotel project, and I was pretty excited about the interior options for the house project.

I glanced at my clock and yelped, realizing I was supposed to meet with Nico and Knox in ten minutes to review the plans and the preliminary cost estimates for a new build on one of the inlets. Thankfully, the meeting was short because Knox wanted to present the design and Nico would discuss the costs.

After a quick lunch, I met with the admiral and his wife and presented my ideas.

His face remained stern but he nodded. "You really grasped my vision, Ms. Wright," he said. "I can't wait to watch Steel Magnolias in one of the recliners."

"Great movie choice," I said with a smile.

He winked. "I spent thirty-seven years as a hard-ass on the seas or with my men. Now, I get to sniffle through tear-jerkers with Millie here."

They were too cute.

"I'll stop by the showroom to make sure we can get the projector I recommended," I said as I walked behind them toward the door.

If only all my projects were as smooth as the admiral's. The next day I spent two hours at the hardware store returning the wrong order for kitchen and bathroom cabinets for a custom-build Nico was heading. He'd been on site, trying to figure out how the contractor managed to flood the upstairs bathroom—and to assess the damage to the structure.

Even with the setbacks on that project, I really enjoyed the work. We managed that job Friday, and I spent the weekend browsing showrooms in Boston. And through it all, my main focus was The Mac. This hotel was one of four signature projects Wright and Associates landed this year—and the boutique hotel would be a showpiece, not just for industry magazines but for our portfolios.

Getting the details right mattered. A lot.

The next week and a half had been hectic, and I hadn't caught a glimpse of Ryder since our dinner together. He seemed to leave before me most mornings, but I arrived home later in the evenings. Tonight I was especially late, but that wasn't completely my fault. My trip out to The Mac site earlier that evening had allowed me to walk the growing exterior of the structure and get a better sense of how to bring that inside the large space, but I came back from the large lot with more than I'd bargained for. As

I'd walked back toward the hotel from the beach, I'd heard yips and shrieks. A small puppy battled a fisher—until the weaselly animal saw me and ran off. Unable to leave the big-eyed Australian shepherd pup with a bloody paw, I found a box in the large onsite Dumpster and brought the dog home.

Before I could change my mind about bothering Ryder, I limped to his door and knocked.

He opened the door, and I noted his wet hair and the way his T-shirt clung to his shoulders and chest. I must have just caught him out of the shower.

His hair was darker—a near impossibility because it had already appeared black—and shinier from the water. His eyes—the same startling sage—hit me in the chest. He had beautiful eyes.

And…I'd been correct about his chest. I stifled a groan. I needed a medical expert not a shot of gorgeous, sleek male. New Aidy wasn't interested in dating.

Ryder gasped, pulling the puppy from the box and snuggling her in close against his chest before I managed to say anything.

Of course he snuggled puppies. He seemed to be an all-species baby snuggler. Dammit. This man was too perfect for me to resist.

"I need your help," I said.

He raised an eyebrow. "I'm not washing your dishes again," he deadpanned.

I shook my head even as a smile tugged at my lips. "I wouldn't have bothered you but the vet's closed."

I went there first, which was why it was close to ten now. I was exhausted, starving, and my ankle throbbed.

"What happened to her paw?"

"She was in a fight with a fisher," I said.

Ryder's eyebrows rose. "This puppy's not even the same size." He headed down his hall toward the bathroom.

I set down my briefcase and purse at the back of his couch. His gaze jerked up to mine as I entered the room. He'd settled on the floor next to the bathtub, testing the water with his wrist while holding the tiny shepherd in his other hand.

"No. But she's very sweet and seems thankful for my rescue. She likes to give kisses."

She started licking his wrist and neck.

"See?" I smiled at the sight. "She can't be very old. Or maybe she's a miniature."

"I wouldn't know."

"You never had a dog?" I asked.

He shook his head. "My dad didn't like them." He turned his head, focusing on the bathtub. "I want to get as much of the sand and dirt off her as possible before I bind up that foot."

He lowered the dog into the bath and, based on her high-pitched yips and the renewed thrashing, the puppy did not like the water.

He glanced up at me, water now dripping from his face down onto his soaked shirt.

I winced as I crouched down next to him. He must have caught my grimace from the corner of his eye because he turned toward me.

"You're hurt, too?"

"I twisted my ankle."

He tilted his head toward the toilet. "Sit there. I'll look at you next."

"I'm fine," I began. The puppy yowled and Ryder focused on her.

Because I wasn't much help, I settled on the closed toilet seat and lifted my leg to the edge of the bathtub, trying not to wince at the slight swelling in my ankle. I frowned, wondering if I'd be able to go to yoga on Saturday.

Ryder's efficiency of movement became apparent as he rinsed the dog and palpated her midsection, legs, and injured paw. The puppy cried at the touch to her injured pad, but those soon turned to whimpers.

"Grab that towel, will you?" Ryder asked.

I reached over and snagged the towel from the rack as he handed me the dripping dog. I toweled her off with brisk strokes, talking softly to her.

"Interesting coat," he said. "Goes with her heterochromia."

I looked down at the dog. Now that she was clean, her coat showed almost blue-gray between the brown. "A blue merle," I murmured.

"What?"

"This coat. It's called a blue merle with brown."

"Why do you look like that?" Ryder asked. His voice was soft, his eyes concerned.

"She reminds me of…" I trailed off and looked away.

"What is it?"

"I always wanted a dog," I blurted. "I sent my parents photos. This…this was my dream dog."

Ryder looked down at the puppy, her blue and her brown eye following his every movement. He gently scratched her small head between the ears. She closed her eyes. Then she yawned, her small, white teeth so clean in her pink mouth. She settled into the towel with a snuffling sigh.

"I'm glad you got your dream," he said so quietly I wasn't sure he really spoke at all. I glanced up, questions on my lips, but they died when Ryder picked up my ankle. He was soaking wet and his shirt conformed to the ridges of his chest. His lashes were spiked together, and his lips were wet.

I caught my breath, committing it to memory. He rose and washed his hands in that thorough way I associated with doctors. He squatted in front of me, tugging my foot into his lap and pulling off my shoe. He was gorgeous—gentle yet commanding as he manipulated my foot. His fingers were long, lean, agile. I liked how they looked against the pale skin of my ankle. His palm was warm as it wrapped around my Achille's tendon. I managed not to tremble—just—as he slid his palm down over my now-bare foot.

"Does that hurt?" he asked.

I just shook my head, worried at how breathy my voice would sound if I spoke.

"You said you twisted it?"

"I tripped. I didn't go down to my knees, just stumbled over a root or rock or something but wrenched it pretty good."

"Good. I think you have a mild sprain. You'll want to ice it and maybe use a bandage, but I bet it'll be tender for a couple of days. Watch for increased swelling or any heat or redness."

I nodded.

He removed his hands from my skin, and I managed to catch my breath. His attention returned to the puppy. He took her from me, setting her on his strong thighs, which flexed under the soft denim of his jeans. After an examination of her pad, he said, "It looks like a puncture wound, so maybe the fisher bit her. I'll put some antibiotic cream on it, but she'll need to see a vet for a rabies vaccine."

He spread the salve with gentle fingers and wrapped her foot in soft gauze, which he surrounded with copious tape. "So she doesn't manage to chew it off."

"Of course."

Ryder worked for another few minutes as I watched. Then, he rose to his feet, the puppy now sleeping in his arms. It was probably hormones, or even biology, but my body responded to the large man holding the defenseless baby with such care.

"She likes you," I murmured.

I did, too, especially after seeing him in action. He grinned.

"This was a lot easier than the ER."

He tugged at his T-shirt causing it to ride up enough for me to see his abdomen and the thin trail of hair between his belly button and low-hanging jeans.

"Less messy, too."

He helped me up and I noted my ankle barely ached, thanks to the bandage wrapping it. I held out my hands, but Ryder shook his head.

"Why don't you let me keep her here tonight? I'll make sure she doesn't munch on the dressings. I'll bring her by in the morning because I'm at the hospital tomorrow."

"Sure."

I grabbed my purse and briefcase, wondering why I had to be attracted to Ryder. Even when we'd shared dinner the other night, and I had enjoyed his company, I'd been able to minimize my response to him. But tonight…he'd dropped everything without question to help me and this small creature. In both interactions, he showed his sensitivity, and each time he did made me want him more, which was foolhardy. And dangerous. New Aidy needed time to complete her thesis, to establish her life prior to the birth of her daughter.

Frustration lashed through me as I tamped down on the growing attraction I felt for Ryder. The timing wasn't right, and I didn't want to jump into something until I was sure I'd taken care of my needs first—something I'd never focused on before.

I turned back toward him. "Thank you," I said.

He smiled. "No problem. You're definitely keeping my nights interesting."

Chapter Six
Ryder

I knocked on Aidy's door around eight, fifteen minutes after I received the call from the hospital. She opened the door, dressed in athleisure clothes like I'd seen on women who were about to workout.

"Come in. Want some tea?"

"No, no time," I said as I stepped into her condo. It looked as inviting as the woman—I meant as the space had before. I dropped my attention to the puppy so I wouldn't stare at how good Aidy looked that morning.

"I'm glad I didn't wake you. I'm sorry this is earlier than I'd planned, but one of my patients has a high fever and abdominal pain."

Aidy's hair was piled atop her head and a few strands caressed her cheeks. She sipped from a large ceramic mug. "No worries. Thanks for keeping her last night."

I smiled, not willing to tell Aidy her pup was a restless sleeper. She'd learn soon enough. Plus, the furball was cuddly and soft and gave the best kisses, so I wasn't about to complain. "Let me know how the visit goes."

"Sure. I'll touch base with you later."

"Give me your number," I said, even knowing as I did so that I was tempting fate. I'd made a point to steer clear of Aidy, hoping it would lessen my fascination with the woman.

"I'll text you back so you'll have mine."

She grabbed her phone off her spotless counter and did as I requested. When I turned to leave, she said, "I made these for you."

She grabbed a large plastic container from the dining table and pushed it into my hands. "As a thank you."

I opened the top. My gaze came back to hers, my eyes rounded in surprise. "Your mom's cookies?"

She frowned a little as she nodded. "You remember those?"

I cleared my throat. My Adam's apple bobbed a second time before I managed to say, "They've always been my favorite. Some of my best memories are eating these cookies in your mom's kitchen."

I leaned forward and wrapped her in a hug. Her breasts pressed lightly to my chest, and my palms slid along her slim back without any conscious thought—I liked her there, so near me, even as I wanted her closer. My hipbone bumped her belly. Shit. Right.

Aidy was pregnant. No way I'd *ever* get involved with a pregnant woman. There was a reason I was a pediatrician, not an obstetrician. I wanted no part of births.

A birth led to my family's demise.

That's why I'd been avoiding her. Aidy fascinated me, and I enjoyed spending time with her—too much—but she was pregnant.

"I'm seeing a woman," I blurted out.

She blinked up at me so rapidly her lashes caught together. "Okay." She scooted back, putting more distance between us. "That's…of course you are."

And now I felt like shit. I'd blurted that out, made what had been a beautiful moment awkward.

"I just didn't want you to get the wrong idea…"

Why was I still talking?

Her lips lifted a little at the corners, but she stared at a spot next to my head. "We're neighbors, Ryder. Maybe one day we'll be friends. You helped me out. I reciprocated. We're even." She walked to her door and opened it; the message was clear. I was dismissed.

"If you're sure…"

"You don't owe me anything, Ryder," she said, her tone firm. But she still refused to meet my eyes. That bothered me.

"Well, um…bye," I said.

"Maybe I'll see you around." She closed the door practically on my nose—my fault because even though I'm the one who created the distance between us, I didn't want to make more.

With a sigh, I opened the container and pulled out a treat. The first bite caused my eyes to close and a moan of bliss to rise in my throat.

They were even better than I'd remembered.

She made me cookies. Not just any cookies—my favorites. The ones I'd missed for over twenty years.

But not even the lingering taste of sugar and chocolate on my tongue could override the acidic taste burning up my throat. I'd upset her, and that had been unnecessary, Especially since she'd gone out her way to be nice to me.

I munched my way through the rest of the treat, hugging the container, still wrapped up in the smell of her skin and hair even though I'd been smart enough to move away. Now, I just needed to *stay* away.

Starting now. I headed toward the elevator as I grabbed another cookie and devoured it. The elevator doors opened and, after a moment—and a third cookie—the car slid downward. Still delicious. Almost as sweet as Aidy's skin.

Up until this point, I'd managed to pretend my feelings for Aidy were the same as they'd been twenty years before. I liked her, sure, but she was Knox's five-year-old sister. A cute kid.

Except now she was a thoughtful, caring woman who'd gone out of her way to thank me for such a simple thing—helping her with the puppy had truly been my pleasure. I'd lain in bed last night with the small ball of fluff cuddled close and dreamed that Aidy was there with us, her arms wrapped around us both.

Because I was an idiot.

Aidy might be smart and beautiful and a hell of a baker, but she was a woman recovering from a broken relationship, still finding her feet.

And I was seeing Margo.

The elevator dinged and I stepped out toward my vehicle, the bliss from the cookie melting away faster than the sweetness in my mouth as I thought about the woman I'd been dating for the past couple of months.

She was sleek, sophisticated, cool. All elegance. Everything that a doctor's wife should be. She also worked in Boston, which made getting together more challenging, especially with Margo's hectic work schedule.

Who would have thought that I, as the doctor, would have the consistent work schedule in a relationship? Certainly not me. But then, I hadn't considered working at a clinic or ever returning to Providence. This town had been my home during my earliest memories, but I'd lived in Boston for much longer. I'd planned to take the position at the office affiliated with Brigham and Women's Hospital, but I hadn't.

Instead, I'd drunk too much beer one night and played the what-if game: What if my father was still in the area? What if I found him? What if I told him I thought he was a terrible excuse for a human being for abandoning his kid as he'd done. Those thoughts swirling through my head, I'd applied for a position at a local clinic. I'd been shocked when I received a response, and even more shocked when I'd scheduled an interview.

Three months ago, I drove into Providence for the first time in more than a decade. Simon Hogue ran my interview and we'd clicked. He was about my age with a boyish charm and natural charisma I found charming even as I envied him his ability to speak his mind.

During my time at the clinic, I found acceptance with the staff, not the competition of my colleagues in Boston. The change was mind-boggling and refreshing. So much so, that during the lunch he'd suggested, I'd touched on my personal tragedy and he'd shared some of his sad history. I hadn't had a friend like that since…well, since Knox.

I hadn't realized how much I missed the connection. How much I craved it.

"Thanks for today," I'd told Simon. "I think I needed it."

Simon had nodded, his gaze serious. "I know this isn't the fast pace of the ER, and it's probably a pay cut from Boston. But I like you, Ryder. You fit here with the group. These hours and our stake in the profits mean we have more control over your schedule and life than you'd have in Boston."

I nodded, not sure what to say.

Simon ran his fingers through his blond hair, causing it to flop onto his brow. His blue eyes turned serious, maybe even a little heavy.

"I was in a similar situation a while back. I had a great offer from a facility in Leeds." He glanced around the diner then his gaze went out toward the ocean we couldn't see from our current spot. "But there's something about this place," he murmured. His smile widened, turned a little wicked. "And I couldn't leave my lovely Bridget."

He'd spoken often of his fiancée and young son—even telling me how comfortable Brendan, the boy, would be with me.

"I need to think about this," I'd said. "It's not what I envisioned for myself." And yet, the position, Simon, even the ease of finding a place to live in a brand new building less than ten minutes from the office, all fell into place. My aunt Zara would say it was fate, a sign I should heed.

Simon had clapped me on the shoulder. "Sometimes, it's the unexpected turns that lead us to where we're supposed to be."

Those words stuck with me as I spent the remainder of the afternoon at the cemetery between my infant sister Molly's graveside and my mother's. In the end, it hadn't been Simon's words or the money or the lure of consistent hours so much as the fact I didn't want to leave my family.

I missed my mother. The only person I might be able to forge a relationship with was my father, but he wasn't here, as

I'd hoped. Not that I really expected him to be. He'd sold our family's house years ago. Still it was time to find him and ask the questions he'd walked away without answering.

The day at the hospital fulfilled my need for the adrenaline-pumping cases I'd left behind when I chose to work at the clinic. I reset a broken collarbone, sewed up a few gashes, and diagnosed a child with pneumonia in addition to the one in need of an emergency appendectomy that had called me in to begin with.

Still, I ended the day energized as my patients rested comfortably in their rooms, reassured parents breathing a little easier knowing their children were receiving the care they needed. I patted the seven-year-old's foot, smiling at his gap-toothed grin as an orderly brought him two containers of ice cream.

Today was a good day.

I pulled out my phone, noting the time with a curse. My dinner reservation with Margo was in an hour and I needed to shower and change.

Aidy had sent me a text earlier with a selfie of the puppy in a park, giving enthusiastic kisses to her chin.

I hadn't responded because I'd told myself I was too busy. But that wasn't true—I simply hadn't wanted to continue thinking about her. She was my neighbor. Margo was my date, maybe even something more.

That didn't stop me from picking up my phone multiple times, desperate to hear more of Aidy's day—to simply hear her voice.

I crushed each urge.

I called Margo and asked her to meet me at my place. Maybe

I just needed to see her in my space, as I now did Aidy and her adorable puppy. Yeah, that was it—Margo rarely came to Providence, preferring to stay in the larger, more metropolitan city where she lived. While we only saw each other a couple of times a month, if that, I knew Margo didn't want kids. She was married to her career, just like me.

But when Margo agreed, my stomach curdled. Because Margo wasn't the woman I was looking forward to seeing.

Chapter Seven
Aidy

Ryder's hug stuck with me almost as much as his comment about dating a woman. I fixated on both, a sadness that he clearly wasn't as into me as I was into him settling over me as I waited to see the vet. The office was in a strip mall near Calliope's yoga studio. Dr. Allende, a trim man of medium height with wavy dark hair, smiled as he walked into the room.

After introductions, he said, "Let's get her checked out."

I swung the box holding the puppy up onto the table, and he pet her, finding her bliss spot behind her left ear before he tried to examine her foot.

"Does this cutie have a name?" he asked as he checked her teeth and her eyes.

"No. I'm not sure I'm keeping her."

"I can give you the name of a no-kill rescue if you decide to surrender her there."

I bit my lip.

"What brand of food should I get her?" I asked. "And does she need shots?"

Dr. Allende turned his head, but I caught his smile. Yes, I'd been seduced by the little dog's mismatched eyes and sweet personality. He and I both knew I wasn't taking her to the shelter.

"Want to try that name again?" he asked.

"Rosie," I said. My mother had grown up with an Australian Shepherd named Rosie, and I wanted to continue that tradition with my own daughter.

He didn't comment as he entered her name and probable date of birth—he thought Rosie was four to five months old. He told me he didn't expect her to weigh more than twenty-five pounds when she finished growing around the one-year mark.

I left the vet a few hundred dollars poorer but with all her shots updated and a bag of kibble. I'd missed yoga, which would have been difficult to practice, thanks to my tender ankle. But I decided to do some of that socializing Dr. Allende suggested and took the pup to Calliope's yoga studio for a visit.

My friends, Bridget, an ER nurse I'd met here a few months ago through the yoga studio, and Calliope, the studio owner, cuddled the dog while I made use of the restroom and bought a smoothie. I wondered if Ryder had eaten the rest of the cookies I'd made him. My chest warmed as I remembered his expression.

I stood in line behind a nice woman I'd met in class last week. Her name was Emmaline, and she had a degree in architecture from RISD. I took her up on her offer to help me do some dog shopping, and we spent an enjoyable afternoon together, though we quickly learned that the puppy didn't understand where to eliminate.

I stared in horror when the dog saturated Emmaline's side. Emmaline swallowed hard and passed me back the puppy.

"I guess that's my cue to call it a day," she said, pulling the dry part of her shirt away from her side. "I need a shower."

"I'm so sorry," I whispered, fingers pressed to my lips.

"Why?" She grimaced. "You didn't pee on me."

"I think this means we have to be besties," I said. "That way, you can tell everyone about your asshole friend with the peeing dog. And I owe you a shirt."

"You're on," she said, laughing. "Good thing Rosie's so cute."

I wondered how Ryder had fared with the pup last night. He hadn't mentioned her penchant for peeing anywhere and everywhere. That had to change, fast. I checked my phone after settling Rosie back in the box—no way I wanted a repeat performance in my car—but Ryder hadn't responded.

I tried to remain upbeat, but the way he'd blurted out his dating status made me think the good doc and I weren't destined for many more cozy evenings spent together.

Dogs were exhausting. Or maybe, more accurately, babies, in any form, caused exhaustion. Whatever the case, I was more than ready to call it a day.

I dropped my keys in the ceramic bowl I'd set on the small wooden table near my door and hung up my purse on the row of hooks above it. I unclipped the pup's purple leash from her matching purple collar and set them on the table.

"All right, girl, let's get you some dinner," I said.

My jeans seemed tighter than they had been this morning, attempting to cut me in half. Definitely time to purchase maternity clothes.

I sent Emmaline a text to let her know, again, how sorry I was that Rosie was so rude. Emmaline texted me back, asking if I'd like to hang out or grab dinner.

Rosie barked.

I focused on the dog. "Are you hungry?"

She barked again and again.

"I'll take that as a yes." I pulled her new bowls out of the satchel along with her food. Rosie yipped and scampered, trying to grab her tail. I laughed at her antics as I filled her bowl.

Someone knocked.

"Aidy?"

Ryder. I opened my door, a smile ready. And immediately regretted it when I saw that Ryder wasn't alone. A sophisticated brunette stood at his side, her bearing regal and her eyebrows now raised up so high I couldn't see them under her sleek bangs.

Sure, I was wrinkled and covered in dog fur, but he'd knocked on my door—while with another woman. I hadn't answered Emmaline about dinner because I'd hoped, stupidly, Ryder would want to spend time with me. *Wasn't I the fool?*

"Yes?" I asked. When Ryder just stood there, I smiled at the beautiful woman who was looking more annoyed by the moment. "I'm Aidy."

Her lips pulled down a little. "Margo."

I didn't bother to say it was nice to meet her because she'd stopped looking at me. *Well, okay then, frosty. I won't be friendly.*

"I wanted to make sure you were okay. I thought I heard…"

"She's clearly fine, Ryder," Margo said.

"Yep. I'm perfectly healthy," I said. "So's Rosie. Thanks for checking in." My tone was chipper, my smile bright and fake. "Have fun, you two."

Ryder opened his mouth as if he wanted to speak, but I was

already shutting the door. I needed it closed before the flame of embarrassment flashed further up my neck and became obvious.

"I don't want the puppy to get out," I said.

While true, I didn't want him to see how much his date upset me.

"Aidy," he began, concern causing his eyes to darken.

That made me think I'd done a shit job of covering my hurt.

Margo tugged at his arm, but Ryder ignored her, continuing to stand there. His frown became more pronounced, as if he didn't want to leave.

"Thanks for the cookies." He lowered his voice. "They were even better than I remembered."

"Thanks for bandaging my dog," I said. My gaze drifted to the stunning woman in the black silk sheath, now tapping her stiletto by the elevator. "You need to go," I whispered.

"I'll check on you two later," Ryder said, clearly unwilling to let the situation go.

"No," I said. No way I wanted him here now that I knew he had a girlfriend. "Go on your date, Ryder. Have fun. I'm not your responsibility."

I closed the door. Much as I was attracted to Ryder, I couldn't trust my instincts when it came to men. I'd thought Jeff cared about me. He'd pursued me with a determination I found flattering. He'd kissed me with a tenderness and passion I'd never experienced.

That attention continued each time he was in town, between fires. I'd loved being his singular focus. Except that supposed focus had been a lie, and he'd hurt me with his cheating. I closed my eyes, refusing to remember our last communication.

I scooped up Rosie, who whined at my feet, and sniffled all the way to my bedroom.

I unbuttoned my blouse as I looked toward my unused bathtub with longing. While a soak might alleviate my achy joints and sadness, I'd read hot tubs were bad for the baby, and so, for the next few months, I was steering clear of my siren-song soaking tub—just as I didn't eat the soft cheeses I craved more with each passing day, or drink alcohol or coffee. Better safe than sorry was my motto.

I closed my eyes and moaned again at the thought of a glass of white wine. Never mind. I shucked my blouse at the hamper and removed my bra, sighing with pleasure at the lack of confinement. I put on a camisole with a thick bra shelf and topped that with an asymmetrical sweatshirt that buttoned at my shoulder. I struggled out of my pants and into a pair of leggings and shoved my feet into my black Sorrel slippers. I wiggled my toes. These slippers were my new favorite thing to slip into each night. The faux fur was soft against my tired feet. I pulled my hair free from its tie. I frowned at the mass of curls that floated around my head and down my back but decided to ignore the mess. Brushing it caused my scalp to ache, and using my flat iron made me tired. Maybe this was why so many new moms cut their hair.

I really wouldn't know.

I texted Emmaline to let her know I'd take a raincheck, too saddened by Ryder's actions to be good company. And then I launched into my thesis.

I had three more sections, each with about five chapters, to go before I could submit it to my advisor. This section focused on energy footprints. Currently, building accounted for about half of all carbon dioxide emissions, and reducing that could be as easy as transitioning to more sustainable materials. I outlined some of the current options on the market, smiling when I made it to reclaimed wood—my personal favorite design tool. The variety in this category ranged from basic oak to tropical, adding character to any residence.

I smiled as I typed. My advisor had been correct—I'd turned in something well beneath my capabilities, but this…this felt *good*. My confidence built as I completed the chapter.

I padded into the kitchen and put on my electric kettle. While the water heated, I puttered around, pulling out my largest mug and my favorite herbal tea blend. I took Rosie outside, telling her how good she was when she squatted in the grass. She flopped down in her new bed that I'd placed next to my sofa, gnawing on one of the teething toys the sales associate assured me would save my shoes from her little teeth.

Soon, the soft scent of mint and lavender from my tea hit my nostrils. I pulled out my notes and reacquainted myself with the topic of how to adapt environmentally friendly strategies into historic renovation projects.

After an hour of research and work, I pushed away from the computer and made myself another cup of tea. This time, I popped in my earbuds and cranked up the music as I sifted through my notes on adaptive reuse. I typed, pleased with my conclusions.

I flinched when the pounding on my door infiltrated my headphones.

I heard someone calling my name. I closed my laptop, effectively cutting off my music and stood, popping the earbuds from my ears.

"Aidy!" The pounding was loud, nearly frantic. I stumbled around my startled puppy, who'd settled at my feet sometime earlier. I winced at the ache in my hips. I must have been sitting longer than I thought.

"Aidy!"

I opened the door but stepped back with a wince just before Ryder's fist connected with my nose.

"What's wrong?" I asked.

He bent down and scooped up Rosie before she managed to bolt out of the door.

"Are you kidding me right now?" he snapped. "I thought you were in some kind of emergency."

"Why would you think that?" I asked.

He slid into my condo, picking up my wrist with his free hand. He lifted it and then stared at his watch on his other wrist.

"Pulse is normal," he muttered. He put his hand to my forehead. "No fever."

He tugged me forward and settled me on the couch. When the puppy whined, he lifted her into my lap. I narrowed my eyes. He expected her to keep me seated. The *nerve* of him.

I started to get up. He placed a gentle hand on my shoulder.

"Sit down. I'll check your blood pressure." He paused, patting his dress pants. "I need my stethoscope."

"Ryder, what's going on?"

"You didn't answer your door. I texted, even called you when

I was at the restaurant, but you never responded. You didn't look good earlier, and…"

My back shot straight. No woman wanted to be compared to another one—especially one who had looked good, like his date. Margo. She'd been stunning.

I tugged my arm free of his grasp. "I'm fine."

"You don't know that," he said.

"You're worried about me," I said, surprise making my own eyes widen.

"I was sure you were unconscious. Or at the hospital." He scrubbed his palms over his face.

I shifted, trying to find a more comfortable position for my numb posterior and my hip popped, causing me to wince. I patted Rosie's head and she looked up at me with those big eyes.

"What time is it?" I asked.

"Nine-thirty."

"Wow. I guess I lost track of time."

"What were you doing?"

"I was working on my thesis. I was really in the zone."

I wondered how many pages I'd managed to write. Hopefully enough to take a big bite out of the work I still needed to complete.

"And you didn't hear me?" Ryder asked with a scowl.

I shrugged. "I had on music." I gestured toward my dangling earbuds.

Ryder stared down at his oxblood dress shoes. They were stamped leather and way sexier than laced shoes should be. I wanted to laugh and cry all at once.

I had it bad for this man's *shoes*. For months I'd been disin-terested, not just in men but in living. Now, thanks to Ryder, I seemed to have been slapped awake and unable to return to my hazy numbness. And, because the universe was still extracting retribution for my youthful sins, he had a girlfriend.

"Yes, I was worried," he said. He stepped in a little closer. "I don't want anything bad to happen to you, Aidy. I care too much."

Chapter Eight
Ryder

I couldn't believe I'd said that. But my heart still galloped behind my ribs, memories of Molly flashing through my head. I refused to allow Aidy's daughter to end up like Molly.

Of course. *Molly* was why I panicked. My breathing evened out and my shoulders eased downward.

Aidy scrunched up her nose. "Why?"

Good question but I didn't want to discuss Molly with Aidy— for many reasons. As I considered how to respond, I took in the lush tumble of hair swirling around Aidy's shoulders and down to the middle of her back. The baby must have woken because Aidy placed her palm against the left side of her small bump and smiled.

"She likes men's voices," Aidy said. She rolled her eyes as the dog jumped from her lap and settled on my shoe. "And, apparently, so does my dog."

I picked up the puppy and settled her in my lap. I liked her tiny weight and wide eyes.

"Really?" I asked, delight dancing over my skin at the thought of Aidy's daughter responding to me. A memory danced through my mind: me, sitting on the couch next to my *walida*'s belly, singing songs to Molly. *Walida*, mother in Farsi, was one of the few words she taught me. That, of course, changed when I went to live with my aunt, who insisted I have a much better understanding of our Iranian ancestry.

Aidy waved her hand, frustration evident in her jerky gestures. "You don't want to spend your evening talking to my babies."

"I'm pretty sure I do."

I caught her emphasis on my, which told me something else: Aidy was sensitive about her daughter's lack of a father figure. Because of her ex? Made sense but I'd also felt the tension between the Wright siblings when I was here the other day. Maybe Knox would give me more details when we met up next week. Surprise rattled through me at how much I was looking forward to catching up with my childhood best friend.

Maybe Aunt Zara's theory that I shut down after Molly's death was correct. She'd said I'd needed to protect myself, and for a while I had—when I was still a child.

But, now, I had friends, relationships. I'd been out with Margo tonight.

Margo.

I pursed my lips as I wondered if she'd forgive my inattention—and if I wanted her to.

"We don't really even know each other," she said. "And you have a girlfriend. She didn't seem all that enthusiastic about you talking to me earlier."

I almost missed the pounding pulse in her neck as she darted a surreptitious look at me, but once I caught it, I was mesmerized. Her voice and face appeared serene, like she was totally in charge, unaffected, but that pulse…it told a different story. One I wanted to explore. Because hell if I didn't like the idea of Aidy Wright being off-kilter when she looked at me.

"I know *you*," I said. "I used to hang out in your backyard, eat cookies your mom baked."

"I don't remember that," she murmured.

Snarfing down cookies with Knox in the Wrights' kitchen used to bring me comfort and joy. My mom made cookies, too, but she always doled them out, one at a time. That experience wasn't the same as eating handfuls of treats while laughing with Knox and Nico and even little Aidy as she trailed behind us, begging to be involved in whatever game we were playing.

I hadn't realized how much I'd missed those moments until Aidy gave me the cookies that morning. They'd been the highlight of my childhood—from a time untarnished by suffering or fear.

Aidy straightened, blinking away a memory. Of her mother? Considering I was thinking about the Wrights, I wouldn't be surprised to find her strolling back down memory lane, too. As she neared her due date, I'd bet she'd be thinking about her relationship with her mom more often.

All evening, I'd been lost in thoughts of Aidy to the point Margo noticed my distraction and called me on it. So, instead of a pleasant night of orgasms, I was, instead, here in Aidy's condo, with my hands buried in puppy fur, wishing I could mutter sweet nonsense to her unborn daughter.

And for the first time that night, I felt…content. No, happy. I was happy.

Huh.

"We've been growing apart," I said.

Aidy assessed me for a long moment. Tension built between us.

"I need to take her down to wee again," she said.

"I'll go with you."

Her jaw clenched but she didn't say no, just collected her coat and the dog's leash. We remained quiet on the elevator ride down and even as we pushed past the doorman out into the chilly night.

"I owe you one," I said. I hadn't planned to tell her this, but I didn't like the idea of anything else between Aidy and me—especially not after I'd seen the accusation and hurt in her eyes earlier tonight when I'd been escorting Margo.

She frowned. "You really don't."

"I really do." I sucked in a breath. "I called Nico that night."

Her confusion was obvious. "When? What are you talking about?"

"That night about eight years ago at Narragansett. It was early summer."

Her eyes widened as the memory dawned. Her cheeks flamed, and my guilt became oppressive. "Oh my gosh! The night Nico showed up? He dragged me out of there..." Her lips pressed tight in a firm line. "That was *humiliating*."

Yes, Nico had gone out of his way to humiliate her, and I'd felt bad about it since, which was part of why I'd agreed to Knox's request that I check in on Aidy that night we ended up having dinner. I hadn't expected to like her so much. To find her so fascinating. To want to spend my free time with her.

I flinched when her hand slapped hard against my chest, but I was relieved. I didn't have to continue my train of thought.

"Oh, my god! You were there? Why didn't you say something? I *totally* needed a ride that night, and while I was glad Nico showed up, he was *such* a jerk."

I scowled. "He *was* a jerk to you. What was that about?"

We watched the dog trample through the brown grass. She sniffed at an old pile of dirty snow. Finally, she squatted. I didn't think Aidy was going to answer me, but she said, "That wasn't the first time. At least that time, I was glad I could let *him* make a scene. I didn't want to be there."

"Why not?"

She sighed. "Tommy took me to that party."

I scowled as I pieced together more of the details. "You were Tommy Henneman's date?"

"Yeah. We'd only started going out that week, and I'd agreed to hang out with some of his friends, but I'd made Nico a promise not to do anything stupid."

She tilted her head back, her eyes closed. "Because I'd been doing lots and lots of stupid things that year. I'd received a full-ride to Rice but nearly messed that up when I stopped trying in my classes the last few weeks of the school year. My teachers were kind about the situation, knowing my parents had just died."

I slid my hand into my pocket so I didn't take her hand again. "I'm glad they were compassionate."

She snorted. "I didn't want compassion or nice or anything like that. I was…"

She sighed.

"Going to the party was stupid—a way to get even with Nico for trying to get me to buckle down. Tommy downed two cups of something within minutes of arriving. He broke up with me when I told him I didn't want to stay—he was scaring me. He said I was too young and too much of a goody-two-shoes to know how to party."

I grimaced. When I knew him, Tommy Henneman had waded through girlfriends faster than most guys changed their socks. Whatever women found attractive in his face and body, his personality lacked. So, Aidy's story didn't surprise me, but it made me feel even guiltier.

"I should have talked to you, asked what the problem was."

She shrugged as she turned back toward our building. "I probably wouldn't have known who you were and wouldn't have said much. I was glad to leave. But Nico was seriously pissed with me that night." She peered up at me. "What else did you tell him?"

I frowned, straining to remember. "I don't know. Just that I was surprised to see you at a college party."

Her shoulders sagged. "I'd hoped maybe you could shed more light on his continued frustration with me."

"Why don't you ask him?"

"It's one of the things we need to work out. I thought we would while I lived with him, but…" She sighed. "I was impulsive and engaged in destructive behavior after my parents died. I know I caused him lots of stress he didn't need on top of our parents' deaths, but I'm pretty annoyed that he won't address the situation directly. If he would just talk to me…" She shook her head.

Chapter Nine
Aidy

The return to the building proved a welcome tension release from the emotional bombs riddling our conversation. For the second time, I'd confided too much. For whatever reason, I was drawn to him, felt safe sharing with him. Even though I didn't want to.

I kept my gaze on the lobby, noting how the vaguely retro lighting elements transitioned nicely with the low-slung mid-century seating. I would have used more geometric patterns to tie the seating back into the soft blond wood end tables, but the darker tone worked well, even if a Scandinavian option would have tied in better.

I peeked at Ryder from the corner of my eye as we waited for the elevator. My brother's former best friend or not, Ryder wasn't *my* confidante. And baring my soul didn't make me feel better. I'd tried that tactic after my parents' death with my then-bestie Gretchen, and a counselor, but nothing seemed to diminish my anguish and rage. In fact, talking about my grief made me lonelier—and caused an increase in my impulsive drive, all of which led to more animosity between Nico and me.

We exited the elevator. Ryder walked to his door, I walked to mine. Rosie plopped her little butt down between us, looking back and forth.

Ryder dropped to his knee and scratched her behind the ear.

"I never had a dog."

Of all the things he could have said, this one pinged me straight in the chest. Was he trying to string me along?

No, I didn't think so. In fact, I didn't believe he had any idea what he did to me. At least there was that small consolation. Because my pride might not hold me tight during the night, warming me and reminding me I was wanted, but it did help me get out of bed in the morning.

"Maybe I could have her over sometimes," Ryder said. He glanced up at me, his expression mirrored in Rosie's.

I gritted my teeth. As if I stood a chance against these two. "We'll see. I mean, I bet you're really busy and all, so we'll just, you know, be flexible."

Ryder's hand paused before he gave Rosie's ears one more good pet. "Sure. Whatever you want, Aidy." Then he rose and went to his door. He opened it and I caught a glimpse of his brown leather couch.

"Good night."

He closed his door.

I went inside my place, and unclipped Rosie's leash. "That was…"

Surreal. The entire night felt odd. But in a good way. Rosie trotted after me, whining. I picked her up and hugged her close. After the much-needed cuddle session, I placed her on the floor of my bedroom. Rosie took a running leap and jumped up on my bed uninvited.

"Well, okay then," I said.

I got ready for bed and soon snuggled in next to Rosie, who

was already snoring lightly. As I slid into sleep, I thought about the gorgeous man who'd spent the better part of his evening with me—not Margo.

The warm contentment vanished as the cold reality hit: my last relationship devastated me, and Ryder, the person I'd connected with most since my return, was dating someone else. He showed me compassion after I told him…my cheeks flamed… after I'd admitted to stupid decisions in my teens. But there was no way I could date Ryder even if he wanted that. I couldn't do that to ice queen Margo.

Jeff cheated on me, and I'd never, ever put another woman through that hell.

Chapter Ten
Ryder

My foul mood lifted when Knox asked me to meet him and Nico for happy hour the next evening. Knox had texted me just after I ended up admitting a nine-year-old boy who was presenting symptoms that pointed toward leukemia. I'd know more in the morning but watching the parents wilt under the word *cancer*— that I couldn't eradicate it and make their son well and whole— made me so angry and frustrated.

We met at a small bar not far from our offices with a distinctly Cheers vibe. That surprised me because Knox had played hockey all through college, and I'd anticipated he'd choose a sports bar.

"Too loud," he said when I told him that. He grimaced. "And too many bunnies."

"Bunnies?" I asked.

Nico slid onto the third stool at our table. "Puck bunnies. That's what hockey players call the girls who are interested in bagging them for a night. Or more."

Again, Knox grimaced. "It's not an issue anymore, Not usually, anyway. Still, Sunday—football day—is better."

"Not your scene?" I guessed.

"Definitely not."

Nico chuckled as he ordered a beer. He'd loosened his tie and rolled up his shirt sleeves. "Did you see Aidy this week?" he asked.

"Yeah. She found a puppy. She brought it over so I could treat its foot."

Nico shook his head. "I know. Like she needs more responsibility she won't be able to handle. She hasn't learned anything in nearly ten years. She moved in the with jerk-off as soon as he gave her a ring, and then a year later, she's home, crying her eyes out because he never wanted to follow through on playing house."

"She's not seventeen anymore, and she planned to marry the guy," Knox said. "If there were anyone she should have been able to trust, it was Jeff." Knox turned to me, a sneer curling his lips. "That douche better not come back sniffing around Aidy again. She was depressed for weeks. I've never seen her that low—even after our parents disappeared."

"How's she handled the pregnancy?" I asked.

Knox shrugged. "I dunno. She gets tired a lot, and she always seems to be at the doctor these days."

"Which is messing up her productivity," Nico said, his scowl building.

"Get your head out of your ass, Nico. She's doing the best she can," Knox snapped back.

"That's the problem," Nico growled back.

I got the sense this was a long-standing argument.

I shoved my hands in my pockets. "Aidy never mentioned you were a dick." I narrowed my gaze. "But you just acted like one."

Nico crossed his arms over his chest. "I push her. She needs someone to make her focus. She's flighty and impulsive."

"And you're seeing the girl she was, not the woman she is." I sighed. "Look, man, I know things aren't great between the two of you. She's hurting over it."

"My relationship with my sister is none of your business," he said, his tone as stiff as his shoulders.

I hated fights. I had since I'd gotten knocked around and broken my nose and collarbone while in foster care. Since then, I'd kept my head down and my mouth shut, but this time, I stepped forward until Nico and I were nose to nose. I was gratified to see I could stare him straight in the eye.

"Maybe if you got your head out of your ass you'd realize she was a *teenager* when her parents died. She was at an age when she really needed her mother, and instead, she got a cold, seemingly uncaring older brother who let her know a *business* was more important than her."

"Who sold the only home she'd known mere months after her parents died," Knox chimed in.

"A man who never once considered what that would do to her psychologically to lose the last connection to her parents."

I avoided looking at Knox, unwilling to acknowledge his surprise at my defense of his sister.

"You have no idea what a pain in the ass she was as a teen…" Nico began.

"Worse than *your* behavior?" Knox shot back. "You were the adult in that situation. Not a seventeen-year-old who was mourning the loss of her whole world."

Oh, fuck. Knox's comment hit me hard in the chest. Aidy shared that terrible experience—we'd both lost our security, our sense of family.

"I saw how you treated her at that party," I said, my voice

quiet. "It was mortifying for all of us to watch. Did you ever stop to think about her feelings?"

"Why do you care?" Nico snapped.

I shrugged. "I just do."

Nico tilted his head to the side as if thinking back, considering. The hands came back up and scrubbed again. "I need to think about what you've said." He swallowed what seemed to be a bitter pill. "Maybe I handled that badly."

Knox scoffed. "I've been telling you for years, man. Aidy's not the problem. Well, not anymore."

Why I took pity on him, I really couldn't say. Except Nico wasn't a total asshole. He was a man who had too much responsibility thrust on him too early. I totally understood because I'd lived it myself.

Instead of buckling under the scary, big world, Nico powered through, all the while becoming more brittle. That prickly, hard-to-break-through exterior protected him from further hurts, and I understood the desire to protect his heart because I had the same urges. Hell, I even acted on them. Case in point: Margo.

I clamped my hand on his shoulder and squeezed. "So, do right by both Aidy and your niece."

Nico drained his glass and threw some bills on the table. I figured he should pay for being such a dick. Knox continued to bore a hole in the side of my head.

"You aren't involved with her, are you?"

"I'm her neighbor and, hopefully, will become her friend. I happen to like her because she's smart, funny, and kind." I paused, shocked by how much I wanted to be Aidy's friend.

But the look in Knox's eye pushed my half-formed fantasies of more-than-friends to the back of my mind. I'd been avoiding them because of Margo—and keeping Margo around had been smart because I was able to say to Knox, "I'm dating a woman."

Though, my conscience niggled. I'd told Aidy yesterday that we were growing apart.

"Aidy messed up a lot in high school and has really worked hard to be responsible since then," Knox said, voice quiet. "Seems to me, she wants Nico to be proud of her. Maybe you stepping in will be able to do what I haven't."

I met Knox's gaze. "Even though Nico doesn't see it, she has her shit together. She found a place down the street to watch the puppy while she's at work."

Knox shook his head. "What she doesn't need is more of Nico's shit." He lifted his beer. "Or a man fucking with her feelings again. She needs a good guy who'll put her first."

I took a long drag of mine. Message heard loud and clear.

Chapter Eleven
Aidy

Silly though it was, I missed Ryder's companionship that weekend. Still, I managed to type out another full section of my thesis
and complete the interior designs for The Mac.

I glanced at the timeline I'd drawn up. We'd have our first
finished suites by the end of next month. Good. If we could keep
to an aggressive completion schedule, I should be able to oversee
the process before my daughter made her appearance.

I stood and stretched. I took Rosie downstairs for her last wee.
She hadn't had an accident all day, so I was starting to think we
were getting the hang of the whole potty-outside deal.

The ping in my email as I arrived back inside had me collapsing
back into my seat with a groan. I glanced over at the door, noting
I hadn't heard Ryder enter his place yet even though it was after
nine. Besides the night of his date, he'd never been out this late.

I glanced at my newest email, unsurprised to see it was from
Nico. Instead of opening it, I rose again and collected the container of cookies I'd put together earlier. I penned a short note
and went across the hall. I hesitated but decided not to knock.
Ryder's life was his business, and just because we'd spent some
time together didn't mean I owned him. That's why I set the container at his door and headed back into my place. I glanced at my
clock as I locked my door.

Goody. Nico would work at least another hour before he shut off his computer for the night. I sighed as I clicked open his message.

I dropped my head to the table at his frustrated reply.

"Why did I agree to work for him?" I muttered. "Why didn't I just stay in Houston?"

Because I needed my big brother. The one I'd hero-worshipped before our parents died.

I needed *that* brother now, but instead, I had a grumpy bear who refused to see my value. Nico's lack of trust in me hurt. And he did *not* like my timeline for the renovations. I rose from the table and pulled out my copy of the blueprints. I went over the list of client requirements. I frowned. "What does he want?"

Nico wanted to be in charge.

Well, screw him. I could handle this project. *I would.* I had built a rapport with the client and I was going to manage all of the details. That was the only way he'd learn to trust me.

I jumped sometime later at the soft knock on my door. I crossed the room and looked through the peephole. I opened the door and leaned against the jamb.

"Ryder."

"I saw your light."

His hair was disheveled, as if he'd run his fingers through it… or a woman had. He leaned in and I caught the faint hint of perfume and beer. I stiffened and my chest began to burn. He'd been with *Margo*—the woman he hadn't wanted to talk about because they were *growing apart*.

Yeah, wasn't I the fool?

At least Jeff never sugar-coated the other women. I'd never known they existed—wouldn't have at all if his sister hadn't sent me the link to that private social media page with her password to get on. That had been an eye-opening experience.

"I was about to go to bed," I said, tone stiff. "Good night."

"Hey, wait."

I'd already shut the door, but I mumbled, "I'm tired."

Then, I turned out my lights and headed to my bedroom, willing myself to fall into a sleep that never came.

I rose early the next morning, that same ache still in my chest. I tossed around my makeup brushes, annoyed by my exhaustion, by Ryder showing up at my place last night after he'd hooked up with Margo, and by Nico's lack of trust.

I dressed and strode out of my place before seven, Rosie trotting at my heels. I was determined to finish my build-out schedule before Nico arrived. I did. Barely. But that's because dropping Rosie off at daycare was much harder than I expected.

She'd yowled as I left, which in turn, caused me to rush back and hug her wriggling little body. Finally, with more tears and crying—from both of us—I managed to leave my fur baby with many promises to her continued welfare.

Nico nodded at me, once. "This is an aggressive timeframe."

"It's two weeks longer than the one you sent to Knox and me internally. I wanted to add a bit of padding in case we had any issues with the electrical or plumbing."

"Smart. And there will be issues. This is your first large-scale project to manage."

I pursed my lips but managed to swallow my retort. A small

victory that no longer seemed worth the effort.

I sent off the revised calendar to Chloe. She approved it, so I set up meetings with the contractor for the next afternoon. Then, I began my renderings for a large beach-front home on one of the inlets.

I called to check on Rosie.

"She's doing great," Daphne, the doggie daycare owner, chirped. "Hold on. I'll use video calling…"

I clicked over to an image of Rosie batting her small paw at another puppy.

"That's Jambalaya. He's also got some Aussie shepherd in him. They really hit it off," Daphne said. "They've been playing all morning. My guess is we're getting to snooze time soon."

I smiled, warmed by my puppy's obvious pleasure in her new friend. "Thanks, Daphne. I've worried all morning."

"Don't. If there's any problem, I'll call."

"Thanks."

I touched the screen, rubbing my finger over Rosie's back through the screen, then clicked off.

And by four that afternoon, I was so tired, I could barely focus on my computer screen.

"You look done in," Knox said.

"I am," I replied, rubbing my hands over my aching eyes.

"Go home," he said.

"Nico doesn't like me to leave before five."

"Well, he's gone for the day, so it's not like he can ding you. And as the other boss-man, I just told you to leave."

"Good to know." I stood as I clapped my hand over my mouth,

stifling another yawn. I dropped my briefcase into my chair and began to fill it with the items I should go over that night.

"He's annoyed about you taking over the project," Knox said. "But he'll get over it."

"When isn't Nico annoyed with me?"

"When you do something right."

"No, he seems *more* annoyed then," I said. Sadness pulled at me. I yawned again. "Nico put me in this position."

"Because you don't stand up to him."

I tossed my head back. "What do you want me to do? Tell him to shove it?"

Knox quirked an eyebrow. "That'd be a good start."

"He's my *boss*. And my older brother."

"Who's treating you like an imbecile."

"Why, Knox? You have to know. Don't play dumb. What the hell happened between us? I know I was a handful in high school. I was so angry, and he ignored me, and I just wanted him to pay attention. I *needed* someone to seem like they loved me…" I willed my lower lip to quit trembling. "I miss him."

Knox hesitated. I'd asked him before, but he said that was a conversation for Nico and me to have. Except Nico wasn't willing to have it with me.

"I'm sorry I was gone then, Aidy-pie."

"You were finishing your degree," I said with a sigh.

"I should have come back to RISD. I considered it. That would have helped. Nico's just…" Knox ran his hand through his hair. "Look. This is between you two. Force the issue. *Make* him talk to you."

I scooped up my bag. "I have. He won't answer, which you also know."

Knox pulled me in for a long, tight hug. He pressed a kiss to my brow. "Get some rest, Aidy-pie. Tomorrow, you can take on Nico."

Chapter Twelve
Ryder

I knocked on the door to Aidy's place a couple of nights later mainly because I missed her. She answered the door, breathless but also relaxed, her cheeks flushed. She looked like she'd just rolled out of bed, all cute and rumpled.

I forced down the image of me picking her up and taking her back to her bed. She bent down and scooped up Rosie just before the puppy managed to dart out of the door. She brought the dog to her cheek and Rosie closed her eyes in bliss as Aidy cuddled her.

Lucky pup.

"What were you doing?" I asked.

"Yoga. Come in and shut the door, please. I don't want Rosie to get out."

"I thought you did that on Saturdays."

"How did you know that?"

"Simon Hogue. His fiancée—"

"Bridget," she finished with a smile. "She's *awesome*."

"That she is," I agreed.

She set Rosie down, but the dog came over to investigate my shoes. Aidy grabbed a water bottle, her gaze dropping to the large paper bag. "Smells good."

"I hope so. So, what's up with the home yoga?"

"I like to exercise," she said with a shrug. "It calms me.

Centers me."

Something in her tone made me think we were rubbing around the edge of a sore spot. She reached for a bright green hoodie that was lying over the back of her couch.

"I wanted to see how you were doing and to see how my favorite puppy's doing." I bent down and set the bag on the floor before I reached over to pat Rosie's head. She'd settled on her little haunches and waited for me to acknowledge her, which charmed me. She leaned into my hand as I ran my hand over her soft ears.

"She's good. She likes her doggie daycare program, thank goodness. She's already made a few friends, but I think she has a BFF. His name is Jambalaya. You should see them play. It's precious."

Aidy side-eyed me as she squatted down and picked up her yoga mat, stumbling slightly as she rose to stand. I grabbed her elbow. She smiled at me, a little sheepish.

"Thanks. I'm not used to the extra weight in front. Or how far I stick out these days." She patted her belly.

"You look great. And I'm glad Rosie's made friends." I repressed the urge to ask more questions about the dog's daycare because it wasn't really my business.

She shrugged. "I look pregnant."

"Barely. I would have guessed you were maybe four months, but you're…nineteen, twenty weeks? I thought you told me you were through your fifth month, but Knox wasn't sure."

Aidy grunted. "That's because he's not particularly interested in the baby's development or how it impacts my life. And he doesn't need to be because his world won't change much."

Probably true, but I wasn't going to say so. Seemed to go against the friend code, and I'd enjoyed catching up with Knox more than I'd expected. Besides Simon, I couldn't really call any of my colleagues friends, so, with Knox firmly back in the pal column, I'd doubled my circle.

"I just started my twenty-first week. So, in a few more weeks, the worst of the danger if she's premature is over." She looked up at me with large eyes, worry swirling in their depths. "Right?"

"Yes, most babies can survive after twenty-eight weeks, but I do suggest you keep that one inside as long as possible."

She rubbed her belly, and I noted it was slightly more prominent—a good thing if she was already at the end of her fifth month.

"That's the goal."

I walked my bags over to the counter. "I was hungry and thought I could return the favor of dinner. I brought lobster bisque. You okay with that?"

"Mmm. It's my favorite."

"Knox mentioned it when we hung out on Sunday, and I had a craving. I thought you might like to eat with me."

She blinked at me. "Sunday night?" Something thawed in her expression.

"Maybe I should have waited longer to stop by again," I said.

"No, no, that's fine. I just…I thought you'd be out with Margo," she said.

"She works a lot. And she lives in Boston."

Aidy cleared her throat, her expression hard to read. "Well, thanks for bringing me dinner. I wasn't really looking forward to the salad I'd planned."

I kept my mouth shut even though I wanted to explain the importance of nutrition for the baby. But that wasn't my place. I was just the neighbor. I swallowed hard as I admitted that I wanted to be more than that. And I really shouldn't. But hearing Nico talk about his sister brought something out of me—a protectiveness I hadn't realized I possessed. It had been awakened when she'd told me about her ex, but Nico's attitude reinforced my need to come to Aidy's defense, to support her. And the more time I spent with her, the more I wanted to indulge the emotion.

Her eyebrows scrunched tight together in obvious confusion. "You're upset about something. *Really* upset."

I hesitated. The few snapshots of newly born Molly that my *khaleh* Zara managed to snag in the NICU…and after flashed through my mind. I wasn't ready to tell her about my baby sister. Bringing Molly up made me raw and something deep inside ached at just the thought. I shook my head.

Aidy let it go and busied herself setting out the food. We settled in at her bar and once again shared a meal.

"How's the thesis coming along?" I asked.

Her eyes lit up. "Good. *Really* good. My advisor approved the first section, and I finished another last night." She picked up a piece of crusty bread and dunked it into the creamy stew. "If I can get Nico off my back long enough, I should have my draft completed in a month, maybe six weeks, which is weeks before my advisor needs it in order to read and get it back to me prior to the end of the semester."

"Sounds like a solid plan."

Aidy shook her head. She nibbled at her bread but set it down with a sigh. "I hate cutting it so close."

"But even if you take six weeks, that'll still be February."

Her mouth twisted as she looked down into her bowl. "I wanted to be finished last semester, but I messed up."

"Oh?"

She clenched her jaw, a move I remembered from her youth. She'd do that when she was determined to accomplish some task her brothers thought she was too baby to do or when she felt strong emotions and didn't want to let them out.

When I tilted my head, I caught the pain in her eyes.

"You needed some time to process your breakup," I guessed.

Her gaze shot to mine. She nodded, the delicate muscles in her throat bobbing. "Nico said…he said I…" She shook her head.

Her brother treated her with such disregard for her feelings. Who did that to a woman who'd just found out the guy she planned to marry abandoned her, pregnant, no less?

Rage curled in my belly, but I set it aside. For now. If Nico didn't come through, we'd have words again. Or maybe I'd punch him. That fantasy of my fist cracking into the skin on his face felt good.

"If I'd stayed focused, I wouldn't be in this time crunch. Nico's right. I'm impulsive, led around by what I'm feeling in the moment."

I looked around at her space—her briefcase and purse hanging above the bowl that held her keys, her phone charging next to it. Her living room had a throw across the couch and a couple of books open on her coffee table next to her laptop. Even her puppy had a bed, though Rosie had taken up residence under our chairs, no doubt on the lookout for crumbs.

"I'm sorry I brought up something so uncomfortable. I just…I don't see you that way. At all."

Her eyes remained wide, a little uncertain. Much as I loved kids, I wasn't big on touchy-feely sensation with anyone who wasn't my patient. Those weeks in foster care changed a lot for me, especially since my time there was punctuated with painful touch.

But with Aidy, touch wouldn't be painful. It would soothe hurts deep within both of us. Except we were neighbors, working toward a friendship, and I was dating Margo. Margo was the woman who deserved my focus.

I cleared my throat as I picked up my spoon, focusing on my meal. That seemed safer than offering comfort when I didn't plan to follow up or follow through with more.

"You're making the most of *this* semester, then. And you'll have yours turned in months before most of the other grad students. Cut yourself some slack. Knox said you're working full time and juggling your studies."

She picked up her spoon and skimmed it over the soup. "Not like I really have a choice. My life is going to be much more hectic after she arrives."

"Do you have a name?" I asked.

She rubbed her hands over her belly, and I noted the stretches and wiggles under her sweatshirt. I relaxed a little at the movements. The baby really did like male voices. "Yes."

"Ah. Is it a secret, then?" I teased.

She remained still for a moment before she met my gaze. "I haven't shared it with anyone yet. My mother's name was Lillian. I want to name this little one Lilia. After my mom."

Lilia. I rolled the word over in my mind as my chest warmed. "That's pretty."

"Thank you."

I sat back in my chair and surreptitiously dropped a small piece of bread to Rosie. Aidy sipped her soup slowly as if savoring every texture and new flavor.

"Tell me about your day," she said.

I spent the next thirty minutes regaling her with the antics of the kids at the clinic. She gasped when I told her about the projectile puker.

"Does that happen often?"

"Enough."

I picked up my water glass and took a drink. No point in telling her she was going to be up close and personal with all kinds of glop. She'd find that out soon enough.

"Do you have a birth coach?" I asked.

She shook her head. "I would ask Bridget since she has medical expertise and would be a good advocate, but with her giving birth herself soon, that seemed selfish of me."

"I'll go with you," I said.

She blinked, clearly startled. "Where?"

"To your appointments. The hospital. I'll be your birth coach. Your backup birth coach," I amended. "In case Bridget can't make it."

She was already shaking her head. "I can't ask you to do that," she said.

"You didn't. I offered." I clasped my hand over hers. "And I meant it."

"If this is because you feel guilty about calling Nico or because you think you owe Knox—"

It was my turn to pause, to consider my words. But I decided to go with my gut. "It's because I care about you, Aidy. And I don't like the idea of you going to these appointments alone, and I definitely am not okay with you delivering a baby alone."

She inhaled sharply and stuttered out a breath. "Okay," she whispered. Her shoulders eased as if I'd just knocked off a huge weight. "I'd like that."

A somber silence settled over us as we stared at each other. "No problem. So, ah, I'll get out of your way so you can work on your paper."

She smiled a little, her eyes brimming with softness. "Thanks, Ryder. For dinner and for being a good friend."

I smiled back, holding it in place until I closed her door behind me. I crossed the hall and opened my door. I closed it and then dropped my head back against it.

"What the fuck are you *doing*?" I snarled.

Of course, I didn't have a good answer. "You need to leave Aidy *alone*. She's a nice woman who just had her heart broken and is about to become a first-time mom. She definitely doesn't want to deal with your unwillingness to deal with birth—why, *why* would you want to be there for hers?"

My compulsion made no sense. I'd hated the OB/GYN

rounds during med school, thankful to move past them. I never planned to witness another birth again. Yet, somehow, I'd just offered to be with Aidy for hers.

I strode into my bedroom, removing my clothes. My shower was long because I had to jerk off to the thoughts of the softness of Aidy's skin and the delicacy of her shoulders. Her fucking *shoulders* turned me on.

Getting off on my fantasies of Aidy was becoming a habit—one I didn't seem able to break. I was so screwed.

I hated that I thought of Aidy and not Margo. But Margo hadn't crossed my mind when I was with Aidy—and not much before. No matter what I'd told Knox last night, Margo and I weren't serious and we wouldn't be.

I ran the towel roughly over my head, hoping it would shove out my thoughts, but it didn't.

I needed to break things off with Margo. That was the only viable option.

Except if I did that, I knew I'd want to take Aidy to dinner. I'd desire more than sharing another meal, and Knox was right: Aidy deserved a man who put her first.

The next night, I called Margo.

"Want to go to dinner?" I asked.

"Are you going to pay attention to me this time?" she asked, her tone dry.

"Of course."

"Well, I have a dinner meeting tomorrow night. You're welcome to join me."

"I'd love that," I said.

Chapter Thirteen
Aidy

Later that week, I arrived at The Mac Hotel site a few minutes early, thanks to another fitful night in my bed. Since Rosie was so happy playing with her buddy, daycare drop off had smoothed out. Now, if I could just stop obsessing about Ryder, I might actually get some work done. I felt like Meredith during season two of Grey's Anatomy, pining for a man who wasn't mine. Rosie and I had taken to curling up together on the couch and watching an episode after I finished my thesis chapter. Sometimes, Emmaline joined us.

Just like Meredith compartmentalized, I needed to as well. Right now, I needed to go over the list of electrical and plumbing changes with the contractor, Marcus. He was a tall, thick man with more salt than pepper in both his receding hairline and bushy beard.

"It's taking longer than we anticipated, baby cakes," Marcus said.

I kept my face smooth but my hands clenched. "Better get on those fixes, then, *baby cakes,* because Chloe will be here in an hour, and I've already sent her a message not to release funds until your staff meets the very doable checklist we agreed to at our last meeting."

Marcus glowered down at me, and I glared back, sick of all

the crap I'd been taking from men in my life.

"I'll see what I can do," he muttered. "No promises."

I tipped my lips up just enough for him to get a flash of my teeth. "Then, no paycheck."

Four men, voices raised, stepped into the building. They were raucous and not wearing their hard hats. Could this day get any worse?

"Ah, good. Gentlemen, I just informed Marcus here that if you don't actually accomplish your weekly goals, you don't get paid. End of story." I put a significant bite into my words as I met each of their eyes. They shuffled their booted feet, and Marcus's forehead mottled.

"Chloe and I will be walking through the interior in two hours. I expect to have progress to show her, and for her to take to corporate. I also expect you to follow safety guidelines and wear your hardhats while on site. If you have a problem with that you're welcome to leave now."

I returned my gaze to Marcus and held my ground. He dipped his chin once, but his lips remained compressed. He could dislike me all he wanted as long as he held up his end of the bargain.

I forced my stiff, trembling legs to move me down the hall and toward the main foyer. I released a puffed breath but squeaked when a thick hand gripped my wrist and spun me back toward a male body.

Marcus.

"You don't get to talk to us like that, little girl."

I drew myself up.

"You're fired."

Marcus snorted.

"On whose authority?" His gaze dipped down to my chest and then further to my belly. He smirked. He lifted his hands to touch my stomach, but I slapped it back.

Fear seeped from my pores, but I straightened my spine, thankful for my heels and the extra height they afforded me. I pulled out my phone and pressed the shortcut to Nico, frustrated I needed to use my brother to get me out of this situation, but smart enough to know I might be in danger.

"On my authority. I'm a partner at Wright and Associates, and this is my project that you've been lucky enough to work on. That changes, now. Get. Out."

Marcus crowded me. "I'm not going anywhere. This is *my* crew, *my* project, but if you're sweet enough, I might forget this conversation ever happened."

Marcus leaned in, a leer on his face. I must have blinked because next thing I knew, Marcus was on the ground and one of his crew members stood over him. Blood poured from the hands Marcus had cupped to his nose and trickled down his chin.

"Th-thank you," I stammered.

The subcontractor looked me over, but without lust in his dark brown eyes. "He shouldn't talk to you like that. Treat you like that."

He tipped his head back and I saw the rest of the crew, about forty faces, six of which were feminine, all with narrowed eyes. One of those women stepped forward and raised her staple gun.

"I'm Lidia, and this guy is Kent. We'll make sure Marcus is off the premises."

Marcus lay still, seemingly in shock.

"I'd appreciate that," I said.

"And for the record, we would have gotten more done but Marcus is a greedy asshole who pulled two-thirds of this crew and put them on another job after you left every day last week," Kent said.

I glanced down at the man still lying on the ground. "Duly noted." I raised my gaze to sweep it over the men and women standing there. "I'm not sure if Marcus told you, but Macintosh is offering a fifteen-percent bonus should you all get this place past inspection and ready for opening by late March."

The group shifted and voices rose in disbelief and anger. Marcus had the sense to scuttle back, but two burly men grabbed him by the biceps and tugged him to his feet.

"He did *not* tell us that," Lidia murmured. "Wonder what else we didn't know."

"I'll catch you up once he's gone," I said.

Kent handed me Marcus's credentials as he glanced at my belly. "You okay?"

I nodded.

"Lidia and Kent, we should discuss your promotions."

"First, we'll take care of him. And we'll make sure the project meets your expectations," Kent said.

I nodded again, my emotional reserves shot. A few others surrounded Marcus and his two captors, leading them toward the chain-link fence that separated the grounds from the worker's vehicles.

"I'll inform site security he's been fired," I said. My voice remained steady.

I straightened and looked over at the rest of the crew. "Anyone else have a problem with me?"

No one said a word. "Then how about you start working toward your bonus?"

The noise level ratcheted up and the crew disbursed—in their hardhats. I laid a hand on my belly, needing to reassure myself my daughter was safe. This was not a part of the process I'd considered, but now, I was going to have to ask Nico and Knox about protocols that would ensure such an incident didn't happen again.

I lifted my phone, shocked to see it connected. I pressed it to my ear.

"Hello?"

"No need to contact security. I've taken care of it." Nico's grim tone flooded my ear, and I leaned back against the wall to steady myself, thankful to hear Nico's voice through the speaker. Not the same as a hug, but I'd take what I could get.

"I also have Angus Jericho on the line with me, listening to what we could of the conversation you were having. Hold tight a sec, Aidy." Nico's voice turned steely. "If Marcus comes near The Mac or Aidy, I'll file charges for assault and trespassing. The Mac security team understands he is not allowed on the premises. And, for the record, Angus, if you don't clean up your mess, I'll bring in a crew from a different city and make sure everyone in the business knows why."

"Understood," Angus's voice drawled. "And, Aidy, for what it's worth, I'm sorry. I'll deal with Marcus."

Unsure how to respond—thank you didn't seem appropriate—I said, "I plan to work directly with Kent and Lidia."

"Whatever you think is best," Angus said.

Nico told Agnus goodbye and then re-focused on me. "Are you okay?" he asked.

"Yes. Fine."

No. Not really. Before I could tell him that or burst into tears, he said, "Proud of you, slugger. You had steel balls."

I wrinkled my nose. Not an image I wanted in my head.

"Aidy?" he said, voice hesitant.

"Yeah?"

"I don't give you enough credit. You're pretty amazing."

I frowned, shocked by his words. I wasn't used to compliments, but my chest swelled a little. Nico cleared his throat. "I'll be there in thirty so we can make sure your new contractors are up to speed."

He sounded like Nico again, a kinder yet still gruff version of himself. Before I could ask him why he seemed more pleasant, he clicked off.

Lidia leaned on the wall next to me. "Thursdays suck," I muttered.

Lidia laughed. "Gotta say, this is the best Thursday I've had since I started with Jericho." She winked. "I always wanted to be in charge."

I snorted as I rubbed my forehead, realizing I was in for hours of additional work. Still, it was worth the time to make sure Chloe and Macintosh Hotels were happy.

"We'll get you the results you want, Ms. Wright," Lidia said. "The rest of the crew—they're good people."

I smiled at her, putting aside the ever-expanding to-do list.

"I'm looking forward to working with you and Kent, Lidia."

And I really, really was looking forward to some Rosie cuddles later. I might project confident businesswoman, but inside, my guts churned with continued anxiety.

Rosie greeted me with her usual enthusiasm, and I spent a few minutes in the car petting her before I was ready to drive back to my place. After completing my thesis chapter and taking Rosie out for her late-evening pee, I collapsed into my bed, and I didn't move until five the next morning. Thankfully, neither did Rosie. For an Aussie, she was surprisingly chill. Probably nine or more hours of playtime at doggy daycare wore her out.

I groaned as I pushed out of bed. My legs felt leaden and my hips cramped, no doubt from my weird sleeping position. I couldn't believe I'd managed hours in that position. But my stomach did because the growls emanating from there were deafening.

After a quick stop in the bathroom, I took Rosie downstairs for her morning wee. Hunger pangs slammed into me, making me dizzy. I really shouldn't have skipped dinner.

Back in my kitchen, I turned on my kettle and opened the fridge. I pulled out a container of yogurt. I dipped my spoon in with a shaking hand and nearly cried with relief when it hit my tongue.

I devoured the container before my water boiled. I stuck my head back in the fridge, searching for something else that would shut off the gnawing sensation in my belly. I found nothing. I slammed the door shut with a grunt. Right. I'd planned to go to the store last night. I'd managed to get by without doing so this week because Ryder brought me dinner.

I glanced at the clock. It was five-thirty in the morning. I was too hungry to worry about niceties. I grabbed my keys and walked across the hall, knocking on his door. Rosie at my heels.

I tapped my foot, irritated with the wait. He finally opened it, hair in disarray, sprouting in all directions from his head, eyes bleary.

"Aidy. Are you okay?"

"I'm not in labor. I'm hungry." I bypassed him and beelined to his kitchen, which was the same clean granite-and-white appliances as mine.

Once again, Rosie followed. I gasped in delight as I grabbed a loaf of bread. I pulled out a slice and shoved it in my mouth, chewing furiously.

"Want an omelet?" he asked.

I glanced back to see him kneeling on the floor, his large hand stroking my puppy's shiny fur. My heart melted and my vagina tried to take notice. But I refused to acknowledge all his bare skin and sleek muscle next to puppy preciousness. I was on a mission.

"You know, some protein to go with those carbs?" he asked.

"Make it quick," I said. "Or I might eat your arm instead."

He chuckled even as he stood. "Give me a sec."

Oh, my. My cheeks flamed as I took in the broad expanse of his nude back. Ryder's broad shoulders tapered to narrow hips, and all the way down, my gaze caught on interesting ridges and swells that slid into the valley of his spine. He worked out. Often. No other way he'd have that body. I stood by my original assessment that he looked like the *Men's Health* model. Only even more defined and sexier.

My gaze dropped further.

"Um, I didn't interrupt anything, did I?" I asked, my eyes still on his fabulous ass encased in the thin cotton barrier of his boxer briefs. Oh, hell, they were Calvin Kleins. I would forever have a deep-seated love for the brand thanks to their perfect framing of Ryder Mackay's ass.

"Yes."

Oh my…he'd brought *her* here.

My stomach tried to turn itself inside out, but then it grumbled. Fuck it. If he were getting action, I definitely deserved this loaf of bread and a good ogling for my fantasies.

He started to turn toward me, and I barely managed to drag my eyes up before he caught me ogling.

"I'm sorry," I said. I shoved part of the slice of bread in my mouth and snagged a banana and an apple from his counter, which I piled atop the loaf of bread. I headed toward the door, saying, "Apologies for interrupting…ah…yeah, well. Bye."

He cocked his head to the side, clearly unable to understand me through my slice of bread and my mumbled shame. Rosie whined. I glared at her.

No, traitor, we could not stay for more petting.

"I was *sleeping*."

I rearranged my loot and took the quarter of the slice of bread from my mouth. I chewed furiously before I was able to say, "I'm sorry I woke you. I'll just take this for now and bring you some replacements later."

"Is that what you said? I couldn't hear the words around the bear rumblings passing your lips."

Mine twitched. "Shut up." I was still ravenous so I shoved the rest of the slice into my mouth. "I'm hungry."

"I noticed. And if you'd let me put on pants, I'll make you a real breakfast."

I sighed. "Fine."

Mainly because I didn't want him to put on pants. It would hide some of his incredible butt. I was definitely a Ryder Mackay glutes fan.

"If you're sure it's not a problem—"

"I don't have a woman here," he yelled back down his hallway.

My stomach soured. Not *this* time. That was the implication.

Nope. I'd appeased my curiosity about Margo. She hadn't stayed the night. But that didn't mean she wouldn't next time, and my jealousy toward her ratcheted up.

This was *bad*. I shouldn't dislike a woman I didn't know. Especially not over a man. Shame washed over me, drowning me in its noxiousness, because I did. I hated Margo because she was with Ryder.

He came back down the hall wearing sweatpants and a T-shirt. As expected, I mourned the loss of his beautiful butt but perked up at the tightness of his T-shirt. It didn't adhere to his front enough so that I could see every single rise and crevice of his chest and abdomen, but I had a great memory that I'd use later.

My hormones had skyrocketed as out of control as my appetite.

"Did you have a date the other night?" I asked.

"Sure did."

I made a noise as I peeled the banana. No way I could wait for the omelet to cook. Missing dinner had been a terrible idea. I said as much aloud.

Ryder frowned as he cracked eggs into a bowl. "Are you always that tired?"

I swallowed my bite before I replied. "I pushed it Tuesday and Wednesday before, didn't sleep well. I was in the office before seven. Plus, Rosie's not the best sleeper."

He whisked the eggs while he poured in a splash of half and half. "I know."

"So, how was your date?"

He glanced up under his lashes at me. "Good."

I bet it was. "Figured," I polished off the rest of the banana and rose to put the peel in his trash can. The soft sizzle of eggs hitting oil made my stomach rumble again.

"Okay, okay, we're feeding you." I patted my belly as I headed back to the stool. "So, you two worked out your issues, huh?"

Ryder pulled out a black spatula and took his time loosening the egg from the bottom of the pan. He tossed in some white cheese and drizzled a homemade bruschetta into the middle. He flipped one-half of the eggs over the other side. Finally, he glanced up.

"Yeah. That's why I saw her again last night."

And just like that, my hunger evaporated. So did my good mood. The few times I'd seen Margo, she'd been so cold, almost calculating. I knew, in my bones, she'd never bake cookies for him. Not that a woman had to make a man cookies, but Ryder soaked up homey-ness like most people breathed air. And, from what I'd gleaned Margo rarely checked in. It was like…Ryder was her prop boyfriend, a trophy to trot out. *See, I'm dating a doctor.*

But she didn't seem to want *Ryder*, the thoughtful, kind man who I'd awakened and was now cooking me an omelet.

I forced a smile. "I see. That's nice."

"Mmmhmm."

I edged off the chair. Nope. I'd thought I could be friends with Ryder, but I was wrong. My chest ached and my eyes stung, and…and I wanted to be the woman who ran her fingers through his hair and the one he took on dates and…

"Where are you going?" Ryder asked.

"Home. The banana and bread finally hit my stomach. Plus, you know, your girlfriend won't like that I showed up before dawn and—"

"My girlfriend isn't here."

"Which is how I know she's not right for you," I shot back.

He settled back, eyebrows raised. His hair was mussed but his eyes lost their sleep look.

"If she loved you, she'd be in that bed with you every night." Like I wanted to be. I lifted my chin. "And we both know that."

"That's my choice as much as it is hers," he said in that calm, I'm-a-doctor-and-in-charge voice, and it annoyed me.

I pressed my hand to my stomach, willing away the desire building there. Dammit. I wasn't really over Jeff's betrayal, and I didn't have a say in Ryder's love life.

"I shouldn't have said anything. It's not my business."

"Aidy—"

"No, Ryder. It's not. And that's why I shouldn't be here, and you shouldn't stop by. All that needs to stop."

"Why?" His brows plunged together, forming a vee over his nose. "We're friends."

I shook my head. "I can't…I don't want to be your friend. And you hanging out has me confused and hurting. That's my problem, and I'm sorry but it's better if we just don't interact."

He seemed stunned. He dropped his gaze and rocked back on his heels, a gesture I'd noticed showed his discomfort. I didn't want him to respond. I didn't want to be even more embarrassed than I was.

"The smell…" I waved my hand in front of me and wrinkled my nose. Then, I turned, calling Rosie. Thankfully, she followed.

I crossed the hall and practically ran into my condo. I locked the door behind me. I snatched Rosie up as I hurried toward my room. I lay in my bed, petting her for a long time.

Finally, when my alarm went off, I rose again. I turned on my Bluetooth speaker and then headed into my bathroom. I slumped in the shower, angry with myself for yearning after Ryder and angry with *him* for making me feel so strongly—when there was no possibility of more.

Chapter Fourteen
Ryder

Aidy was definitely avoiding me. She had been ever since I told her Margo and I were staying together. I replayed her words again. *If she loved you, she'd be in that bed with you every night.* The sadness in Aidy's eyes when she said that, before she disappeared—taking my loaf of bread and an apple with her—reminded me of the look in her eye after she took in my hair and rumpled clothing the other night. Discomfort slithered through my chest.

I didn't like Aidy being upset, and I knew she was because she told me so: *I can't…I don't want to be your friend. And you hanging out has me confused and hurting.*

I liked even less knowing I was the reason for it.

But I was because I chose to hide behind a relationship I no longer wanted to participate in—one that should have been comfortable and easy. The expectations were low. *If she loved you, she'd be in that bed with you every night.*

Margo wasn't. Not because Margo hadn't suggested staying at my place or hers because she had—as I'd done in the past. But I hadn't been able to take her up on her offer because Margo wasn't Aidy. And since I'd met my neighbor, I wasn't interested in Margo, which told me a lot about how messed up my mental state was.

And now, more than a week later, I hadn't caught a glimpse of my neighbor, and I was frustrated. I had things I needed to say to her.

I'd even tried coming downstairs around the time she used to bring Rosie down for her last nightly walk, but Aidy must have changed that part of her schedule, too.

She was better at avoidance than a damn spymaster. Maybe she honed those skills during her rebellious teenage years. Not that it mattered; I was going to catch her eventually.

I cast a quick glance at her door as I pulled out my keys. It was Saturday morning, the day of her prenatal yoga class—the one she attended with Simon's wife, Bridget. I lingered in my front entry, waiting to hear her head out.

I closed my eyes and tilted my head back. "You promised her brothers you'd look out for her, and you're doing a shit job of it."

Thanks to my close proximity to my front door, I heard her door click open. I held my breath, counted to ten and then opened mine. She dropped her keys into that voluminous gray purse she always carried as I nodded at her. I bent down to pet Rosie, who licked my wrist enthusiastically.

"She's grown," I said.

"Yes."

Aidy wore stretchy black pants that did amazing things to her backside and a ruffly red hoody that covered up whatever top she wore to workout.

I rose and she began the short walk to the elevator. We waited for the car, and I could smell the soft fragrance drifting from her, soothing some of my raging desire.

I rubbed my hands over my face, nerves wracking my midsection. I should just say what I wanted to, get it over with.

"Are you off to an exercise class?" I asked. The elevator doors slid shut behind us.

"Yes," she murmured. She fiddled with the zipper on her hoody. Tension swelled in my chest, causing my shoulders to stiffen.

Aidy didn't say anything else, so I looked back down at my phone where I had a slew of messages.

One was from Simon.

I'm stuck on a consult that looks like it's going in for emergency surgery, and Bridget needs a ride home from yoga.

Instead of texting him back, I called him. I wasn't a texter. I didn't like the impersonal nature of the communication, which seemed strange even to me because I was a loner by choice.

"Of course I'll pick her up," I said as soon as Simon answered. "I'm about to get in my car. Just send me the details."

"You're a lifesaver," Simon said, then rattled off the details faster than I could process. "I'll text you," he finished, out of breath.

"Good because I didn't catch all that. And it's not a problem," I replied. "Happy to help. Talk later."

I tried hard not to glance over at Aidy as she exited the elevator, Rosie trotting happily beside her. I sure as hell refused to check out her rounded, plump ass that was encased in shiny black material as she walked in front of me. She had the beginnings of the pregnancy waddle I'd noticed while I worked in L&D, but she still maintained nice proportions. From the back, I'd never know she was carrying a baby.

I forced my gaze away as she strode toward her sedan.

"Hey, Aidy," I called.

She turned to look at me over her shoulder, her hand on her car's doorframe.

"I'm picking up Bridget there in an hour. Want me to take you and bring you home?"

She squinted at me. "I have to run a couple of errands. But thanks."

"Yeah. Sure. Um…we should catch up soon."

"We don't have anything to discuss, Ryder. You're dating a woman, and I…" She shook her head as she settled into her car seat. Rosie stood up in the passenger seat, paws on the window.

Aidy closed the door before I formed a response. I stood there for a moment, staring at her taillights before I pulled out my car keys and unlocked my vehicle. I sighed, wishing I'd handled that morning last week and this one better.

I headed to the gym. Much as I wanted to get out on the ice, I worried I'd lose track of time, so instead, I headed to the weight room. I finished my fifth round of squats, heaving for breath when I glanced up at the clock. I cursed, realizing I might well be late. I wanted to be there to help Bridget out of the class. Not that she thought she needed the help, but I did. And Simon expected me to do so.

I swiped away the sweat from my face and neck as I hurried to my car. Thankfully, I found a parking spot nearby, and stopped short, just inside the door of the studio, when I saw Bridget talking to Aidy. Rosie was blissed out on one of the sofas, eyes closed as two women pet her. They laughed at some quip Aidy made while I hovered by the door, unwilling to interrupt Aidy's happiness.

Both women were curvy, due in part to their pregnancies, but Aidy's bone structure was more delicate. And she'd pulled all that glorious red hair in a bun. As I watched, she released it from the clip. I held my breath as the shimmering, glossy strands unwound…and stayed in a cascade from a sleek ponytail. I release my breath, a bit saddened I hadn't gotten to see all that hair tumble down her back and over her shoulders. Probably a good thing, though. My heart may have stopped, or my eyes might have bugged out of my head.

Dammit. My reaction to Aidy was entirely inappropriate. I'd planned to tell her that we should go back to hanging out, to being friends, but clearly, I wasn't capable of seeing her in that light.

I wanted her.

Bridget caught sight of me and waved then, so I waved back, unwilling to move from my spot by the door because I worried I'd want to invade Aidy's space. And that wasn't acceptable. She'd made it clear she didn't want to hang out, and I needed to respect that.

Bridget continued to talk for another minute, her smile as wide and genuine for the younger woman as it was for me as she made her way over, her blonde ponytail bouncing a little as she moved toward me, her hand supporting her belly. I eyed her, hoping she didn't decide to pop out those twins in my car.

"Too shy to say hello to Aidy?" Bridget teased.

That was the impression everyone had of me—that I was shy. I did nothing to disabuse them of the notion because the alternative, the guy who refused to talk to people, to let them in, seemed like an asshole even to me. Though, the unwillingness to connect with others was much closer to the truth. I'd found the fewer conversations I had, the fewer relationships I built. Because people left. Even the ones who said they loved you like my parents. They just…left.

So, getting close to people wasn't smart. If my parents couldn't stick around, why would others, especially when they didn't even have the blood tie as an obligation?

"How long have you known her?" I asked.

"A few months. She started yoga here right after she moved back to Providence." Bridget tipped her head. "She said you were friends with her brother before you moved to Boston."

My gaze slid back to Aidy where she sat next to a brunette, who had Rosie in her lap. "That's true. Who's she talking to?"

Bridget glanced over. "Emmaline. I assumed you knew her—she and Aidy are close. So, you two aren't friends? What about as kids?"

I shook my head. "There was a five-year age difference. That was huge back then."

Bridget nodded, seeming thoughtful. "Simon and I are about five years apart."

"You met as adults. I think Aidy was in kindergarten when I moved."

"Ah. Well, she's all grown up now," Bridget said with a sunny smile.

I gritted my teeth, wishing Bridget would stop feeding my fixation. My mind flashed back to Aidy's eyes as she darted out of my apartment last week.

"You ready to go?" I asked.

"Sure."

I stayed next to her side through the doorway and into the small lot behind the building. I opened Bridget's door and helped her settle into the passenger seat.

"She's so talented," Bridget gushed when I settled into my seat. "I asked Simon if we could have Aidy come in and help with our remodeling project. We're going to wait until after the wedding, of course, because I don't want the babies breathing in all the dust and stuff, but she's already talked me through a couple of ideas that would really help with the flow of the house."

Even though I enjoyed Bridget's company, I tuned her out, needing to clear my head. Then I helped her from the car and up the steps to her house.

"Want to join us for dinner tonight?"

"I can't. I have a date."

Bridget wrinkled her nose. "Well, if your plans change, you're welcome to stop by. We're having tacos."

"Thanks." I hugged her and waited for her to close the door before I walked toward my car. I turned back when I heard the door open behind me.

"Just thought you'd want to know that I invited Aidy. And Simon invited Sean."

For the second time that morning, I stumbled. Bridget didn't comment but since I nearly planted face-first on the sidewalk, I knew she'd noticed.

Sean near Aidy—no fucking way. He was the other pediatrician in our practice and a couple of years older than me. The clinic staff tittered about his attractiveness, and he was actively looking for a wife, which he hadn't found, in large part because he was always tossing out pickup lines.

I clenched the steering wheel the whole way home.

Chapter Fifteen
Aidy

I happily accepted Bridget's dinner invitation, glad for the opportunity to connect with more people. I hadn't made an effort to
reach out to any of my old friends. At first, I'd been too heartbroken and then too embarrassed by my situation. When I realized
they all knew I was home and hadn't reached out to me, well, that
told me everything I needed to know about the people I'd once
considered my closest confidants.

So far, my circle of female friends included Bridget, her friend
and our yoga instructor Calliope, and Emmaline. Cultivating
a friendship with a mom who already had a kid sounded like a
pleasant experience.

I spent the afternoon building and testing my idea for an
eco-friendly flooring material that could provide a seamless
transition out onto the deck I wanted to cantilever over the inlet.
The problem was the building joists that would support the deck
needed to be double-length inside the building envelope, which
caused issues with the sleek exterior lines the clients preferred. I
managed three different to-scale models and rechecked my math
to ensure the weight loads were within the necessary parameters.
I was leaning toward ceramic wood, which lasted longer than
traditional decking, handled more extreme weather and looked
fantastic, but needed to offer a more conventional option. Finally,

I settled on a solid-oiled teak. I loved the richness of the wood, which would add a nice lushness to the interior and fade to a softly-aged, gray-tinted wood over time, thanks to outdoor exposure to sun and seawater.

I hoped the client would like the ceramic wood option because it would be killer on their deck—plus, the manufacturer I'd contacted said that nearly ninety percent of the material was recycled, which would drastically reduce the home's carbon footprint.

I knocked on the door, tugging at my skirt. The dress crept up, showing more thigh than I remembered, probably because of my expanding belly. I smiled at the attractive blond man who opened the door.

"Aidy," he said. The British accent caused a slight ripple of pleasure over my skin.

I smiled, a little nervous around the very attractive doctor. Our interactions to this point had always been at the yoga studio.

"Nice to see you again, Simon. Thanks for inviting me to dinner."

His return smile was devastating. "Glad to. Just know now that I plan to pick your architect brain."

"Aidy! So glad you could make it," Bridget said, wiping her hands on a towel as she walked out from the kitchen, her smile a beacon of happiness.

Every time I saw her, I had to swallow a groan. How her stomach managed to keep growing defied my imagination. Bridget tipped her head up and accepted the kiss Simon placed on her lips. Well, if my lover and baby daddy looked like Simon—and looked *at* me like Simon looked at Bridget—I'd be euphoric, too. That thought soured my mood, because my last lover hadn't wanted our child or me. And Ryder…no, I wouldn't think about him. Every time I did, embarrassment licked hot over my chest and heated my cheeks.

"Your house is lovely," I said, pulling myself out of my funk.

"We want to stay here so our son Brendan can be with his school friends," Simon said.

"But the place needs updating. I'll show you around," Bridget said.

Simon patted Bridget's bottom as she passed. I smirked. Those two were too cute.

The house was a typical two-story Cape Cod. There were three bedrooms and two baths upstairs in addition to the formal dining room, living room, powder room and kitchen. The intriguing piece was the small apartment off the kitchen.

"Simon rented that from me," Bridget said, her smile growing. "I'd met him before, but the constancy of him around then is what really built our relationship."

"Oh?" I smiled at her dreamy look. "What do you plan to do with it now?"

"That's why I have you here. So we can figure out the best use of space. Going from a family of three to a family of five will push us to the seams in the main home."

I nodded as I walked around the space. "Are you interested in more play space for the kids? Bedrooms? An office?"

"Yes," Bridget said with a laugh. "I don't know if the babies will each want their own room eventually, but I do want Brendan to remain comfortable, and Simon could use some additional space to work. Right now, he uses what was his old bedroom as an office."

I'd noted that, which was why I asked about the office.

"But I do know we have to get this carpet out of here, stat. Every time I walk in here, I sneeze." She shifted her weight, hands going to her belly. She leaned closer to me. "I don't come in here often because sneezing can cause all kinds of leakage."

"Okay. Let me think about some options, but I'd recommend pulling the carpet and putting in bamboo flooring. No matter what you use this space for, the bamboo will offer some cushioning and reduce those allergies you mentioned. Plus, it looks great and is very durable, which allows for great versatility."

"And it's easy to get?" Bridget asked.

"Absolutely. I'll send you the best place as well as the name of my preferred installer."

"Fantastic. Thanks, Aidy," Bridget said, leading me away from the offending carpet—and potential pants-wetting experience.

As we walked back into the kitchen, I heard Simon talking, followed by a laugh—one I knew well. My shoulders tensed as I slowed my pace. Simon, a tall, sandy-hair man and Ryder Mackay stood in the kitchen. I gritted my teeth against my growing annoyance when I saw he'd brought the lovely Margo with him.

Chapter Sixteen
Ryder

Aidy's cool gaze slid over me, reminding me of the distance she'd created between us. When her gaze paused on Margo before shuttering completely, a twinge of discomfort pinged through my chest.

"Ryder!" Bridget said with a smile. "I'm so glad you could make it. And you brought your date. Hello, I'm Bridget."

As Margo introduced herself, Aidy's jaw tensed and she fixed her gaze on Sean. I felt a growl building in my throat. I didn't want Aidy anywhere near Sean.

I shoved off the counter and walked toward her.

I pressed a kiss to Bridget's cheek. "Good to see you," I said to Aidy.

"Yeah, you, too," she responded, her tone dismissive. She glanced around me. "Hello, Margo. Nice to see you again."

That rejection riled me. I wanted to pull her into my embrace and kiss her cheek. I must have leaned in because her breath caught and her eyes flashed up to mine. She scuddled back, her cheeks reddened as her eyes widened.

"You know this lovely lady?" Sean asked, stepping in close enough to Aidy to nudge me out of the way. "Ryder, you must have been cleaning up."

Aidy jerked back from both of us, confusion causing her brow to wrinkle. "What?"

Simon and I groaned. Here it came: the terrible one-liner Sean thought was charming—but *so* wasn't.

"I'm Sean Davenport. And you must be a broom because you've swept me off my feet."

Aidy smiled but it was strained. "Aidy Wright. Ryder's my neighbor," she said, responding to Sean's earlier comment.

"And friend," I said. "How's Rosie?" I asked.

Aidy tucked her hair behind her ear and her pulse leaped in her throat. "Good. That's my new puppy," Aidy added for the rest of the group's benefit. "She's hanging out with Tina Murkowski."

She stated that like I should know who that woman was. But I had no clue. Before I could ask, Aidy said, "Our neighbor down the hall."

I hadn't bothered to meet anyone but Aidy, though I wasn't surprised that Aidy knew most of the people on our floor. She might not be the most outgoing person, but she had an engaging personality and a genuine interest in others that drew people to her.

"Margo, what's new in Boston real estate?" Aidy asked, turning her back on me.

My hands fisted. She really wanted to play *that* game?

Margo raised a narrow eyebrow. "Well, actually, I acquired the Ames building listing this week."

"The one with the Roman arches and carved details over the doors?" Aidy asked, her gaze turning keen.

Margo nodded. "Yes." Margo's smile warmed. "I've never met a nurse interested in buildings."

Aidy blinked. "I'm an architect."

Margo waved her hand. "Much better than nursing, I'm sure."

Bridget's platter clattered on the counter as I winced.

"Dinner's ready," Simon said, shooting me an angry look.

"Nurses are some of the most important people in the medical profession," I said, meeting Bridget's gaze, mine filled with apology.

"Well, I suppose—" Margo began.

"Like Bridget, here," Aidy stepped in, both literally and figuratively, wrapping her arm around Bridget's shoulders. "She's an ER nurse. She single-handedly saved my best friend's life when she was in a car accident a couple of years ago."

"Who's that?" Sean asked.

Margo downed her glass of wine, her cheeks bright pink, her glare at me accusatory. "You could have mentioned she was a nurse," she hissed.

"I didn't know you thought so little about the medical profession," I said. "Seeing how I'm a doctor and all."

We were the last to be seated, which left us at the end of the table, me at the foot while Margo was settled next to Bridget. Simon still appeared miffed, and I was at a loss for how to overcome Margo's unkind comment.

"What's the deal with the Ames building?" Aidy asked from Sean's other side.

"It'll need some extensive internal remodeling for the client I have in mind. I'll contact Rohr and Clement about it Monday. They're the best," Margo said.

"I happen to think the Wright firm creates the most spectacular designs," Bridget said. "Aidy here is in charge of the fabulous new Macintosh Hotel build."

Margo picked up the bottle of wine from the table and refilled her glass to the brim.

The rest of dinner was better, but, for Margo and me, in our first foray into meeting my friends, it was a disaster.

Aidy caught my eye briefly, a flicker of sympathy in her gaze before she turned her attention to Sean, who'd asked her about Rosie. She and Sean launched into an animated conversation about puppies versus human babies, while Margo leaned closer to me.

"We should go soon."

I sighed. No way I was getting out of tonight unscathed. Margo was refined and sophisticated, but she insisted on getting her way. Typically, I was a roll-with-it guy, but I didn't want to leave Aidy here with Sean.

Dammit.

I'd admitted I wanted Aidy, but I'd acted like a fool— I'd been stringing Margo along so that I didn't have to admit to my attraction to Aidy. No, it wasn't Aidy; it was the fact she was pregnant that terrified me.

So, I'd brought Margo here to…what? Make Aidy jealous? She'd already told me she was hurt by my dating Margo. And now Margo was going to be angry with me when I refused to leave. My behavior didn't sit right with me. I'd been wrong—possibly even hurtful to both women.

By the time we'd finished dinner and Sean made four different comments about Aidy's eyes, I couldn't stand the tension his remarks caused in me. I rose, taking all the plates to the kitchen where I set them in the sink. Simon followed with an empty water pitcher.

"I didn't realize you had a thing for her," he said, his voice pitched low enough that we wouldn't be overheard. "Watching your misery almost makes up for your date's rudeness to Bridget in her own home." He scowled. "No, it doesn't."

"You're right. Margo should apologize, and if she doesn't, then I will to Bridget before we leave, which we'll do as soon as I finish these."

I turned on the tap and began to rinse the plates.

"You don't have to do that, mate. We invited you to dinner."

I continued to load the dishwasher. "Considering I'm about to head out, I figured it was the least I could do."

Simon sighed. "For what it's worth, I'm sorry I invited Sean."

I glanced up at him, a smile curving my lips. "And I'm sorry I invited Margo."

"Me, too."

We shared a chuckle.

"He's acting like a wanker," Simon added.

My smile widened. "He always does. Those pickup lines are—"

"Cringey," Simon finished. "Epic bad."

I nodded. "Near as bad as Margo's behavior."

Simon slapped me on the shoulder, letting me know in man-code that I was back in his good graces.

"Well, thanks for washing my dishes. I'll walk you and your date out."

I went back into the dining area long enough to apologize to Bridget, mainly because Margo was blinking blearily and swaying in her chair. She'd polished off the bottle of wine and not touched her taco. I leaned in closer to Bridget.

"I'm really sorry about her," I said.

Bridget smirked. "She's going to wish for my medical knowledge tomorrow morning."

"My aunt used to always say natural consequences were the best ones to learn from."

Bridget pecked my cheek. "Your aunt sounds smart."

"She's a surgeon." I winked at her as she burst into giggles. Good. Bridget wasn't going to stay angry with me either—as long as I didn't bring Margo near her again, which I wouldn't do.

Tonight had been a painful lesson for me but one well-learned. Now, I just needed to get Margo home and inform her I wasn't going to see her again.

I turned to Aidy and Sean. When her gaze met mine, I could have sworn I saw misery swimming in their depths, but I simply gave her a quick nod.

"Give Rosie a good scratch for me," I said. "See you Monday, Sean."

I hefted Margo from her chair and left.

"Did tonight go as badly as I think?" she asked, her voice cool but the words slower, as if she were taking more time to form them.

"Worse. You managed to insult everyone there."

"I was nervous," she snapped. "I didn't know that…that woman would be there."

I gripped the steering wheel. "That woman?"

"Don't play stupid. Your neighbor."

"Her name is Aidy."

"I don't care what her name is." Margo crossed her arms over her chest as her lips drew down in a pout. "She made me—"

"I'm going to stop you right there," I said, my tone cool. "Normally, I find interrupting others quite rude, but no way am I going to let you blame someone else for your bad behavior."

She gasped. "My bad... You think I acted..." she continued to sputter. I really should get her some water, but that meant dragging out my time with her in the car.

Though dread settled in my belly, I continued to drive into Boston. The sight of the city brought a pang to my chest. My aunt and uncle didn't live far from Margo's converted loft. I'd rather visit them, sit at their table and watch them interact than tell Margo I couldn't see her again, but I owed her a face-to-face conversation.

I stared with longing at the exit that would take me to my family's house. Tomorrow, I'd spend the afternoon with my *khaleh* and Tarek—just as I did every year on January 29th. It was my family's least favorite day of the year, but no matter how much we disliked the traditions Zara put in place twenty-plus years ago, we never failed to meet together and follow through on going to the cemetery in Providence. Having my aunt and uncle's support was the only way I could get through the trauma that started with my baby sister's death.

I skimmed over my mother's death, as I always did. Zara had asked me once, after I completed my pre-med degree, if I'd blocked my ability to feel anything where she was concerned. I hadn't known what to say then and I still didn't now. Margo stared out of the side window, her silence stony.

I managed to find a parking spot within a block of Margo's place. She walked in front of me, and I noted her line was straight and she didn't wobble in her heels. Maybe she wouldn't be hungover in the morning.

She opened her door and tossed her keys into her bag and dropped her bag by the door before she kicked off her heels. I hadn't realized the little touches in Aidy's place that kept her organized until I watched Margo's haphazard strewing of her belongings. I bit back a snort as I remembered Nico's insistence that Aidy was impulsive and flighty. If he would just see the woman I did…

Margo turned to face me.

"Would you like a drink?" she asked.

"No, thanks," I said. "Maybe you shouldn't…"

"I really should."

I slid my hands into my pockets. "If I could—"

She opened a bottle of red and pulled down a wine glass from her chic, all-in-one countertop bar. "You really can't, Ryder. I'm not interested in a man who thinks about another woman while he's on a date with me. And I'm *definitely* not interested in a man who takes me to a party because that other woman is there."

I shoved my fingers through my hair. "You're right. I messed up."

The wine glugged into the glass, and I swallowed back a suggestion for her to drink a glass of water. Margo was an adult. But I did need to ask, "Are you going to remember this conversation tomorrow?"

"Yes. And it's going to sting then, too."

"Fine."

She shrugged as she headed to her couch, tucking one of her

long legs beneath her and lifting her wine glass. She didn't bother to tug down her skirt, which had ridden up, but I studiously avoided looking. She raised her eyebrows in a "get on with it" look. Her normally soft pink lips were puckered in frustration. The contrast to her normal serene exterior made me wonder if I really knew Margo.

I decided I didn't, and that had been just fine with me. The sex had been fine.

I wanted more than *fine*.

I wanted a connection. Like the one I'd started to build with Aidy.

Margo sipped her wine, the ruby color flowing down the side of the large bell as she set it back on her coffee table. Margo was a stickler for the proper glass, just as she was particular about punctuality and keeping promises. It's one of the details that first attracted me to her.

She settled back against the cushions, her gaze vaguely polite. Underneath, her eyes simmered with frustration. I sucked in a breath.

"I can't see you again," I said.

"I agree. This isn't working. I need a man who understands how important my time is—to me and to my business."

"What's that supposed to mean?" I asked, affronted even though I told myself not to rise to her bait.

"It means I'm not interested in being second in a relationship."

The longer I stared at her, the more I realized she'd never been unflappable; she'd been disengaged and disinterested in *my* life and *my* career. She'd liked the power couple persona we exuded as long as I made concessions to work my schedule around her needs.

She'd find another man. Either one to match her in her business or one who was more than willing to let her take the lead. Either way, that wasn't me.

She took another long drink of her wine.

"Well, then, I guess us parting is for the best," I said.

She rose from the couch and walked to the door. She opened it and met my gaze with her own brown one, her eyes as cool as always.

"Bye, Ryder."

For the first time in weeks, my neck and shoulders eased.

"Bye, Margo."

Chapter Seventeen
Aidy

Sean leaned in closer and said, "Your eyes are so bright, they must have been stars stolen from the sky."

I managed, barely, not to roll my eyes. He seemed to be waiting for a response. My not eye-rolling was my response.

When Ryder left, I gripped the edge of my chair so hard my fingertips went numb. Bridget seemed troubled throughout the meal, her mouth tightening when Simon and Ryder disappeared into the kitchen. I assumed she didn't want to be left in here with Margo, but the other woman simply stared into the distance, rolling her wine glass between her soft hands topped in a French manicure.

Bridget inhaled sharply and looked down, catching my white-knuckled fingers, and her gaze softened. She tossed me a soft smile before she asked if we wanted dessert. Much as I craved solitude, I'd enjoyed Bridget and Simon's company, and it wasn't their fault Ryder was an ass and his girlfriend an even bigger one.

I liked spending time with them—they were warm with their affection, and Simon had a wicked sense of humor. Sean... not so much.

As soon as everyone finished eating their tres leches cake, which I barely tasted, I insisted on helping Simon with the dessert dishes. I noted Bridget looked less than pleased sitting in the living room with Sean.

"Thanks for your help," Simon said, wiping his hands on a dishtowel.

"No problem. I don't mind doing dishes." Well, I did with a burning passion, but I wasn't going to tell Simon that because he'd invited me to dinner. But more importantly, dish-duty kept me from spending more time with Sean. I might crack a tooth if I had to hear one more bad pickup line.

"May I ask you something?" Simon asked.

I nodded, already bracing myself for the question about Ryder.

"Ryder mentioned he knew your family. When did he live nearby?"

My shoulders eased away from my ears. Oh. That was much easier to answer than the weird tension I felt like Ryder and I wafted whenever we were near each other.

"He lived two houses down when we were in elementary school."

"So you knew his parents?"

I met Simon's gaze. "I was five when he moved. I don't really remember him at all."

"Pity," Simon muttered.

I tilted my head to the side. "Why?"

Simon shook his head. "There's something there, in how he treats the babies. I wondered if…" He shook his head. "Never mind. We all have our reasons for what we do."

I fiddled with the side of my skirt, unsure what to tell Simon. "He had a rough go," I said, my tone soft. I'd always known

Ryder's history—my family would talk about him like a long lost relation for years after he moved. But since I'd gotten to know him, since I was pregnant myself, I wanted to hug him tight. But he wasn't mine.

"Figured," Simon said. "Bridget thinks he needs adopting."

I smiled. "He just might."

Simon gazed at me speculatively. "And you're not up for the job?"

"I'm not Margo," I replied, my tone stiff. Cue my bad mood and the reason I'd put up with the pickup lines throughout dinner.

Simon's eyes remained clear and steadfast when he said. "No. I think you could be more. You'd be his friend."

I steadied myself on the counter. "We are friends," I said, my voice soft.

"Are you?" Simon asked. He peered around the corner into the dining room. "I need to rescue Bridget." He grimaced. "I had no idea Sean knew *that* many bad lines."

When we returned to the dining room, Sean rose and said he planned to head out.

"Want me to walk you to your car, Aidy? You can give me your number on the way."

Simon's words ricocheted through my head. *You'd be his friend.* A piercing pain slammed into my chest. I wanted to be more than just Ryder's friend, which was why I was avoiding him. More importantly, I *didn't* desire Sean, and if I couldn't have the man I wanted, then I wasn't willing to settle. Not ever again.

I shook my head. "I'm not ready to date or even hang out. I'm still dealing with the fallout from my ex," I blurted.

Why would Sean ask me in front of Simon and Bridget? I must have given off vibes that I was interested. My face burned with mortification.

Why did these types of situations have to be so awkward?

"I'm…I'm sorry," I whispered as I met Simon's knowing gaze. I hoped he understood who I was apologizing to—and why.

Because I wasn't thinking about Jeff or Sean. My mind fixated on Ryder. I'd been so aware of him during dinner. Each of his scowls when Sean paid attention to me caused a faint thrill in my chest.

Was that mean spirited? Maybe. No, probably. But *I* wasn't the one who'd brought a date, and I was just going to have to continue to ignore him until my attraction dissipated.

Unfortunately, that didn't seem likely, no matter what my brain told my heart.

Chapter Eighteen
Ryder

I woke to the trilling of my phone. I grabbed at where it should be on my nightstand, missed and groaned again as I forced my eyes opened and searched for the offending noisemaker. I jerked upright as the time registered: after ten.

Shit! I couldn't be late today. I fumbled for my phone, cursing as my head bumped my nightstand, nearly oversetting the lamp.

This situation was all Aidy's fault, I decided. Sleep eluded me for hours because I'd arrived home late last night, and no light showed under Aidy's door. I worried she was still with Sean.

I'd stood at Aidy's door, stewing until I heard the faint sound of Rosie's paws on the hardwoods. If Rosie were home, then so was Aidy. The fact that no one spoke gave me hope Sean wasn't in there with her but didn't keep images of the two of them together from plaguing me for hours.

My phone stopped ringing just as my fingers brushed over the surface. I picked it up and put it to my ear.

"Hello?"

"Ryder! Are you ill? I knocked on your door but you never answered."

"Sorry, *Khaleh*. I'm so sorry! I never heard the door."

"No worries, *azizam*. I just wanted to make sure you're okay. Your lovely neighbor, Aidy, and I are making a quiche."

"Aidy? Quiche?" My brain struggled to orient around the words.

"Yes, she'd just arrived home as we were knocking and invited us over for coffee," Aunt Zara said. "And the sweet girl had all these delicious items from the farmers market, and I told her how you liked quiche, and now we're making one."

I scrubbed my hand over my face as a strange noise trickled from my throat.

"But the smell of eggs upset her," I murmured.

"What?" Zara asked.

Aidy hadn't left because of the eggs. She'd left because she'd been hurt, feeling like I'd strung her along. Why was all this so much clearer *now*? I'd needed this information last week.

"Uh…"

"Why don't you take a shower? We're about to pop the quiche in the oven, so you have a while before we're going to eat." Zara lowered her voice. "And that gives me more time to talk with Aidy." She switched to Farsi and added, "She is the sweetest young woman!"

Part of me wanted to nip out my aunt's joy but the rest of me needed a long, hot shower and time to assimilate the upcoming trek to the cemetery.

"See you in a few minutes."

"Great! And bring a pot of coffee," Zara said. "Aidy only has decaf, and I'll get a headache if I drink that."

I smiled. She was such a surgeon. We'd practically lived on coffee and vending machine candy bars while I worked at the hospital. Good to know not much had changed.

I said goodbye and tossed my phone on my rumpled sheets. I stood, stretched and groaned as my muscles protested. I headed into the bathroom, hoping the hot water would perk me up.

No such luck. My eyes ached and my steps lagged as I dressed and made the pot of coffee. I collected my wallet, keys, and phone, then made my bed before the coffee pot burbled to a stop. I decided to carry the carafe over because it was easier than balancing three mugs.

The laughter filtering through the door surprised me. I knocked, hard and fast, in the spurt of threes I preferred as the urgency to separate Aidy from my aunt growing with each passing second.

"Ryder!" Zara smiled as she threw out her arms. I just managed to move the coffee pot before I was wrapped in a big hug.

I sighed out some of my confusion and frustration into my *khaleh*'s hair as I held her with my free arm.

"Good to see you," I said.

She pulled back enough to cup my cheeks in her palm. They were soft but rough at the same time—those doctor hands that required constant scrubbing. "I missed you, *azizam*," she said, her voice solemn.

When she said that, she reminded me of my mother. I clutched her hand, needing a moment to breathe through the pain of that loss. If Mamma had survived, my life would have been so different. Family meant everything to Samirah Hadid, just as it did to her older sister, Zara.

I'd been lucky in ways many of the kids in the system weren't. My *khaleh* wanted me and was willing to upend her life to create a home for me. Still, the transition into her life had confused me, not just because my aunt had a different last name, but because, while secularized, she still adhered to the family's Persian roots. I'd struggled for months with the traditions I didn't understand, having been wholly indoctrinated into my father's American culture. Daman Mackay had no patience for my mom's heritage, which, as I'd learned after living with my aunt, caused friction between my parents.

My mother hadn't expected to get married, which was why she'd accepted Daman's proposal. That had caused a rift between the sisters; Zara had wanted Samirah to marry a man supportive of her Persian history.

Aunt Zara's eyes took in the dark, painful shadows this day always brought forth, and I swallowed down my own emotions.

Tarek stood behind, a steadying presence, just as he'd always been. He and my aunt met when she went to his firm to get financial advice and set me up a college fund.

He'd asked her and me on their first date. I'd been an absolute shit, not interested in sharing my aunt's attention. But Tarek was kind and thoughtful, and he'd won us both over within a few weeks.

Now, I couldn't imagine my life without him—didn't want to. He was a good man. One of the best. And I'd often wished he was my biological dad, not Daman Mackay.

"So, you've made friends with my neighbor, huh?"

Zara perked up. "She's an absolute doll," she whispered, again in Farsi. "So is that puppy. My goodness! We should have gotten you a dog." Contrition flitted across her face.

"I didn't need a dog."

My uncle Tarek grabbed the pot of coffee from my hand, patting my shoulder as he stole my caffeine. I took a few steps into Aidy's apartment, intent on getting back my much-needed coffee, but Zara stopped me with a hand on my arm.

"I *really* like her, Ryder," she said.

Her eyes were intent on mine.

"I'm glad. Aidy's great." I choked on the words—not because I didn't believe them but because the situation between her and I remained uncertain. To cover my nervousness, I squatted to greet Rosie, whose eyes closed in bliss at my soft pats.

"She's had a difficult time and yet she's flourishing. That tells me she's tough and motivated. Plus, even pregnant, she's a total babe."

I choked. "Wh-what did you say?"

Zara rolled her eyes. "She's gorgeous. So, don't mess this up by being your normal standoffish self. Even if you're just friends, she'll make you a good one."

Great. My *khaleh* was Team Aidy. Not that I expected any less. Aidy managed to enchant people with minimal effort. Well, not Margo, but then I wasn't sure Margo could be charmed.

"And did you see her models? She built them yesterday, she said. For a renovation project. I'd never seen that material before but now I want to extend our deck to create an outdoor summer room. That ceramic wood would be perfect. Aidy said that it's supposed to be better than the super-decking material that's advertised on TV."

I glanced over at the three models lined up on Aidy's sideboard. She brought home plans often, but I hadn't seen her create small-scale models before. Her attention to each element impressed me, and I picked one up, noting the details both to the beams that cantilevered the deck, making the overhang more visually appealing and the glass-sided half walls that would reduce strong winter winds.

"Quiche is ready," Aidy said. She met my gaze for a fleeting second. "Hey, Ryder."

I held up the model. "This is amazing."

"We'll see if the client agrees when I meet with them on Monday," she said as she disappeared behind the counter. A moment later she reappeared with a large, steaming pan. The aroma wafting from it caused my mouth to water.

"Aidy knew you hated black olives so we left those out, but it is a to-die-for quiche Provençal," Aunt Zara gushed.

My favorite. I loved the mix of tomatoes and feta in the soft, fluffy egg. Tarek handed me a mug filled with coffee and the other to Zara. We both sipped, though I felt Zara and Tarek's eyes on me.

So far, minus my late start, the day seemed pretty good. I had one of my favorite meals, hot, delicious coffee, and the people I cared about most in the world together in one room.

I paused, the coffee halfway to my mouth as I realized what I'd just thought. My aunt and uncle, sure. But…Aidy?

She smiled at me as she handed out the quiche, and I finally stopped lying to myself. Yes, *Aidy.*

Chapter Nineteen
Aidy

Ryder remained quiet throughout the meal, his gaze focused on his plate. He ate but not with the gusto he had during our previous shared meals, and the longer we sat together, his aunt chattering about her work, the worse I felt about my stunt at the party. If Ryder cared for Margo, then I shouldn't give him hell about that.

Ryder's aunt and uncle insisted they clean up. Once they cleared the table and moved into the kitchen, I leaned in toward him.

"I'm sorry." I kept my voice quiet.

His gaze rose to mine, and I bit back a gasp at the pain swirling there. No way *that* could be my fault.

"I'm not sure what you're apologizing for, but don't worry about it," he said.

"For ignoring you this past week. For embarrassing myself at your place. For sitting next to Sean last night."

"You deserved every bad pickup line you had to listen to," he said. But there was no heat behind his words. He seemed… drained.

"Ryder, I'm concerned. What's going on?" I rested my hand on his forearm just above his wrist. Warmth spread into my palm and tingles shot up my arm. I cursed my stupid body for not feeling this level of tingle for Jeff. And I'd planned to marry him.

"My *khaleh* didn't tell you why they're here?"

"What does 'khaleh' mean? And was she speaking Arabic earlier?"

"Farsi."

"You speak it, too?"

At his nod, I crossed my arms over my chest and huffed. "How come you haven't spoken it to me?"

Confusion flitted over his face. "Why would I? Do you know any words?"

"Because that would be…" I managed to bite my tongue at the last second. *Hot.* That would be so hot to hear Ryder whisper love words in the musical language.

"Be what?"

I shook my head. "I assumed your family was here to see you," I said, changing the subject. "And you didn't get in until late, and I worried you were upset with me, so I invited them here. I hope I didn't make the situation worse."

He stared at me for a long moment, taking in my chapped lower lip and the worry I couldn't hide. His aunt and uncle laughed at something and dishes clinked.

"I was pissed last night, mainly at Margo," he said. "And I treated you poorly before. I'm sorry about that. I should have been honest with you from the beginning about my relationship with Margo."

That sounded…ominous. Like a brush off.

I squeezed his arm. "We're friends."

He raised an eyebrow and his lips shifted like he wanted to say something. Instead, he lifted his hand to his mug, effectively removing my palm from his skin. I frowned.

"Okay, *friend*. Are you going to see Sean again?"

My stomach clenched at his emphasis. I wanted to search his eyes but he dropped his gaze to his coffee mug like it held secret wonders.

"I didn't give him my number, and I don't want to, no."

Because of these stupid tingles I had for Ryder even if he were dating another woman. No point in me saying so and making our current conversation a repeat of the other morning. Heat crept up my face. I wasn't sure I'd ever live that down.

I'd just have to continue to avoid him…at least when he was with Margo.

Ryder picked up my clenched fist and tucked his palm against mine. "I'm glad. I would have needed to resist the urge to punch Sean, and the guy's nice."

Shock waves rippled through me—both because of the touch but also because of Ryder's words. He'd just basically told me he'd be jealous of his colleague. But that didn't make sense.

"Except for his pickup lines," I said, trying to lighten the mood. "Those were a deal-breaker."

"Oh?" Ryder raised his eyebrows. "So I shouldn't ask you if it's hot in here or just you?"

Heat crept up my cheeks. Dammit. When Ryder said that to me, I wanted to squirm.

Thankfully, the kitchen faucet turned off and Ryder's aunt and uncle returned to the dining area.

"Are you ready?" Zara asked.

Ryder's complexion paled as he firmed his lips. "As I'll ever be.

Let's do this."

Adrenaline sizzled through me, but I stayed quiet, unsure of how to interpret the dynamics between the three of them.

Zara turned toward me, her gaze sweeping down to touch on where my hand was joined with Ryder's. Her eyes lightened as they rose to mine, and she smiled.

"Thank you, my dear, for such an unexpected pleasure this morning. Going to the cemetery is always a challenge, but you made this anniversary much more bearable."

Anniversary? Cemetery?

I smiled at Zara, but my lips felt numb. Was this about Ryder's mom and little sister?

My hand settled over my belly in a protective gesture, as if my touch would keep the baby inside me safe. Zara's eyes filled with tears.

"Well," she said, grabbing her purse from the bench by the door. "We should head out. Thank you for a lovely morning, Aidy. I'd love your recipe."

"Of course," I said. Ryder rose to follow, but I scrambled after him. "Could I talk to you for a minute?"

He glanced at his aunt and uncle before nodding.

"We'll meet you in the car," Zara said.

I squeezed my fingers together. "Are you...are you okay?"

More guilt settled over my shoulders as I realized I'd been so wrapped up in my little drama over my feelings for Ryder, I'd never asked him about his broken family.

"Not really. But we do this every year. To honor Molly."

"M-Molly?"

Ryder's face crumpled, appearing more haggard. "My baby sister. This was the day she…this should have been her birthday," he said. "But it's also the day she died."

"Oh my God." I swayed on my feet but still managed to wrap my arms around him before he finished the sentence. My own baby took that moment to wake and stretch. Ryder chuckled, placing his palms on my belly.

He knelt down and pressed his cheek to the side of my abdomen, speaking too softly for me to hear the words. Then he looked up, his eyes bright.

"Come with me."

"What?"

"To the cemetery. We only stay long enough to clear Molly's grave and change out her flowers. My mother's, too."

He rubbed his palm over my stomach each time Lilia kicked, but his gaze stayed on mine.

"I've hated the entire winter season, even the holidays, since Molly and my mother died. This is always a hard time of year for us, but you've made it bearable. You've made my aunt laugh today."

"I…" My thoughts scattered.

But going to visit his baby sister and mother…that felt intimate.

"I…"

Ryder's large, warm palm caressed my belly in soothing circles. His eyes pleaded. He understood loss, just as I did. It had ripped his family apart, as it had mine.

"*Please.*"

Chapter Twenty
Ryder

I sat next to Aidy in the backseat of my uncle's Mercedes SUV, as uncomfortable as I'd been when he drove Tina Jin and me to the movies for my first-ever date when I was fourteen.

Aidy seemed to read my unrest, and she gripped my hand in hers, resting them both on her leggings-clad thigh as we pulled through the cemetery's gates. I hated this place. Not for what it was—for what it represented. Within a week, I went from the excitement of meeting my baby sister to the pain of losing first her, then my mother. My father couldn't cope with the grief, and I turned fearful and bitter. For the first time in my life, I lashed out. Six months later, my father dropped me on my mom's sister's porch and drove away.

But all the bad things in my life started with the loss of Molly. I'd been so excited to have a sibling—more excited than my parents. I'd already planned out the daily schedule so that I could feed her at least twice. In my nine-year-old head, I'd built this fantasy where I'd get to read to her and teach her how to climb trees and fly a kite. I'd had a whole laundry list of fun things a big brother should teach his little sister.

I clutched Aidy's hand tighter as the SUV rocked to a stop.

We unbuckled in silence and exited the car. Zara and Tarek led the way to the grave, the two of them bending toward each other. I continued to clasp Aidy's hand like it was a lifeline. Because it was.

I touched the carved headstone that was bigger than Molly ever managed to be. Molly Parissa Mackay. I slid my fingertips over the word on the plaque my aunt added fifteen years ago. The words were in Farsi, not English. I traced the letters: *Maliheh*. It meant beautiful. My mother went along with the name Molly to appease my father, but she sometimes called Molly "Maliheh."

I hadn't understood at the time, of course, but when I was older, Zara explained that my mother struggled with fertility, and Molly had been a late-in-life baby. That put them both at a higher risk. A risk that ultimately caused their deaths.

Aidy stood behind me, face pale as she took in the tiny grave. My aunt had purchased large bouquets, just as she did every year, and I'd brought something of my own, as I did each visit. I'd found a Rhode Island quarter with Molly's birth year on it. I squatted down in front of the marker and pressed the quarter into the soft grass. "That's for you. I figured we'd buy a gumball with it when you were big enough. I can't believe you'd be twenty-one today. Way past gumballs."

Aidy shifted, both her palms pressed to her belly. I wanted to take her in my arms but, at the same time, I wished I hadn't given in to the rash decision to invite her.

"What about your mom?" Aidy whispered.

I pointed to the plot next to Molly but didn't go over. Zara had moved there. She spoke before she nestled a pretty bouquet of tulips against the grave marker.

"What about your parents?" I asked.

Aidy jerked a little. She licked her lower lip, a trait I'd noticed when she was nervous. "Their bodies weren't found."

"That's rough," I said. At least I could come and touch some permanent marker related to the sister I never even got to hold.

Zara finished fussing at my mother's grave and rose to her feet, Tarek offering his arm.

"I could use a drink," she said. The tip of her nose was bright red as were her eyes, but she managed a smile as she took my uncle's hand and they walked back toward the vehicle. I ushered Aidy in front of me, but she stopped after two steps.

"Can I…" She cleared her throat and her lashes fluttered toward her cheeks. "Would you mind if I said something to Molly?"

"Sure."

Aidy stepped gingerly to the graveside. She ran her palm over the smooth granite and squatted down, causing the soft-boiled wool sweater she'd worn to ride up her trim thighs. I stepped back so that she could have some privacy but, thanks to the breeze, her words carried.

"You're very lucky he was your big brother," she said. "I know what I'm talking about because I have two of them, and I'm not sure either would visit my grave often, let alone bring me presents. I hope my daughter is half as blessed with the men in her life. You were and are so loved. I hope you can see that."

I shoved my hands into my pockets, fisting them as I rocked back on my heels.

"And…and, well, if you can, would you help me watch over my daughter? I'm terrified of giving birth, but I think I'm even more scared about raising her. Maybe, with your help, we can make sure she has all the opportunities we both wanted. I won't forget you, Molly. I promise."

Aidy rose with a grunt and headed toward me as I pondered her comments.

It felt natural—right—to wrap my arm around her shoulders and brush tendrils of her hair from her cheek. It felt even better to have her with me, in my place, while my aunt fussed over the photo albums that contained our family's only link to Molly. But when Aidy excused herself to spend time on her thesis, I decided to give her space.

Because I needed time to think about what my relationship with her was—and what I wanted it to be.

Chapter Twenty-One
Aidy

I spent the afternoon working on my thesis and finalizing next week's schedule on The Mac Hotel with the contractors. At six, I rose and headed into my kitchen, Rosie at my heels. I used to be a day-to-day shopper, preferring to go into the store and see what struck my fancy. But with my increased workload and subsequent exhaustion, I'd found the hours spent feeling up produce wasteful, so I'd been trying to purchase food in large enough quantities to minimize my trips to the store to once per week. I opened my fridge and wrinkled my nose.

I had food, but I didn't want any of it. This was why I used to shop daily. I'd never managed to stick to a list or to a food schedule. By the time I brought the food home and put it in my fridge, I no longer found half of it appetizing.

"Maybe you'll like kale," I said, looking over my shoulder at Rosie. She plopped her butt down and wagged her tail.

"Yeah, probably not."

A knock on my door jolted me out of my zoned-out fridge staring and I meandered to answer it, shushing Rosie's mad little barks, all the while hoping the food in my fridge would magically morph into something tasty.

"Nico," I said, gripping my door. "What brings you here?"

His shoulders rounded forward. He wore a cable knit sweater

under his Peacoat and dark dress slacks. Clearly, my brother knew how to relax on a Saturday.

"I'd like to talk."

I opened my door wide enough for him to enter. He strode in but hesitated at the sight of my dog. Rosie showed her manners and sat for him, and he surprised me by picking her up and carrying her to the couch. He settled her into his lap and Rosie sighed with contentment.

I also hesitated before I shut my door. My knees wobbled a bit.

"If this is about The Mac, I'll re-work the sub-contractors, but I don't—"

Nico continued his long, slow strokes down Rosie's side. "No. You're doing a good job there."

My eyes widened. I licked my lower lip and winced at the rough skin. "Um, do you want a drink?"

He smirked. "Got any Scotch?"

I shook my head. "No reason to cause temptation." I pointed at my belly.

"I'm fine." He muttered something else under his breath that I couldn't catch.

I sidled over to my chair and settled on the edge. "What's up?"

Nico rubbed Rosie's ears in an absent-minded fashion. His gaze seemed far away.

"You wanted a dog."

I sent him a questioning look.

"When you were little. You always wanted a dog."

"I did." What did that have to do with Nico's surprise visit?

"You're good with her. She's healthy. Happy."

"I like to think so."

His frown deepened but he looked more upset, his eyes shadowed. "I was angry."

I needed a moment to gather my thoughts. We were doing *this,* right now. And Nico held my snuggle-giver. "At me?"

He squeezed his eyelids tight. "No. That our parents disappeared and stuck me with you." He winced, his expression pained. "But at you, too. If you'd been six months older, I wouldn't have had to move back to Providence and take over Dad's firm. It could have been sold or something."

I frowned. "Why didn't you ask me to move to Manhattan?"

Nico's shoulders drooped. "I couldn't. I'd been living with a woman in a one-bedroom apartment."

"Oh."

Clearly, I didn't know enough about my brother.

He met my gaze, his hazy. "I'd planned to marry her, but then, it all went to shit."

That was pain swirling in his eyes. Guilt caused me to settle hard into my chair. "I'm sorry I was the cause of your breakup."

He barked out a laugh. "You weren't. She decided to steal my renderings to move up in the company—after she accused me of sexual misconduct."

My eyes widened. "What the… Where is she?" I rose from my seat, jaw tense. "What's her name? She and I are going to have words."

Nico settled back against the couch, a smirk forming. Rosie scrambled up his chest and licked his chin. "You sure do get feisty."

"I'm pissed," I snapped. "No woman should falsely accuse a man of sexual…"

"Harassment. Later, after I was fired and had no choice but to stick it out here in Providence, a few other men came forward to show she'd used the same tactic on them. By then I'd invested the money from the sale of our parents' house into fixing the company's cash flow and was able to hire Knox. We were profitable, and, thanks to a lot of sweat equity, we became sought after."

"I had no idea about any of that," I said, sinking back down into my chair once again.

"I didn't want you to know about Amanda." Nico picked at a nonexistent fuzz on his pants. "I was embarrassed and angry."

I leaned in and covered his hand with mine. "And hurt."

He met my gaze and nodded.

"She sounds like as much of a peach as my ex," I muttered.

With this information, I was finally able to understand Nico's aggravation with the situation—which I'd thought was me. He'd been heartbroken and grieving, not just our parents, but his whole life—and the loss of his girlfriend.

"I started thinking about it—the similarities." He gestured between us. "And how impatient I was for you to put yourself back together. It's taken me years to get over Amanda. Why should you need any less time?"

Possibly because of one sexy neighbor, but I kept that thought to myself.

"You, coming home in September started opening my eyes. But that frustrated me all over again. I'd gotten over Amanda—so

I thought—and I didn't want to dissect my feelings. I didn't want to *have* feelings."

I sighed. "I'm sorry."

Nico stopped petting Rosie and she jumped out of his lap, wandering back toward the kitchen. "Not as sorry as I am. I was a terrible big brother, then. I should have realized you were acting out because of the pain, the grief. Not because you wanted to further punish me and ruin my life."

I compressed my lips against the onslaught of emotion. Today had proven eye-opening in many ways. "I was scared and angry. And stupid." I squeezed my eyes shut as shame burned over my skin. "*So* stupid. You were right to call me impetuous."

"You were also only seventeen. I should have insisted you spend more time in therapy or asked more questions. Something. Anything except wallow in my own stinking shit."

I sighed as something in my chest resettled into place—something that had shaken loose when the police came to my house to tell me they'd found my parents' capsized sailboat. "We've had a bumpy go."

Nico sat forward, linking his hands between his knees. "We have."

"So dad was in debt?" I asked.

"Massive debt, Aidy. *Massive.*"

My jaw dropped.

"He'd leveraged the house and the business after some of his projects fell through." Nico's lips thinned. "I had to sell the house to get the firm through the year. That's after I dumped all my savings into it."

"I had no idea," I whispered.

"I didn't want you to know. At first, I thought you weren't old enough."

At my exasperated look, he smirked. "Until today."

"I hope I'm an asset to the firm, Nico, but if I'm not, you can tell me. I'll look for another position—"

"You'll do no such thing." His smile broadened and a look of satisfaction slid over his face. "Thanks to The Mac Hotel deal that you are running so well, we've had multiple inquiries for boutique hotels. Even a couple of restaurants. They all have big budgets. I mean Manhattan-sized budgets."

"But it's taken this long to get the firm into financial solvency?" I asked.

Nico shook his head. "We started making a profit the year Knox came to work for Wright. We definitely had enough, but the past eighteen months has seen us move to a whole new level. So, don't worry about the money. It's there."

"Okay. But, seriously, if…"

He placed his hands on my shoulders. "You're an asset to the firm, Aidy. We're lucky to have you."

I blinked back tears. "Thank you."

He stood. "I know we need to talk more. And we will. But…" He rubbed his hand on the back of his neck. "Can we do it another time? I'm not used to…"

He hadn't even taken off his coat.

I rose as I nodded. "Can I give you a hug?" I asked.

He wrapped me in his arms, and I squeezed my eyes shut, hugging him back. He smelled of the same soap he had when we were kids. I inhaled the scent—my eyes misting a little.

"What the hell?" Nico stepped back, eyes wide.

"That's the baby." I took his hand and placed it on my belly.

His wide-eyed gaze met mine and his smile warmed with pure joy. "That's amazing. She's strong."

I winked. "Like her mama."

Nico's smile softened. "Just like her mama."

He removed his hand, cleared his throat, and strode toward the door. "See you Monday, Aidalynn."

I rolled my eyes but couldn't keep the grin from breaking across my lips. "See you then, Boss Man."

His chuckle remained in the air even after he'd shut the door.

I hugged myself, happier than I'd been in months.

A knock sounded a moment later, and I flung open the door, expecting Nico to be there, wanting to talk more.

"Ryder," I exclaimed, taking a small step back. He'd changed into a white Henley with black sleeves and his feet were shoeless, encased in gray wool socks.

"What are you doing here?"

"I thought we could eat at my place. As a thank you for your hospitality toward my family earlier. And…" He shoved his hands in his jean pockets and rocked back on his heels. A faint flush topped his cheekbones as he mumbled toward the floor, "I don't want to be alone."

I wanted to say no because we'd had an emotional day. I needed space from him—space to regain my equilibrium—but his honesty tugged at my heartstrings and I couldn't help but agree.

"Let me grab my keys. Is there anything else I need?"

"Rosie."

I collected her leash and pulled my door shut, making sure it was locked. "I need to take her downstairs for a potty break."

"Do your brothers or a friend have a key to your place?" he asked.

I frowned. "Why?"

"Well, if you get incapacitated or need medical attention, if someone close by had a key it's better than the EMTs having to bust down your door."

I dropped my hands to cradle my belly. "Oh. I hadn't thought of that." I gnawed on my inner cheek. "If I gave you one, you'd only use it for emergencies?"

He turned a sly glance in my direction. "Why? Are you worried I'll interrupt your naked time?"

Well, I was *now*. Not that I spent that much time wandering my apartment nude. Just semi-nude in as few clothes as possible. During the last week, my body temperature seemed to have gone up ten degrees, and I felt like I was mired in the tropics in the middle of summer. And that was before my skin became overly sensitive and my libido kicked in, causing clothes to make me even hornier.

My face must have shown some of my thoughts because Ryder's eyes widened. He cleared his throat, his gaze dropping to my larger-than-usual breasts before wandering lower, clearly trying to make out my shape under the long black tunic and fleece-lined yoga leggings. My weekly yoga kept my legs and arms toned, but there was no way to miss my growing bump. Not that I wanted him to—my impending motherhood brought me as much joy as it did trepidation.

As soon as we hit the patch of grass outside, Rosie did her business, which allowed me a moment to regain my poise.

"Just for emergencies," he rasped.

The husky quality in his voice caused me to shiver.

"I'll think about it," I said, knowing I'd hand him my extra key tonight. No way was I having my door busted open. Plus, on some level, I liked the idea of Ryder thinking about me in my apartment, the taboo woman next door.

That seemed much better than the sad single mom, so I decided to stick with my original fantasy.

"Nico left right before you stopped by," I said.

"I saw him," Ryder said. "It's part of why I stopped by. I wanted to make sure you were okay."

Oh. Well. That was sweet.

We headed back upstairs. Just before the elevator door opened to our floor, I leaned in and pressed my lips to his cheek. "Thanks."

He cleared his throat, his gaze dropping to my lips. He inhaled through his nose before turning on his heel. He strolled down the hall toward his place. He opened the door and walked straight into his kitchen, which mirrored mine. My mind automatically started to assess his space. It suited him, but the before mentioned dark, overstuffed furniture also lacked inspiration. He needed an area rug and a coffee table. Maybe a table behind his couch to help delineate between his entry and main living space.

Oh, stop me now.

I was designing his home,

I pressed my lips together, holding in the feel of his skin a moment longer as I removed Rosie's leash.

"What's for dinner?" I asked.

"How do you feel about falafel?" he asked.

I smacked my lips as I stepped into the space and washed my hands. "I have a longstanding love affair with falafel."

He smirked. "Really?"

"I lived in Houston. One of my favorite places to eat was an Iranian restaurant."

He raised an eyebrow. "You're serious?"

"I adore kibbeh and dolmeh."

He grinned wide even as he shook his head. "*Khaleh* is going to love hearing that. We're Persian," he added.

"Persian?"

"Iranian. My family left the country back in the seventies during the revolution, but my aunt insists we call it Persia because that's what her father called it."

Clearly, I needed to read up on Iranian history.

His gaze dropped to my lips and the easy teasing between us turned hotter. Awareness crackled. I tensed.

Ryder was seeing a woman. I was the convenient, *pregnant* neighbor. There was no way the man wanted me when he could continue to bone the beautiful brunette. Her ass and mine were no longer in the same ballpark, let alone zip code.

I dropped into the chair at the bar, feeling deflated. "What does *khaleh* mean? You never told me this morning."

"Aunt," he said.

Just as Ryder accepted my change in topic, I let go of the obvious chemistry building between us.

"Were Zara and Tarek feeling okay when they left?"

"As well as can be expected. Zara helped me make this masterpiece we're about to devour."

I smiled. "Smells delicious. And I already know your aunt makes a mean quiche."

Ryder chuckled. "She said you made it."

I waved my hand. "I'll tell you what I told her—the important part is that I get to eat it."

He grabbed plates and then proceeded to dish up the falafel and pita. He added a healthy dose of hummus and a large helping of green salad.

Ryder settled into the seat next to mine and I was thankful we were at his bar so that I didn't have to look at his gorgeous features and try to concentrate on keeping my face devoid of my awareness.

"I do love salad."

"I know."

"Salads are healthy," I defended.

"So is tofu or brewer's yeast, but you wouldn't make a meal out of it."

I wrinkled my nose and dug into the flavorful dish in front of me.

"That's why I have you," I mumbled around the bite. I swallowed. "To be my food police. Because this," I pointed my fork at my plate, "this is delicious, and I want more."

He offered a long-suffering sigh. "It's a tough job but someone has to deal with you. I guess I can be your food pusher."

I chuckled. "That's a worse term than food police, but probably more accurate."

"Want to watch a show after dinner?" he asked.

I dropped my gaze to my plate. "I don't think that's a good idea. But thank you for dinner."

I smiled as I gathered up my plate, even though Ryder wasn't finished eating. He was dating Margo. Ryder seemed to be attracted to me, which I liked but couldn't act on.

I rose, walked to the kitchen, and set the half-eaten meal on the counter next to the sink. "I'll see you around."

"Aidy, wait."

I blinked back tears. I was disappointed that Ryder would hang out with me while with another woman. I didn't want him to be anything like Jeff. Perhaps I'd built Ryder up into something more than he was.

He rose, coming to stand between me and the door.

"I broke up with Margo because I can't stop thinking about you."

"What did you say?"

I stared up at him, trying to process his rushed words. He shoved his hands into his pockets and rocked back on his heels. He looked both bashful and hopeful. Something bright answered in my chest.

"I broke up with Margo because I can't stop thinking about you," he said. He pulled his hands free and cradled my cheekbones with his thumbs.

"But—"

"We ended the relationship after you broke in and stole my bread and licked me all over with your gaze."

"I did not," I gasped.

"Oh, yes, you did." His gaze burned into mine. He inched closer. "That look—*so* hot."

"She was with you at dinner last night."

"Because I'm an idiot. But I stopped thinking about her the moment I first saw you. And I should have broken up with her then—or when you were here that morning for breakfast…and I definitely had to stop seeing her after she was horrible to you and Bridget."

I remained rigid against him, every muscle vibrating with tension. His thumbs slid down to the corner of my mouth. I startled. I needed to say something. My tongue peeked out. Ryder's breath changed. I met his gaze, which had heated further. My body softened, inched closer to his.

"I don't understand." Not about Margo. I got that he broke up with her. I didn't understand why he was telling me he had or what he wanted from me now. If he wanted to fundamentally change our relationship. Pursue something romantic.

Shut that train of thought down, Aidy. Shut it down.

I wiggled from his embrace. "I thought…I thought I was lusting after a man in a relationship. Do you have *any idea* how that made me feel?"

"I'll tell you." I jabbed my finger into his chest. "Jeff cheated on me. I found out after…"

Never mind what it was after. "That made me feel stupid, blind, and like I wasn't enough. Then you…" I pressed my eyes closed. "Then I met you and you were nice, and I felt like we clicked. I didn't know about Margo right away, and I started to think…" I shook my head.

"You've messed with my head, Ryder. I don't know if it was intentional or not, but I struggled because I wanted you, and you were with another woman, and that put me in the position of hurting Margo. Don't you see that?"

I studied his eyes, which had darkened as I spoke. With my words, his body tightened as if he were pulling into himself.

"I'm sorry, Aidy. I didn't realize how you felt."

I reached forward, clasped his wrist. A shiver of awareness drifted up my arm, zinging down into my core. "I know. That's why I'm telling you." I straightened. "New Aidy is proactive, mature."

His lips tugged up. "She sure is."

My smile grew at his compliment. "And New Aidy has responsibilities. She's trying damn hard to make sure she makes the right choices."

He tilted his head. "You know it's weird you talk about yourself in the third person, right?"

I shrugged. "What you need to understand is this isn't just me anymore. I'm a mother...almost a mother. And I need to make good decisions for my baby. I'm all she has."

Again, Ryder seemed to pull inward. What about me having a child caused him to do so? He worked with kids, infants. I puzzled over that but left it for now.

"Just, do me a favor, okay? Think about what you want. Please. Because I care about you, Ryder." I rose up on my tiptoes and brushed my lips across his cheek. "Which means this, between us, could be great. Or it could really hurt."

Chapter Twenty-Two
Ryder

Simon and I went to lunch the following Tuesday while I was still mulling over Aidy's parting comment. We ended up at a seafood restaurant with a view of the bay. I ordered the lobster bisque, thinking of Aidy as I did so.

I settled back in the broad, leather chair and sighed. I hadn't seen her since the night I asked her over for dinner. She was giving me space, which I needed but didn't want. I'd broken up with Margo because I wanted to be with Aidy. But she was having a baby, and babies died, and I wasn't sure I could watch Aidy suffer from that loss…and my head remained jumbled, uncertain, while the rest of me was unhappy.

"I wanted to tell you again how sorry I am for Margo's behavior…" I began.

Simon shook his head and I trailed off.

"That's on her, not you, and you already apologized. So, Bridget has a guy installing new bamboo floors this afternoon," Simon said. "They were Aidy's idea. She said if we turned the space into a nursery and playroom, the floors would offer more give than traditional hardwood and be easier to clean. While farther away from our room than I wanted, I have to admit, turning the apartment into the girls' space is smart. We can eventually partition it off into their own rooms and they'll share a bathroom, leaving Brendan with his own." He grinned. "Aidy has great vision."

"She does. And most of the materials she uses are eco-friendly. Her thesis is all about these materials."

"Thesis, huh? How's that going?"

I shrugged. "We haven't talked in a few days. But last she told me, she was about halfway through it."

"What does Margo think about you spending so much time with your neighbor?" he asked.

Right to the point. That's why I liked Simon so much. Aidy did the same thing. And…I was back to thinking about her. Not that I ever stopped, really.

"We broke up."

He raised his eyebrows. "After you came to dinner at our place?"

"Right after. No way I was going to be with a woman who insulted my friends."

He stared at me for a long moment before returning his attention to his lunch.

"What?" I asked.

He crunched one of his fries. "I can understand the initial attraction. Margo's attractive. She's also cold and calculating."

"You met her once and you know all that?"

"Yep. But her bigger problem is she's got a skinny arse and hard eyes."

I chuckled as I dug into my lunch because Simon wasn't wrong. The bisque was light and flavorful. I dipped in a chunk of crusty bread. Damn, that was good.

"You shouldn't trust a woman whose bum is nonexistent. Or looks like a boy's."

"Please, continue with your sage advice, Dr. Hogue."

He shook his head. After a long sip of water, where he watched me with those miss-nothing blue eyes, he asked, "What happens if Aidy's ex shows up?"

I leaned back, pushing away my mostly-empty bowl. My earlier hunger dissipated with Simon's questions—and the concerns they brought forth. "What do you mean?"

"I mean, the man has rights to the baby. He and Aidy have history."

"How do you handle the situation with Bridget's former husband?" Ben had died a few years before Simon moved in with Bridget. But his death had caused them a lot of problems, nearly destroying their relationship before it really began.

"With Brendan, I need to tread carefully. I can't try to take Ben's place. Even if Ben was an epic wanker."

"So is Aidy's ex. He's not going to pop back into her life."

Simon, who had gone all British and ordered fish and chips, dragged a fry through his ketchup.

"I wouldn't be too sure." He met my gaze. "The past has a way of rearing its ugly head."

I wiped my hands on my napkin and tossed it next to my bowl.

"What's with you, man? Why all doom and gloom?"

"I've seen how you look at Aidy," he said.

"Oh? How's that?"

"Like she fascinates you—like she's all you see."

I stared down at the remnants of my soup, needing a moment

to catch my breath. Aidy *did* fascinate me. Probably too much.

"I care about her."

"And I care about you," Simon said, leaning forward. "Which is why I'm butting in with my manly arse, putting it square where it doesn't belong, and telling you to tread easy. Bridget and I agree, Aidy's in an emotionally tenuous place. She stated as much when Sean asked for her number the other night."

I gripped the edge of the table to keep from popping him in the mouth. Simon was my *friend*. Not that he was acting much like one at the moment.

"I'm…annoyed you said that about her."

"You're flat-out raging at me, and you should be. I'm overstepping." Simon leaned in, forearms on the table. "I like Aidy. A lot. She's funny and smart. Kind eyes." He paused, and I knew he was thinking about her ass, but he kept that thought to himself. "But she's also about to be a new mother, and there is *nothing* that rocks your world like parenthood."

"And you speak from experience," I sniped. First he drops this emotional BS on me and then he might as well of come right out and said that he's looked at my—*Aidy's* ass.

"I may not be Brendan's biological father, but I *am* his father now and, yes, it changes relationships."

"Duly noted," I said, my tone dry.

Chapter Twenty-Three
Aidy

I settled onto my couch, thankful I'd been able to talk my brothers into hiring my new yoga bestie, Emmaline. With her starting soon, I wouldn't have to worry as much about the company, which let me focus on other…things.

Hmm, maybe hiring Emmaline wasn't as good of an idea as I'd thought. I picked up my book and began to read. This was an indulgence I hadn't been able to enjoy in years, thanks to late nights from classes and my thesis. But now, now that I'd *completed* my paper earlier tonight—pending my advisor's comments, of course—I could carve out some time for my guiltiest of pleasures: sci-fi romances.

I'd fallen into the space world when someone, probably Ryder, knocked on my door. A glance at my clock caused surprise to ripple through me. It was nine-thirty. Nope. Nothing good happened this time of night. Sure, sexy, wonderful, naked things happened, which I'd just been reading about, but not *good* things.

Mainly because I had to press pause on my sex life, which I'd been obsessing about with horrifying frequency ever since I'd caught Ryder in his tight boxer-briefs.

Fantasies of Ryder in his underwear that morning I had barged in his apartment for food had only been the beginning. Over the past few days, my body seemed to rev up at even the faintest hint of something sexual. I'd read libido overdrive was a common occurrence during the second trimester, but I was officially in my third. My hormones didn't seem to care about the date, though.

After I ogled the delivery driver's butt in his tight brown pants as he settled packages next to our secretary's desk, I'd figured something must be wrong with me. But that was nothing—*nothing*—compared with the throb in my sex when I'd stared at Ryder's taut behind under his blue cotton scrubs just that morning. I'd never seen him in those before, and my desire told me I'd gone too long without an orgasm. So, I rectified the situation—with Ryder starring in my fantasy that caused me to come so hard I saw stars.

That was a first for me. I'd always considered sex…nice.

But that Ryder-driven orgasm ripped through me and took no prisoners, leaving my body limp and so satiated, I slept hard for nine hours.

While the great night's sleep and languid feeling the next morning made me want a repeat, Ryder's role in my fantasies left me feeling guilty and ashamed. I had no right sexualizing him. But once I did, within moments of that release, I wanted another.

It was only after surreptitious and carefully-worded online searches that I'd begun to realize my raging libido was normal—not my fixation on Ryder. That was still wrong. So very, very wrong.

But the need for sex? The thickening of my blood, and the desire to be filled up? The way my nipples rubbed against the padding of my bra? Apparently all normal during pregnancy. I was a hormonal hot mess, and each day my raging need worsened.

That's why I'd taken to reading erotica, hoping a book boy-friend would give me the same release as Ryder. So, time to focus on the hot, tall alien with a big dick.

"Aidy, I need to talk to you."

I grunted, removing my hand from my shorts. My face flushed. I was a serious perv. The ache between my legs strengthened and pulsed. I scowled at the door, scowled at Ryder's voice, scowled at the world I lived in that made the man of my fantasies continue to annoy me, especially when I'd been so close to relieving the problem.

"I'm busy," I called back. "Working on my thesis."

Such a lie. I shoved my Kindle behind my couch's cushion, as if hiding it there would make my near-orgasm wither.

"Bridget had the babies," he said.

"What?" I squealed. I jumped off the couch and rushed toward the front door. "They're all healthy right?" I asked.

He nodded, beaming. "Two beautiful little girls."

"Yes," I yelled as I threw myself into his arms. "I'm so excited. I can't wait to meet them."

His arms wrapped more firmly around me, tugging me closer to his body. Rosie ran around us, barking. She was too cute.

Before I could try to focus on my puppy, my body softened against Ryder and my mind drifted back to his mostly naked body I'd seen that morning I'd stolen his food. And with that image, my core heated, my thighs clenched. I stumbled back.

"Yeah, so. Wonderful. I'll…I'll stop by tomorrow. Which hospital?" I tucked my hair back behind my ear, trying to regain some level of poise. My body ached for him. *Ached.* My nipples thrummed with the need for him to touch them.

He tilted his head to the side. "Are you okay?"

I waved a hand. "Fine." My voice sounded choked. I tugged at my shirt and sat back down on my couch, plopping my computer into my lap. I sat back against my e-reader, hoping I'd turned it off. I had, hadn't I? No time to look.

I willed the lust swirling through me to go away.

It would. After I got rid of Ryder and finished what I'd started.

"Are you upset with me?" he asked.

"Nope. Everything's cool."

Except for my body. It burned. For him.

Stupid body. I was hotter now than I'd been reading about two dragon warriors taking their fated mate. I'd chosen that story because all the reviews said it was smoking hot.

"I haven't seen you in three days."

"You didn't want to see me a couple of days ago," I reminded him.

Ryder scowled. "That's because Simon…Never mind. I got over it. Why haven't you been answering my calls or when I knock?"

"I've been busy," I said. My tone was short, cross.

"I've been at the hotel site most of each day and then finishing up renderings on the interiors for three other projects. And I need to complete my thesis. It's coming along."

I winced at my word choice. Could anything I said not be taken sexually right now? Maybe he didn't catch it. I lifted my gaze and drank him in, from his disheveled hair—I'd come to learn that the neat style of the morning was always wrecked by afternoon because he couldn't keep his fingers out of it—to his rolled-up shirtsleeves that showed off impressive forearms.

I closed my eyes and covered them with my own arm, hoping that blocking out the sight of my personal porn-star would alleviate the ache between my thighs. No such luck.

The situation escalated when he gently tugged my arm away. Zips of heat traveled down my arms, caressing my aching breasts and warming my core.

"Are you having Braxton-Hicks? Are you hurt? Is it the baby?"

"I'm fine," I pouted. "You don't need to wait on me."

Don't leave. Don't leave. Please touch me so I can come.

"You're flushed. Do you need some water?"

"I *need* to finish my paper." No, I didn't. But it was a good excuse, and I was grasping because I wasn't gasping. Hell. I was in So. Much. Trouble.

Ryder headed into the kitchen, opening my fridge and bending down to pull out one of the cans of sparkling water.

Of course, bending over like that gave me an up-close and personal view of Ryder's taut posterior in his dress slacks. The thin material pulled tauter as he reached forward and I bit back a groan, trying not to imagine myself sinking my teeth into the firm muscle there.

I lost.

Worse, he heard me.

Double worse, he came back to the couch, where I could smell the faint hint of his body wash or aftershave. Whatever it was, my pheromones were in love and wanted more. The pulse between my legs turned to an all-out throb—the one I'd almost worked through before he knocked.

"Thanks," I managed to say.

"What's wrong, Aidy? You're clearly out of sorts."

"Nothing." If only that were true. "It's getting late. I should get to bed."

"You are not fine," he grumbled.

My daughter woke and started dancing as if she, too, were happy Ryder was here. The little traitor. I wouldn't *be* in this position if she weren't whacking out my hormones.

After two attempts to rise, I managed to haul myself upright and I started down my hallway.

"Where are you going?" he asked.

"Bathroom."

I slammed the bathroom door. I dropped my forehead to my hands and tried to breathe. Oh, God. I was a flaming inferno of desire. How could I get him out of my house? Maybe I didn't need to. I'd masturbate in here. I dropped my head to the door, trying to remember the scene I'd been reading before Ryder interrupted.

I slipped my hand under the waistband of my pants and over my rounded belly. At the first flick of my fingers over my sensitized clit, I groaned. I slammed the back of my other hand against my mouth, but, like a damn bloodhound, Ryder heard me.

"Aidy? What's wrong? Seriously, I'm worried. Do you need to go to the hospital?"

And because I was pregnant and horny, I flung open the door and yelled, "I need to orgasm."

I was too worked up from the brief moment of stimulation to control the words flying from my mouth. I sagged against the door frame, my face flaming, my body even hotter.

"I'm like a fourteen-year-old boy all of a sudden. It's all I can think about and…" My jaw dropped open. "Are you *laughing* at me?"

He rearranged his features, but hilarity still lit his gaze. "Uh, no. Because that would…that would be wrong."

He leaned down, toward me, holding my gaze, making my pulse pound and my clit throb. "I can help you with that."

"*No!*"

He blinked at my fierce denial.

"Why not?"

"I saw your last girlfriend, Ryder." I waved my hands at myself. "And I do *not* look like her."

His eyes softened. "You look gorgeous. I've been drooling over your ass for weeks."

I clamped my lips together, my willpower weakening at the hungry glint in his eyes. But…but…there's no way he could want me over Margo. I managed to shake my head again.

"I'm not talking to you about this anymore." My shoulders sagged, and I fought back the tears that seemed to well up between one blink and the next. "I'm mortified and turned on, and I didn't even know those emotions could coexist."

Ryder took a step closer and placed his palm near my head. He leaned in and nuzzled my ear, then down my neck. I jumped when he pressed a kiss to the side of my throat, working his way back up to my jaw. I turned my head on instinct, unable to think about anything other than having his lips on mine.

He didn't disappoint. In fact, he was an even better kisser than fantasy-Ryder, and *that* guy had been a fucking maestro.

But real-life Ryder kissed me with both gentleness and passion. The juxtaposition between the softness of his lips and the rough need barely restrained caused my heart rate to speed up and I whimpered, trying to get closer.

He kept his palm planted on my wall while the other made its lazy way from my rib cage, over my waist, to my hip. He gripped my thigh and raised my leg so that his thick erection lined up against my hot, needy center. I moaned, hating the wool of his dress pants that kept me from feeling him against me—from having him fill me.

"I don't think you need to worry about my desire for you," he whispered against my ear. He pressed himself against me, and I gasped, grinding back in an effort to get more friction.

"But this isn't about me," he said in a voice that sent shivers of pleasure down my spine. "It's about you."

He slid his big hand up the back of my thigh to my waist. Before I could process what he was doing, his hand was inside my leggings and panties and his fingers were delving between my damp curls. I kept myself well-manicured down there, but, as my pregnancy progressed I'd become too sensitive to handle waxing.

I tried to pull back, embarrassed, even as my body betrayed me, and I rubbed myself with shameless abandon against the pads of his fingers.

"You weren't kidding," he said. He sounded choked. "You're *really* wet."

I whimpered as he slid two fingers inside me. His thumb hit my clit and he pressed against the sensitive nub in a delicious, slow circle. I rose on my tiptoes, trying to absorb the sensation, trying to process that Ryder was touching me.

"Shh. I have you," he crooned. He wrapped his free arm around me, his hand splayed over my butt cheek, his warm breath drifting over my neck. My breathing sped up as I gripped his biceps and rolled my hips.

"Please. Please, please, please."

"You want more of this, Aidy?" He pulled his fingers from my hot center before pushing them back in. That felt criminally good.

"Y-yes."

"Or do you want this?" He pressed harder with his thumb against my clit as he massaged my sensitive flesh. I couldn't respond because pleasure curled along my spine, expanding.

"What do you need, sweetness?"

"Both," I gasped. "All of it."

His smile was wicked, and his eyes gleamed with such heat, my breath stuttered. Then his mouth was on mine. I tried to arch my hips, but Ryder kept me still, working my body like he'd known it for years. My skin prickled with heat and my mouth fell open as my head thumped against the wall. He dropped soft kisses along the column of my throat.

I clung to his forearms as the orgasm ripped through me, a powerful force that would have knocked me from my feet if I weren't secure in Ryder's arms. I shook and convulsed around his fingers. Finally, spent I managed to open my dazed eyes and meet his.

He leaned his forehead against mine.

"That was the hottest moment I've ever experienced," he murmured.

My body sang as pleasure drifted through my limbs, thrumming from my core.

"Can we do it again?" I asked.

Chapter Twenty-Four
Ryder

I pressed my throbbing erection against her soft thigh. "You better believe we're doing that again. I love how you break apart in my arms."

I slid my fingers out of her wet heat, biting back a groan. Much as I wanted to sink my aching dick into her welcoming warmth, we weren't ready for that yet. I closed my eyes and inhaled, trying to get control over my raging need.

I should ask her what she wanted, how this would change our relationship. I took her mouth instead.

I slanted my head and deepened the kiss as she opened for me. Her tongue dueled with mine, rubbing and touching as she made soft noises. I fucking *adored* her vocalizations.

I pressed her back against the wall, my hands sliding up from her hips to capture her breasts. They heaved and my palms itched to pluck her tight little nipples poking through her bra and shirt. I kneaded her skin. She dropped her hand to my zipper and it hissed downward one soft click at a time.

When her warm hand cupped me through the thin layer of my underwear, my eyes crossed. I yanked her closer, kissing her harder. She slid her hands under the elastic of my boxer briefs and gripped my rigid flesh. I canted my hips forward into her silky fist, letting her stroke my whole length.

I gritted my teeth and held my breath as she rubbed her fingertip across the slit at the top. I groaned, lost in sensation. I pulled back a little, and her hand loosened. I pressed forward and she pumped her hand down my length. She maneuvered to get her other hand between us, and she cupped my balls, rolling them against her palm.

My spine began to tingle, and my hips thrust into her warm hand. She whimpered as I pumped again, my teeth clamping on her ear.

"You have to stop," I said.

"Why?"

Another pump.

Heat coiled in my gut.

"Because I'm going to come."

"Hard?" she asked. Her tone was breathy.

I panted, staving off my release.

"Aidy, you don't have to—"

"I do. I want to feel *you* come apart in *my* arms."

She squeezed me as pleasure arrowed into my cock. I spurted all over her hand, quaking. My knees weakened, and I slammed my free hand against the wall so I didn't lose my balance and hurt either of us.

"Fuck. *Fuck.* That feels so good."

I took her mouth as I continued to come. The intensity of my initial release eased. I looked down into her bright, big eyes and my chest went light, easy. I caressed her cheek before dropping another, softer kiss on her swollen lips.

She looked down at my softening dick and took in the wetness on her arm and my dress pants. "Oops."

"Definitely *not* an oops," I said. My voice felt scratchy, but my body was sated, my muscles loose and easy. "I'd say we both needed that."

She turned her head and those gorgeous bottle-green eyes met mine. She looked into one eye, then the other.

"But you just broke up with your girlfriend." She frowned, clearly not liking the idea of me with another woman. Not that I blamed her. I hated the idea of Aidy with another man. After seeing her with Sean…I shuddered. Nope. I couldn't. This passion was *ours*. And we'd see it to the end.

I shoved my dick back in my boxers, wincing at the wetness on the cotton. I zipped my pants though I'd much prefer to shuck them completely. We needed a bed next time we were together. And nakedness. I had so much of her to explore.

Her lips were still plump and pink from my kisses and her cheeks flushed from the earth-shattering orgasm I gave her. Her hair fell in a thick cloud of waves, framing her face and over her shoulders, tumbling to her heaving breasts.

Fucking hell. She was gorgeous.

"I didn't want to complicate our relationship with sex."

Definitely not the right thing for me to say. Her back stiffened and she turned to march back down the hall. She whirled, hands fisted at her sides. "How can we be…" she paused, considering. "How can we be *friends* if I can't trust you to tell me the truth?"

I stepped closer and slid my hands up her arms to her shoulders. I leaned in, watching her pupils dilate as I did so.

"I will *always* tell you the truth. But there will be some topics I don't want to discuss. Fair enough?"

She rested her forehead on my collarbone. "I'm not sure."

"What would make you sure?"

"You being honest with me." She stepped away from me and began tugging on her hair. I bit back a whimper as she tucked it away in some kind of bun. I wanted my fingers in the silky mass *right now* as I pumped into her soft, giving body…

She scowled. "You know my ex-fiancé left me the moment I told him I was pregnant. You have to realize I have trust issues."

Her mouth pulled together in a tight pinch. There was more to the story than him walking out the door when she told him about the baby. Much as I wanted to push for more information, I didn't because I hadn't been forthcoming about my past.

"I'm not ready to try another committed relationship, Ryder, but I do deserve your respect and your honesty. If you can't give me those, please leave now."

Her shadowed eyes gave her away. Well, that and the pulse in her neck that always seemed to beat faster and harder when I was around. Her voice was neutral as was the rest of her face, but her eyes seemed to bleed emotion as her pulse fluttered.

I shuffled closer, needing to stem the emotion in her eyes and reassure her as best as I could. I wasn't sure just why Aidy brought out all these turbulent emotions in me, but she did. And right now, I felt…tenderness, which was a new and scary emotion.

I pulled her into my arms as I took a breath and offered her what I could.

"Margo and I broke up after the dinner at Simon's. The

whole time I've known you, I haven't been able to stop thinking about you."

"I'm not sure that makes me feel better."

"Then, how about this? I was so jealous of you giving Sean your attention that I considered stealing his stethoscope or jumping him in the parking lot."

She chuckled even as she readjusted her length to snuggle in closer to me, and contentment slid into me, soft and sweet—like stepping into a warm bath.

"I wasn't ever interested in Sean."

"Not even when he asked you about love at first sight?"

She snorted. "Did you hear the next line? 'Not sure? I could walk past you again.'"

I chuckled. "That's so bad."

I felt her lips curve against my chest. "Don't make me laugh. I wasn't kidding when I said I have teen-boy hormones raging through my body. Laughing makes it worse."

Warmth tumbled through me. I liked Aidy like this—soft, teasing. I wanted more time with her. I was beginning to think I'd always want more with her.

"Does that mean I get to touch you again soon? Have you touch me?"

She hummed while I waited, content to hold her. "I'll think about it."

"You do that." I pressed a kiss to her temple. "I'll take Rosie outside."

Her smile warmed my chest. If someone had told me last year I'd be walking a puppy that wasn't mine, desperate to get back to a woman pregnant with another man's child, I would have laughed in their face. I'd learned the hard way not to get attached.

Yet, here I was, loving every second of this life I'd never dreamed I'd wanted.

The ding of the elevator caused me to turn, heart already racing with joy, a smile curving my lips to greet Aidy. I hadn't seen her yesterday, and I was desperate to hold her in my arms again.

She didn't step out. Instead, a tall, lithe male walked toward me. He was about my age—making him a few years older than Aidy—with sandy blond hair and amber eyes. His rangy build screamed athlete and he ambled forward like a man used to getting his way. He smiled when he saw me.

"Hey," he said before he turned to face Aidy's door. He studied it for a moment and then lifted his hand to knock.

"Who are you?" I asked.

He turned toward me, brows pinching together at both my rude question and aggressive tone. I couldn't help it. I didn't like him standing there, at Aidy's door. I didn't want her answering it, and I definitely didn't want her letting this guy into her place.

And I didn't like that I didn't like that. Sure, I'd given her an orgasm and she'd reciprocated, but we hadn't left our situation with a clear understanding.

So, no, I didn't want another man encroaching on my...

Shit.

I didn't know what we were, which left me little control over the situation. But that didn't mean I didn't care about her, about us, together, deeply. Because I did. I wanted an us. I'd never wanted a relationship this badly.

I looked forward to seeing her smile, the way it lit up her whole face. I liked the way she threw her head back when she laughed. I adored how excited she was when she discussed eco-friendly materials and the health and environmental benefits of them. I enjoyed how she tipped her head when she listened to me talk about my day. I loved the way her long hair shifted over my neck when she rested against me. How she smelled, the softness of her breasts, the faint snore in the back of her throat when she was exhausted…

Everything about Aidy appealed to me, drew me in. I was falling for her, had been for a while. So, the longer I stared at the blond dude, the more jealousy ate at my insides.

The elevator dinged again. Both the blond guy and I turned to face it. Aidy was laughing at something Knox said, and the two of them continued to grin at each other. She exited the car, her gaze bouncing off me as her lips curved upward further, her eyes alight, before widening when they landed on the man standing nearby.

"Jeff."

My scowl had to match Knox's. But I doubted her brother could hate the guy more than I did.

Aidy stopped in the middle of the hallway. Knox stepped closer to her.

"What are you doing here?" she asked.

"I came to see you," Jeff said with a smile. A dimple flashed. Aidy seemed flustered. Knox scowled. I'm pretty sure I did, too.

"Oh, well. Um…why?"

Jeff glanced at Knox, then at me. "Can we talk?"

She patted her hair, a gesture I'd come to realize meant she was nervous.

"I'm taking her to dinner," Knox said. His tone was deeper than usual, his stance wider, more aggressive. "We're celebrating the completion of her thesis, which means she's done with Houston and you. So you need to leave. Lose this address while you're at it."

"You finished your thesis?" I asked. "That's great."

Aidy turned to grin at me, and, for a moment, it was wide and happy.

Jeff broadened his stance. "I need to talk to *my* fiancée."

"Ex," I rumbled, joining the fray even though I could tell Aidy was getting irritated with all the posturing. Knox shot me a chin lift, letting me know he appreciated me putting Jeff in his place.

"You'll have to change your plans," Jeff said. "Aids and I have things to discuss." He glanced over at me, then at Knox, and with each breath he seemed more nervous, as if unprepared to take on both Knox and me. Good.

"I don't think so," Aidy said, regaining her composure. "If you'd wanted to ensure I was free for a conversation, you could have called. Or texted…or, I don't know, not abandoned me months ago."

"Do you really want to do this in the hall?" Jeff's gaze darted around.

"I can't imagine inviting you into *my* home," Aidy said.

Score for her. It was Knox—the soft fucker—who messed up the situation, giving Jeff an unneeded leg up.

"I'll hang out with Ryder while you explain to him that he's a shit and you never want to see him again," Knox said. He walked over and clapped my rock-hard shoulder. "Which will happen in the hallway."

Aidy's lips compressed in a tight line as she glared at Knox. Her gaze met mine and emotions swirled before she turned that glare onto Jeff.

I opened my door, pocketing my keys. Knox stopped on the threshold and faced Jeff. "You have ten minutes. Then, I'm taking my pregnant sister to dinner. And you are *not* invited."

Knox walked into my place, and I had to hide my smirk of satisfaction at Knox's parting shot.

"You okay?" I asked.

Aidy clutched her briefcase in a tight hold. Without thinking, I edged in closer and slid it from her shoulder. She let me take it. She glanced up at me, her eyes wide and filled with regrets. Why? Did she regret Jeff being here? Or me witnessing this discussion?

She licked her lips and nodded.

"Are you fucking him?" Jeff asked as I stepped into my place. I left the door open, wanting to hear Aidy's reply.

"You're involved with her," Knox said.

Dammit. He was messing up my ability to hear Aidy's response.

"No man tries to kill another with just his eyes unless he's involved," Knox said. "And you…you're dating that real estate woman in Boston."

I ran my fingers through my hair. "Nope. Haven't been for a while."

Knox shoved me. Hard. "That's my sister," he said.

"I know," I snapped.

During our years of friendship, Knox and I wrestled; we'd even punched each other over a turtle we'd found in a pond—I'd won that fight and the turtle—but I'd never felt the same kind of aggression roll off him before.

"She's *pregnant*, dude! Aidy needs a man in her life who doesn't do casual relationships, like yours with that real estate chick, and she doesn't deserve the emotional chain-yank like that…that…Jeff out there."

"*I'm* a fucker and *he's* Jeff?" I asked. I clenched my jaw shut, trying to hold in my frustration.

"Yes, you fucker, because you *know* Aidy's special, and there's no way she's dumb enough to let Jeff back into her life."

Because I needed a moment to process, I walked over to my fridge and pulled out two micro-brews. But I couldn't squelch the feeling I might be losing the most important relationship of my life. Perhaps because of that, and the fact my heart slammed into my chest, I pushed out the next words.

"What if I *really* cared about Aidy?"

Knox froze with his beer bottle an inch from his lips. He set it down and stared at me, gaze probing. "She's a few weeks from having a kid, man. That changes things—relational dynamics. You know that better than I do."

Yeah. And Aidy being a single mom, the likelihood of her dealing with postpartum depression went up.

"She's not in a good place to start something, especially not with a guy who can't imagine sharing her Thanksgiving table more than once."

I squinted, picturing myself at a table laden with a holiday meal. Aidy and I sat across from each other, as we had at her table, eating quiche the day we went to the cemetery with my aunt and uncle. We laughed, happiness brightening our expressions, which softened when we looked at each other. The baby slept, tucked in my arm.

I could picture another holiday scene, this one when Aidy's daughter was older, looking up at me with bright, happy, bottle-green eyes. More and more scenes flashed past me, making my breath quicken and my heart race.

"What if I can? What if I can see the two of us together years into the future?" I licked my lips. "And we're happy."

Knox punched me hard in the arm. Hard enough to pull my mind out of my visions. I blinked at him, slightly disoriented, missing the warmth that even now faded from my chest.

"I better be at those holidays, fucker, or you are *not* happy."

"Yeah…yeah, you were there. Carving some roast."

Knox slugged back his bottle of beer. He set it on the counter with a soft *ah* and then smacked me hard on my shoulder. Dammit. He was in a violent mood or he'd played hockey for too many years. So had I—with Knox during those early years. My dreams to play on the same NHL team with him faded the moment the doctor told us there was nothing more he could do to save Molly.

That's when I created my new dream—to go to med school and save kids' lives.

"All right," he said. "But only if you *really* see this as a long-term thing, Ryder."

He punched into the heart of the situation. At least this time, it was figurative, but this emotional wallop hurt more—as he'd intended it to.

I got it. If Molly was alive, I'd be just as protective. More so, probably.

Chapter Twenty-Five
Aidy

"Are you serious right now?" I asked. My tone was low, and it felt snarly. I liked it.

I crossed my arms over my chest and stepped back, needing as much distance and physical barrier between Jeff and me as possible.

"I have a right to know if you're—"

"You gave up *any* right to know *anything* about me the moment you walked out on me." I drew myself up and glared.

"I had to go to my job, Aidy. You know, the one that pays for my nice apartment that you used to live in."

I narrowed my eyes at his sarcasm.

"And your job kept you out of phone range for six months? It kept you so busy you couldn't call, text, send an email?

He scrubbed his hand over his face. "I *was* busy. Those fires in Australia—"

"Have been out for months."

"I had to get home, go through some training…" He trailed off and he looked to the ground.

"And the woman you were sucking face with in Brisbane?"

He swallowed hard but didn't say anything.

"What about the photos of your fire crew with those women in California four months ago? Or the ones in Wyoming the month after that? The ones in Nevada? There are probably more, but I've quit looking."

"How did you…"

I smiled but it was cold. "Because you never wanted me to know about *that* page? Your sister knew."

His lip curled and he cursed.

"My sister?" Jeff shifted. "I… Look, that's all over—"

"By my count, there were *seven* other women you kissed, fondled, and, according to your sister, had sex with while I wore your ring."

"Now, you're counting?" he snapped back. "It has nothing to do with us, Aids. You're having my kid."

I straightened my spine. "Your lack of faithfulness has everything to do with us. And the fact that you're here now, questioning my relationship status, really pisses me off."

"You're pregnant with my child."

"No. I'm pregnant with my child. *Mine*." I stabbed my finger at my chest.

My shoulders sagged. I'd been such a naive fool to have fallen for Jeff's attention, for his sweet words and clearly practiced seduction. Worse, until I met Ryder, I hadn't realized what was missing from a relationship—like communication. Caring.

"I thought I was in love with you," I said, shocked by my complete blindness. "You were so thoughtful when we started dating. I really thought that would last—that I'd be happy *married* to you."

"Yeah, I did, too."

I narrowed my eyes. "And you planned to continue to bed women wherever you were that month?"

He stood taller, bracing his arms wider. "Sex is a basic function, and it's not like I can turn off the desire just because I'm in a different state or country—"

My jaw clenched so tight, I hoped I didn't crack a tooth. "Then, I guess you answered your rude question to me."

He frowned. "You're not a man. It's different for you."

"I'd be very, very careful with what you say next," I warned.

His jaw clicked in that stubborn way of his that told me he was about to dig in his heels. "I have a right to know what you're doing to my baby."

I drew myself up. "I've talked to a lawyer, and she said you don't. Especially since you didn't bother to show up for six months but did leave the note stating you wanted me out of your place. She said it's as good as a renunciation of your rights."

The note, which I'd memorized, was now in my lawyer's file.

Gotta meet up with my crew. I thought I wanted to be with you, but I'm not ready to be a father. I want to make sure you're okay, so I left you some cash if you need it—you know, in case you realize being a parent isn't right for you, either. We both get to choose here, and this is my choice. I hope you make the right one for you.

Jeff

I forced myself to meet his gaze. "I'm having a girl."

At Jeff's widened eyes, I continued, "Yeah, a daughter. She's going to want to do dance classes and to play with dolls and dress-up and have her hair braided and…" I hadn't liked any of those things but I kept up my litany of little girl activities, hoping to prove my point to Jeff—that he didn't actually want to be involved with a female child, just to continue to have some hold over her and me.

Jeff's face paled and his Adam's apple bobbed.

"I…I…a girl?" He swallowed again, his face turning green. "You can't just cut me out of the kid's life."

"My daughter's life. She's a person," I said. I was tired. Why wouldn't he just leave? I was starting something with Ryder—something rich and mature and beautiful. But Jeff's appearance could very well mess up my nascent romance with Ryder.

I squeezed my eyes tight, willing some of the messiness to disappear.

"I changed my mind. If you're doing this, Aids, I wanna be involved."

"But I don't want you to be. It's been months! Please go back to Houston, Jeff. Leave the baby and me alone. We're better off without you."

The door behind me creaked open and Knox stepped out. Part of me ached because I wanted Ryder, but another part of me was thankful I didn't have to see him again. This confrontation was already painful and embarrassing enough. I didn't want Ryder to know about the other women—how easily Jeff had tossed me aside as if I were a used napkin.

"You ready to go?" Knox asked me. He stepped in close, checking in with me.

I smiled a little to let Knox know I appreciated his big-brother intimidation.

"I'm ready for Jeff to go—and stay gone," I said. My tone was as level as my gaze.

Jeff's jaw clenched again, his nostrils flared.

"Fine. But I don't like this, Aidy."

"Too bad. You told me to make a decision, and I did. Which was to move on without you in our lives. Honor that."

He opened his mouth, clearly wanting to say more but set his jaw, walked over to the elevator and jammed his finger on the button several times before looking around. Spotting the door to the stairs, he marched to it, flung the door open, and strode to the stairwell. I sagged against the wall and tried to steady my racing heart.

Knox pulled me into his arms. "You did good, there, Aidy-pie. Really stuck to your guns."

I sniffled as I laughed, and it felt good, so I laughed again. "Since Mom and Dad died, I've chosen emotionally unavailable losers who will never put my child or me first."

Knox steered me toward my door, a faint frown on his face.

"Maybe you did in the past. For the same reason I picked shallow women who wanted to fu…bed a hockey player and never bother to learn anything about me. It was safer that way," he murmured.

"Safer." I considered his words. With a shrug, I said, "Well, this still hurts. So I guess I didn't pick the wrong type well either."

I heard the faint click of a lock engaging behind me and turned to see my briefcase leaning against the wall next to Ryder's shut door.

Ryder hadn't stepped out to talk to me. I set my jaw, grabbed my briefcase, and met Knox's gaze head-on.

"But this is New Aidy, and she's not going to do that ever

again. Also…do you mind if we stay in?"

"Whatever you want, Aidy-pie."

Emmaline called then, promising to bring cookies and comfort food later after Knox left. Good, I needed some girl time and to download.

Chapter Twenty-Six
Ryder

After placing her briefcase outside, I managed to shuffle my weary body to my couch. I might be cautious with women, but Aidy and I were building toward something. Something good.

Right?

But worry niggled. I'd been desperate to pull her into my arms even as I wanted to run away. Those were so mutually impossible that I froze. But some of what she'd said to Knox resonated. Like her, like him, I had the same unwillingness, inability, whatever it was to maintain deep relationships. Look what I'd done to Knox, the kid who had been my best friend for years—ignored his overtures for friendship when he'd written to me and struggled to let him close once more. And if I continued my pattern, I might well hurt Aidy even worse than her selfish, cheating asshole of an ex.

I gritted my teeth. I couldn't bear the thought of that. And it wouldn't just be Aidy—my standoffishness would hurt her daughter. No way in hell I could break Aidy's daughter's heart.

I sat there, in the dark, trying to understand why it felt as though I was the one who'd just had his heart ripped from his chest.

But it didn't dissipate.

I tried to ignore the feeling. Aidy brought up the conversation the next evening as I met her and Rosie in the elevator from the parking garage.

I cupped the back of her head, my fingers tangling in the silky hair at her nape and brought her in for a hug. She nuzzled in closer. "I'm sorry, Ryder. I'd hoped he'd never show up. I'm just so embarrassed I was with him, that I'm sharing a child with him."

Her eyes glistened with unshed tears. My chest ached as I pressed a soft kiss to her temple. "I dated Margo because she was safe," I murmured.

Aidy rested her head on my pec, and my body relaxed. I wanted her there—craved this quiet time with her.

"Yeah, but you didn't link yourself to her forever."

"No, I didn't. But I've watched you handle each crisis as it comes. Honestly, I'm in awe of your resilience."

"I don't feel strong," she said, a puff of breath hitting my neck. I shifted, not wanting her to feel my arousal.

"Stay with me?" I asked.

"I have to deal with Rosie…"

"I'll do it. Just…I want you in my bed. I want to hold you. To prove I'm not an emotionally unavailable loser."

Those words caused me to wince. She lifted her head, studied my face. "You heard? I'm sorry I said that."

When I opened my mouth to reply, she pressed a finger to my lips. "I'm sorry because I wasn't thinking about you. I've never seen you that way. I've never once thought you were like Jeff."

Those words, plus the sincerity in her gaze buoyed me. I led her to my room but left her to ready herself for bed when I saw the shyness creep into her eyes. The moment I slid in next to her,

I pulled her into my arms, and I held her as she slept, content. Throughout the night, I revisited the pain of my mom and sister's death—and of my father's abandonment.

Having Aidy there, next to me, where I'd wanted her for so long, gave me a grim determination. I wasn't losing this, losing her.

The only way to not be like Jeff was to *not* be like him.

I slid into sleep, her soft breath bathing my chest and my heart calm.

I woke late, to an empty bed. Right. Aidy had an early morning at one of her construction sites. Damn, I'd wanted to talk to her this morning about her doctor's appointment—she'd mentioned it at Simon and Bridget's. I needed to be there—to prove I was better than her ex.

So I rearranged my schedule and walked up to her building just as she exited. She had her head down and nearly smacked into me.

"Hey," I said as I clasped her biceps to keep her steady.

"Ryder. What are you doing here?" She extricated herself from my grasp and continued to walk.

"Going with you to your checkup."

"You are?"

"Yes." I ran my fingers through my hair. "Please."

"Don't you have patients?"

I did. But going with her, to this appointment, seemed much more important. "Sean will cover them," I decided.

She raised an eyebrow.

"He owes me."

"Why's that?"

"Because he used one-liners on you," I muttered. "Because he asks me about you."

Aidy stopped walking. She turned to face me. She sucked in a big breath. "You were jealous of me talking to Sean?"

"Yes. I was."

Her eyes widened as a smile tipped her lips. "Good."

"What?" I reared back, but she caught my collar.

"I'm glad you were jealous. I've wanted to pull out Margo's hair for weeks." She settled back on the balls of her feet.

"With you, everything is different," I said. "This isn't like dating a woman with a kid. This is brand-new and scary—for both of us." I took a breath. "But I want to be with you."

"You do?"

I wrapped my arms around her just as I'd wanted to do. "Yes. That's why I'm here. I'm going to have to tell you some things, but I'm not ready yet."

She studied me. "Okay."

"Taking this—us—slow…" I squinted down at her. "Tortoise slow, I mean. That's probably smart." I pressed my forehead to hers. "I don't want to mess us up. We matter too much to me."

"Okay," she whispered.

I grinned. "Good."

She grinned back. "And I'll give you an out in case you decide my life is too much for you."

I raised my eyebrows. "You *do* remember I work with babies all day, right?"

"And you want to come home to one who's fussy and needy after working around them all day?"

I mulled that over. "I'm not sure. I can tell you the idea never appealed before."

Her shoulders slumped, so I cupped my hand over hers, turning it over. I laid my palm on hers and I stared at our joined hands for a moment. "I don't know how to do this," I admitted. The hand-holding, the rightness of her touch against mine—caring this much for another person.

I touched the corner of her lip with my free hand, letting my finger trail down her cheek to her neck. I kept my touch light as it stopped on her pounding pulse. "You make me feel so much."

I tugged her gently and we walked in silence for a couple of blocks before she pulled me into a doctor's office. She signed in while I claimed two seats. Because it was just after lunch, we were the only people in the waiting area. I texted Sean, letting him know I needed some extra time. He agreed to see my two o'clock if I wasn't back.

Good thing my schedule today was light.

The nurse called Aidy back, raising her eyebrows when I stood and walked in with her.

"This is my friend, Ryder," Aidy said. "He's a doctor," she added. Maybe she thought that made it seem less weird that I was with her. The nurse pursed her lips and nodded. "Let's get your urine sample and then I'll do your weight and blood pressure."

Aidy entered the bathroom while the nurse led me to an exam room. I settled into the chair, eyeing the female reproductive posters on the wall.

Aidy came into the room and went to the scale and waited until the nurse told her to get on. After she took Aidy's blood pressure, she helped Aidy lay down so that she could listen to the baby's heartbeat. When the sound whop-whop-whopped through the room, my eyes misted. There was a baby inside her, making that sound.

I counted the beats, as I'd been taught. I squeezed my hands together, my chest aching as I thought of Molly. My story wouldn't repeat with Aidy or her daughter. I'd be there for Aidy and her baby. I'd be a much better man to Aidy's daughter because I'd be there for both of them each and every day. No matter how big or small their problems, they'd know they could come to me, that I'd listen, and if they needed it, I'd help. I'd show Aidy's daughter the affection she deserved—that all children deserved.

The nurse started to pull the gel away and I lurched forward so that I could touch her hand.

"Another minute," I asked. My throat was raw as emotion clogged it. "Please."

She glanced at Aidy, who nodded, her eyes coming back to mine as the fast heartbeat whispered around the room.

"She's perfect," I said.

Aidy squeezed my hand harder as if cementing the connection between us. With a ragged breath, I welcomed it.

Dr. Yao, a tall, lithe Asian woman entered the room, barely sparing me a glance as she went over Aidy's details.

"Everything looks good, but you could gain some more weight. I rarely get to say this, but add more ice cream to your diet."

Aidy's jaw dropped but I grinned.

Dr. Yao swept from the room. I glanced at my watch. We'd

been there twenty minutes, but somehow, everything in my life had shifted.

"Fast visit," I muttered.

"Because everything looks good."

I studied her from the corner of my eye as we began the walk back to her office building. "Will you have dinner with me tonight?" I asked.

"Why?"

"So I can feed you ice cream," I said with a wink. "Gotta be sure to follow doctor's orders."

Aidy shook her head, but the smile had returned, which lifted my spirits.

I dropped her at her office door with a kiss on her cheek. I inhaled her scent, needing to carry a small part of her with me. A sense of peace I'd never felt before settled over me—as if I'd found my place. With Aidy and the baby.

I hustled back to the clinic, my steps lighter than they'd been. I passed Simon in the hall.

"Are there any houses for sale in your neighborhood?" I asked, stopping in front of him.

Simon shrugged. "You'll have to check the listings. Though, I'm not sure you want to live in a community that's a mix of young families and retirees. We're boring."

"I think I might want to be boring, too," I muttered as I pulled on my white coat and grabbed the stethoscope from my desk.

That was looking more appealing with each passing day.

Chapter Twenty-Seven
Aidy

"You don't have to do this, you know," I said after a decadent meal of chicken parmesan.

He'd spent the night in my bed yet again, putting up with my tossing around. I loved every minute of our time together. I craved his touch, his gaze, his lips and tongue, and his fingers, but…I was self-conscious because I wasn't slender or sleek. I was pregnant. Very, very pregnant.

He frowned as he gathered the plates. "Do what?"

"Wait on me."

His shoulders bunched. "You don't like it?"

"Oh, I love it," I said. "That's what worries me. I think I might love it too much. You're spoiling me, Ryder."

He set the plates down, came over, and wrapped his arms around me, pulling me upward until I was plastered to his front. He brought one hand up and tipped my chin. "Good. I like spoiling you. Spending time with you, Aidy…" Something softened in his eyes, and his face brightened, making him look younger. "You make me happy." He smiled.

I grinned back. "You make me happy, too. Next week, I start my weekly appointments with Dr. Yao," I said.

"I bet you're glad to get to this point."

I nodded. My belly swelled past my breasts, and this week, I'd lost sight of my feet. My swollen feet. I sighed.

"Something hurt?" he asked.

"No. Just generally uncomfortable from having a human stashed in my midsection."

He chuckled as he led me over to the couch. Rosie opened one eye but otherwise remained in place. Doggy daycare always wiped her out.

"I heard back from my advisor today," I said.

"And?"

"And he loved my paper. We're working out an option for me to present it via Zoom or something so I don't have to fly to Houston."

After Ryder sat, he placed my legs in his lap and removed my shoes.

"Do you think that will work?"

"I hope so. I've been worried about traveling."

He didn't rub my aching arches. Whatever he planned to say weighed on him. I waited, my heart pounding.

"You know Molly died as an infant, but I don't think I ever told you she died during childbirth," he said.

I fell back against the arm of the sofa. The rawness and the pain in Ryder's face made it much more real. "Oh, Ryder. I'm…I don't know what to say."

"No one told you?"

I shook my head. "I don't remember my parents mentioning that, no, and it's not like Knox is really communicative about personal stuff—what he calls gossip. I wish I had known. I can't imagine how hard being around Lilia and me must be." I gripped his hand. "And you've come to my doctor's appointments. That's why you wanted to hear her heartbeat."

"Yes. I'm worried about you...about the same thing happening."

I swallowed with difficulty. He had the medical training, not me. "Do you think it's likely?"

He shook his head. "No. I really don't. It's actually not uncommon to have the cord wrapped around the baby. But, in Molly's case it wrapped around her legs and neck, so there wasn't any slack. That's what cut off her air supply."

He met my gaze, his troubled, and I sensed it was for sharing this story with me as well as about his grief.

"It's not like it is today. They didn't have that level of monitoring."

"And your mom?" I needed to know...even as I didn't want to. Still, Ryder was talking, sharing. Maybe for the first time.

He stared down at his clenched fists. "My mom hemorrhaged. She'd been high-risk—she was in her mid-forties when she became pregnant, and it wasn't an easy pregnancy. I didn't know that at the time—she wouldn't have told me as I was so young myself. But she told Zara. Anyway, she struggled the whole time, not like you—you're so healthy and young."

"Ryder. Thank you for the reassurance, but just tell me."

He sighed. "There were complications. She died two days later."

The story was worse than the sanitized version Knox had told me. I stared at Ryder, unsure what else to say, how to soothe him.

"And yet you're here with me."

"I'm so drawn to you, Aidy." He raised his head, his sage-green eyes a mirror of old pain and fresh hope. "Maybe it's like Zara says, and you're my second chance."

"I don't want you to feel obligated to me," I whispered.

"That's what I'm trying to tell you. I *need* to be there. I need to be in that room with you. It's…I just need you. And…and I think I need Lilia, too."

I struggled upward and pressed my lips to his. There was nothing sensual about it. Just a way for me to say, I'm here, I see you, I understand. I'm with you.

He responded, his hands dropping to my hips. The kiss was light, sweet. Perfect. I inhaled his scent, tingles shooting through my body.

I was falling hard for Ryder Mackay. He was the man I'd always needed: responsible, thoughtful, compassionate. He tended to think before he spoke, a trait I found incredibly alluring, probably because I was so challenged with that skill. I couldn't stop my heart from beating a little harder—just for him.

"Okay," I whispered as I pulled back. "I'll make sure you're there."

He leaned his forehead against mine. "Thank you. But that's not the only thing I wanted to say."

I hoped my heart could handle whatever else he needed to tell me.

"I've always kept people at arm's length."

"Well, that's understandable, after what you experienced with your sister and mom."

Ryder shook his head, his brows tugged in tight. "No. That's hard. But my dad dumped me on my aunt's porch six months later, saying he'd come back for me when he was in a 'better place.' He never did. The bigger problem was that my aunt wasn't in the country, so I ended up in child protective services—in foster care—until she was found."

Blood pounded through my veins, and my throat ached with the need to scream. I wanted to tell Ryder his dad was a selfish prick, but that wasn't what he needed to hear.

"That must have been very challenging."

His eyes pleaded with me. I wasn't sure if he wanted me to drop the subject or wrap him in my arms. I opted for the second choice. "Come to bed."

He relaxed against me, almost as if he'd been holding his breath—expecting me to ask him to leave. He couldn't think I would do that, could he?

"I'd like that. After I take Rosie downstairs."

I had to kiss him again, which meant Rosie didn't get outside for another ten minutes. I pondered his story while they were gone. He'd been nine when he moved, ripped from his family, everything he knew. I hadn't handled my parents' deaths well, and I'd been almost twice his age. My heart ached for the small boy, and I couldn't fault the coping mechanisms he'd built to protect himself, just as I couldn't fathom how difficult opening himself up to me tonight had been. Ryder was trying so hard to form connections between us.

I needed to give him back the one I knew he craved.

When he joined me in bed, I pressed my back to his chest, reveling in his warmth, and the feel of his arms wrapped around me. He pressed a soft kiss to my jawline.

"You're the best part of my day," I whispered. "I look forward to seeing you, listening to your day, holding you."

I started to turn so that I could embrace him fully.

He rested a palm on my shoulder to keep me still. "Aidy, I…"

"I want to be with you," I said.

Ryder studied me. "I'm not trying to get in your pants. Not until you're comfortable."

"You've already been all up in my pants."

His white teeth flashed in the dim lights, and his chuckle caused my skin to pebble with pleasure. "True. I like what's in them, too." He slid his other palm up the outer edge of my thigh and dipped his fingers inside the edge of my loose sleep shorts. I shifted my legs, restless, wanting more of his touch. Needing him.

He slipped his fingers under the gusset of my voluminous panties and sighed as he found my warm, ready center.

"You're so ready for me."

"You turn me on."

"I'd really like to be inside you, Aidy."

I hesitated, my concern about my changing—growing shape—making me feel awkward. But, no, Ryder and I shared something special. Real. "So would I."

He rose up on his elbow, his fingers continuing their tortuously slow glide. "You sure?"

"I've been thinking about it—you—in me forever." My blush flamed across my cheeks.

He leaned down and pressed his lips to mine. They were soft, sensual, easy. A faint sound emitted from my throat as he slid his tongue into me in tandem with the rhythm of his fingers.

Once again, I tried to turn, but Ryder shook his head. "No. You shouldn't be on your back." He removed his fingers, and I whimpered. "I can definitely work with this."

He shoved off the covers and proceeded to get me out of my shorts and panties in one clean motion. Cool air hit my exposed skin and I fought the urge to cover my rounded middle. Ryder was about to see me completely nude. *Without any clothes and with the lights on.* I'd avoided this with more care than a Kardashian without makeup.

Ryder scooted closer and pressed kisses to my hip, his tongue sliding onto the curve of my belly.

"You are so fucking gorgeous," he murmured.

"I think I'd feel better if you were naked, too," I said. I panted softly, both from arousal and from my attempts not to be embarrassed by my roundness. Sure, I'd heard the truth and passion in Ryder's voice, but I struggled to accept his version of my body.

He shucked his pajama pants and T-shirt, then slid off his boxer-briefs, giving me a healthy view of his solid, hair-dusted thighs and taut abdomen. His erection jutted out, bobbling a little as he settled next to me. He slid his hands up my body, cupping my full, aching breasts while he took my mouth in another longer, drugging kiss.

I twisted enough to get my fingers into the hair at his nape, but my other arm remained at my side. Much as I wanted to touch him, that was impossible from this angle. So, I let Ryder kiss and caress me. I tensed when he unbuttoned my top, pushing the sides wide and feasting on the side of my breast. He avoided my nipples, no doubt because he knew they were sensitive, but trailed his lips down my ribs and back to my belly. Again, I tensed. He lifted his head and met my gaze. His eyes glittered and, this close, I could see his dilated pupils. His breath sawed out and he pressed his erect flesh into my thigh, causing me to moan.

"I have never seen such a beautiful sight. I wish you'd believe me when I tell you I love your body."

"Ryder, please."

He tilted his head as he lifted my top thigh and arranged it on a pillow. He slid two fingers back inside my core. From this angle, all I could do was relax and take him. I loved how gentle he was, only to turn demanding and press against a spot inside that made fire shoot outward, enveloping me in a haze of need.

"I want. I need. Be *in* me."

He grinned and it was wicked and so damn hot; I shifted, trying to ease the ache in my core. Then, his grin slid off his face.

"I don't have any condoms."

I paused. We stared at each other. My breath remained ragged. His touch drove me crazy.

"Well, it's not like I'm going to get pregnant."

He smiled again as he shook his head. "I'm clean."

"So am I," I said.

He pressed a kiss to my shoulder as he eased back behind me. "I know. I've been to your appointments."

He lifted my front leg higher and angled himself behind me so that his tip bumped again my clit.

"Are you sure you want this, Aidy?"

"*Yes*." Not only did I want him, I never wanted him to stop loving my body. Heat rushed over my skin in a thick, lush wave.

He slid inside me, my body more than ready to take the heavy push. I dropped my head back and looked up at him. His eyes were closed, and his jaw tensed. I raised my hand and pressed it to his cheek, enjoying the feel of the rasp of his burgeoning beard against my soft palm. We were such contrasts. Him tanned, dark, large. Me, pale, seemingly delicate against him as he gathered me closer and pressed in deeper.

"I've never felt anything so good as you."

He pressed kisses to my jaw and neck as he slid out before gliding back in. He took his time, each move measured, as if he were memorizing the feel, as if he wanted to remember this moment later.

I breathed through the emotion that realization brought. My fears had nearly overwhelmed me, making this moment impossible.

Ryder's loving evoked too much pleasure, too many emotions for me to remain passive, and I pressed back and down onto him, gasping as his cock hit that magical spot inside me.

"Oh."

He dropped his hands to my hips and hit the spot again. That caused my breath to speed up. He nipped my ear, which sent a delicious shiver that coiled in my low belly, right where the pressure was building.

He pumped in and out, slow, steady, showing me how much he adored my body with his hands and lips and tongue. I quivered and gasped, the side position allowing him to set our pace—and the touch. He built us up, the fever inching, inching with each shift of his hips, each flick of his tongue.

I lost coherent speech when he found my clit and rubbed it softly as he slid inside me. I clutched at the pillow, pressing my hips back, trying to force him to take more of me, faster, harder, more.

"Relax. I've got you."

He cupped my breast, holding me back against his chest, his heart pounding into my shoulder blade.

"I've got you."

I eased my muscles and he continued the smooth motion. I soared higher, then higher still, wound so tight, I suddenly feared the unraveling. I struggled a little, but he continued, unhurried, rooted deep, moving his hips in a seamless, tireless motion.

The tension coiled tighter, my body bowed. He lifted his head and kissed me, his tongue as insistent and steady as his cock. I felt him swell inside me, the first faint shudder ripple over his sweat-soaked skin.

He pinched my clit, hard. I screamed into his mouth as the tension exploded, sending pleasure rippling into my toes and fingers while still centered in my core.

He held himself inside me, letting the first wave overtake me. Then he moved. This time, his finesse gone as he slammed his hips into my bottom, clearly chasing his own release. Again, then again, before he swelled more and with a guttural moan, he emptied himself into my body, his hand still clutching my breast. My orgasm had slowed to lush pulses and I sighed, easing back into him.

He held me, his heart pounding even harder against my back, his arms over my body, sheltering me.

I fell asleep with the realization that this, *this* was what love felt like. For the first time in years, I was cherished.

Chapter Twenty-Eight
Aidy

Ryder and I spent every evening over the next two weeks together, much to Emmaline's disappointment. While she and I lunched together each day, Ryder was the one I looked forward to seeing each night.

He stood outside my office building, waiting to walk me to my doctor's appointment Wednesday.

"Thirty-four weeks," I whispered. "Not too much longer."

Ryder held my hand as I turned my face up to the weak March sun. At least the temperatures had warmed, making finish work on the exterior of The Mac possible. The project should wrap up in the next week, and I couldn't be happier.

"You're looking great, Aidy," Dr. Yao said. "Keep it up."

"And the ice cream?" Ryder asked, a smile tugging at his lips, his eyes dancing.

"If she likes it, sure," Dr. Yao said. "So, you're going to be her labor coach?"

Ryder nodded, his face relaxed. I bit the inside of my cheek to keep from tearing up. He'd made such great strides, working so hard to power through his fears. For me. Was it any wonder I was smitten?

He walked me back to my office and pride swirled through me. I was holding hands with this gorgeous man. Out of all the women he could be with, he chose to be with me.

He kissed me, soft, sweet, as he dropped me at my building's door. He rubbed one of the tendrils of hair that had escaped my chignon between his thumb and forefinger and then he tucked it behind my ear.

"I'll see you at home."

I beamed up at him. "Can't wait."

He brushed his lips against my cheek once more. "Me either."

I walked inside to find Emmaline and Nannette, our assistant, at her desk. "How'd your doctor date with McDreamy go?" Emmaline asked, her eyes laughing.

"Dreamy," I said, smiling at her. "We need to discuss the last of the plantings at The Mac."

She nodded as she fell into step next to me. Emmaline had a few inches on me and a mane of dark curls that she'd secured today in a low, sleek ponytail. She reminded me of a Latina version of Marilyn Monroe—something I'd teased her about once until I realized she was sensitive about her looks.

"The peonies arrived while you were at your appointment and I gave the okay to have them installed."

"Perfect." I clapped. "We can drive over first thing tomorrow to see if Lidia's been able to install the last of the trim and shutters."

"I'd like that."

"Cool. Let's do breakfast, too, if you want?" I asked.

Emmaline smiled. "I can always eat."

I presented my thesis that following Tuesday, and my nerves melted as the smiles on the committee's faces grew. I sighed a pleasured breath as I realized I wouldn't have to worry any further about my degree. A huge weight tumbled off my shoulders.

In May, I would receive my master's degree. I texted Ryder as soon as I finished, and he met me in my condo, Rosie, in a big red bow, and with a glass of sparkling cider. On my table sat a huge bouquet of petite roses in an array of pinks, reds and yellows.

"Oh," I whispered.

"I'm so proud of you," he said, beaming. "You totally kicked ass, Aidy. You're an M. Arch."

As tears began to stream down my cheeks, Ryder's face fell. He set the glass down and shoved his hands into his pockets. Before he could rock backward, away from me, I threw myself into his arms.

"This is so sweet. So perfect." I pressed my lips to his and he wrapped me in his warm embrace.

Rosie danced around us, barking. By the time we pulled apart, now breathless, Rosie had managed to tug off her bow and it trailed behind her, wet and chewed.

Ryder and I burst into laughter. "She's so fun," I said. "I'm glad I rescued her."

"You've been an amazing fur mommy."

I beamed up at him. "I have, haven't I?"

He smacked a kiss to my lips. "Yes. You hungry?" he asked.

I smiled into his eyes. "For you."

His gaze softened. "We'll get there, but let's feed you and Lilia." He dropped to his knees, nuzzling his cheek to my belly. "Hi, baby. I missed you today."

I ran my fingers through his thick, dark hair, my heart melting all over again as I marveled at this man. He might be shy, but once past his walls, he surrounded me in affection.

After dinner, we loved each other for hours.

Life was good—really good. I'd never been happier.

Ryder called me after seven the next evening. I'd arrived home about twenty minutes before because Emmaline and I had stayed at work late, trying to complete some updated renderings for a beach house remodel. We hadn't figured out a way to tie in the request to use reclaimed barn doors with the open concept main floor yet, which left me out of sorts even with Rosie snuggled into my side.

"How are you tonight, sweetheart?"

Warmth flowed over me at the sound of his voice. And that endearment? My smile grew wider.

"I'm good. You?"

"Irritated. I have to do some work tonight," he said, regret pulsing through his words. "I'm fairly behind on some of my notes for a couple of patients. I'll probably be up late, so I'll just stay at my place tonight, so I don't wake you."

That warm glow evaporated. "Sure. Of course. Whatever you need."

"Would you rather I came over?" he asked, tentative. "I didn't want to presume."

"Yes." The word burst from me. "I want you here."

I wanted to tell him how much last night meant to me, his holding me all night, how waking to his kisses made my day special.

"Then, I will. As long as it's not too late. You need to sleep, Aidy. See you later."

I needed *him* more. But I didn't say that because Jeff hadn't liked my girly side, as he called it. When I'd wanted to snuggle, he'd roll away.

But Ryder tucked me close, held me tight. Made me feel desired, special…loved.

I tossed my phone onto my couch, causing Rosie to flinch, and scowled. My back and hips ached and the idea of making my own dinner nearly had me skipping the meal. I struggled to my feet, my achy body causing me to pout down at my feet I could no longer see.

I made myself a salad. Some habits proved too ingrained to quit. I stabbed at the lettuce and crunched through carrots. I tossed Rosie a few and she ate them with the same half-hearted enthusiasm. She kept glancing at the door, clearly waiting for Ryder to come in.

Even my dog was in love with him. Not that I could blame her. I set my fork down and rubbed my eyelids. I was in love with Ryder. This was…this was *bad*.

I was *so* in love with Ryder Mackay. Head over ass, stupid in love.

I rose and dumped the remainder of my meal into the trash, then put the plate in the dishwasher. I sponged down the counters, the table, and the unused stove. I glanced around, looking for something else to clean or straighten.

Nothing.

I settled on the couch but couldn't get comfortable. I stood and walked to my bedroom, lying on my side with a pillow under my belly. Maybe a book would help.

After ten minutes, I gave up on that, too. I scowled as I rolled over. Just as uncomfortable on that side. Fine. I'd eat my way out of my mood. What suited this situation? Chocolate? Ice cream?

I grabbed my purse, slinging it across my body, and then collected my keys and phone. I wasn't sure what I wanted, but I knew staying here wasn't going to find it.

Ryder opened his door, smiling at me.

"I didn't know you were home," I tossed back over my shoulder. Could he see that I loved him? *Please, no*. I needed to process first…figure out how to tell him…

"I just got in. I was coming to see you once I set down my stuff."

"Oh."

His sigh brushed the hairs on the back of my neck. "I couldn't even make it a couple of hours. My concentration was shot. I missed having dinner with you."

Rosie yipped, scratching at my door. Ryder unlocked it and loved on the puppy, who closed her eyes in ecstasy. *I feel ya, sister.*

"I missed you, too, and my salad was terrible. I'm never going to be able to eat one again, thanks to your food pushing."

His lips quirked but he didn't say anything. He gently pushed Rosie back into my place and pulled me into his arms. I settled against him, my heart rate slowing back to a normal pace.

"Why are you out here?" he asked.

I shook my head. "I don't know. I wanted some chocolate? Or creme brûlée? Or ice cream."

Something to distract myself from freaking out about my love for you.

He pressed his knuckle under my jaw and tipped my head up. "Let's go get it for you," he murmured.

I sighed. Really, there was never any doubt I'd love him—not if he were so agreeable to my moods and needs. He locked my door before he wrapped his arm around me and led me to the elevator. Now, if I only knew that he wanted me and my daughter—not in this moment but long term. I wasn't sure how to ask him if he planned to be around not just tomorrow but next year and every year thereafter, as I wanted him to be, and that left me antsy.

While Ryder circled the store with his shopping buggy, I waddle-walked my pregnant tush into the refrigerated section with my own cart, wondering if I could go back for a second sample of the coconut milk ice cream. I was eating for two and having a bit of a mental breakdown, after all. But that skinny bitch doling out the tiny paper cups side-eyed me as I picked one up. I snorted in indignation. Fat-shaming a pregnant woman was *wrong*.

Fluid gushed down my legs as I reached for the yogurt. I gasped, grabbing the shelf and watching the labels swim in front of my eyes.

I shifted my feet and stared at the growing puddle of liquid pooling around my now-wet tennis shoes. Well, the tips of my tennis shoes. The rest of my feet, ankles, and well, entire lower half was blocked out by my belly.

My thirty-five-week pregnancy belly.

Which was why my next thought wasn't about how much stronger the next contraction would be; it was: *This couldn't be happening*. Then, the contraction hit, ripping through my belly.

I heard a strange clatter and only after the tunnel vision of agony faded did I realize the noise was coming from the cart I clutched in a viselike grip.

Too late I realized the vague, achy clamp on my belly hadn't been the pre-labor. Nope. I was *having* a baby. In Whole Grocers.

I let go of my death grip on my cart to drop to the floor and curl into a smaller, tighter ball. I wanted my mother. She should be with me.

Tears stung my eyes. A face slid into my line of sight and I gasped, too out of breath to shriek at the invasion of space.

"That was a strong one," the woman said.

Her weathered skin contrasted beautifully with her calm dark eyes. Salt and pepper hair surrounded her pretty, aging face and thick laugh lines grooved into the sides of her eyes and around her mouth. Her lipstick was a shade too bright that reminded me of a date color. Her warm, tanned hand held mine, and I stared at it, focusing on her short, clean fingernails even as the contraction rippled over my taut stomach.

"Your water broke, huh? I told the boy stocking the Kombucha to see if there's a doctor in the store. And I called 9-1-1."

"There is. Ryder…my…"

Another contraction barreled through me and I gasped, going rigid. I must have gripped her hands because the woman's face contorted much like mine—into a grimace of discomfort—as I tried to remember what I was supposed to do.

"Breathe," she said in a soft voice that I managed to hear over the blood rushing to my ears. "Breathe through it."

I whimpered even as I gnashed my teeth.

And then the contraction eased.

I felt another set of hands on my shoulders, easing me onto my back, and I turned my head only to blink, then blink again.

"Ryder," I whimpered, relief washing over me. "The baby."

"I know, sweet girl. I thought we'd agreed to do this at the hospital with Dr. Yao."

"I want to—take me. Please?" I growled the last word, gnashing my teeth as another contraction slammed into me.

"I'm Lillian," the woman on my other side said. "She asked for you."

"Yes," he said. His voice remained steady, but his eyes were too wide, his lips pressed tight. "We walked here, Aidy. I don't want to leave you long enough to get the car."

As he spoke I whimpered but kept my jaw locked, my eyes seeking his as a new pain tried to rip me apart. I panted as the contraction rippled down into my limbs, which shook and twitched. No wonder women opted for sedation or other drugs. No one should have to do this without numbing. Actually, no one should do this awake. I wanted to be knocked out.

"Did you call an ambulance?" Ryder asked someone behind me. His hands shook.

"Yes, sir. They said they're working on it. Something about a pileup on I-95 and a house fire on Blackstone.

His jaw tensed, making it look even more chiseled, if that were a possibility.

"I'm sorry," I whispered.

I was forcing Ryder to relive one of the worst memories of his life.

His gaze softened as he met mine. "Babies come when they're ready," he said.

But *he* wasn't ready. He was supposed to hold my hand. I was supposed to prove that labor could be safe—to create a better experience for him. I wanted that, desperately…until another contraction hit, and I had to power through the pain.

"Ryder, you can go," I blurted. "I don't want you to have to relive your sister's…"

He took my hand. "I'd never leave you," he said, flashing that soft, sweet grin that caused his dimple to flash. Damn that dimple. It was my weakness, and Ryder knew it.

He closed his eyes for a moment and emotions flitted over his face. When his lashes fluttered upward, determination settled in his gaze. "We're doing this, Aidy. I'm delivering Lilia and you're both going to be *fine*."

"What's your name, sweetheart?" Lillian asked.

"Aidy." I gripped her hands, my eyes wild, my lip quivering as I imparted my news. "The baby…it's too soon."

Right now, all I could think about was the magical date I'd circled when the baby would be full-term.

I continued to thrash my way through the contractions.

"Let's get you breathing," Lillian said.

Ryder glared at her. "You have some training?"

"I'm a midwife."

Some of the tension seemed to ease from his shoulders and jaw. "Great. I'm so glad you're here to help."

I gritted my teeth as the pain crested. Couldn't they bond later—after the pain dissipated?

"Those are close," Ryder murmured. He looked past me, no doubt at the growing crowd. "I need some boiling or sterile water and more clean towels," he said, looking somewhere over my shoulder. "The rest of you should back up. Give the lady some space."

He rubbed my knee. This could not be happening. Even my brain, which seemed capable of developing all kinds of scenarios where Ryder Mackay was concerned, never, *ever* fathomed such a terrible turn of events.

"I do not want you looking at my hoo-ha. If a baby comes out, you'll never want to actually do me again."

He chuckled. He leaned in close. "I'll always want you, sweet girl."

"Do you see what I'm dealing with here?" I said to Lillian, gesturing wildly toward Ryder.

"Oh, I sure do." She smiled. "You should probably just give in, my dear. He seems pretty determined to get his way."

I crossed my arms over my chest, and my legs at the knee, wincing slightly at the sticky wetness that continued to seep through my panties.

"Nah uh. This is not romantic or sexy or…oh, shit! I'm having another one!"

Chapter Twenty-Nine
Ryder

Aidy was in active labor. Intellectually, I knew us having sex last night or me missing dinner with her hadn't caused Aidy's daughter to decide to press her way into the world right now, but my heart raced and my palms sweat, and Aidy's resistance was freaking me out, big time.

"Why don't we work on breathing in nice and slow," Lillian said. She did a breathing exercise that Aidy followed.

"Good. Now, let it out just as slow. Again."

While Aidy followed Lillian's example, I managed to keep my fingers on Aidy's arm long enough to calculate her pulse. It was elevated, which was to be expected, but I really wanted to check her blood pressure. Without my stethoscope, I couldn't. Just as I didn't have the correct equipment to monitor fetal distress. I checked my phone, but my SOS to my friend at Newport Hospital hadn't been answered.

"Anyone get through to 911?" I called out.

"They're trying to free up an ambulance," a voice said from behind me. I turned to look over my shoulder. It was a smallish man who reminded me of a hamster, right down to his twitchy little nose. He pushed his glasses up toward his beady eyes. I glanced over and noted his name was Don and that he was the manager.

"Thanks, Don. Could you keep trying? She's in preterm labor. Can you relay that for me? Also, I need someone to head over to the first-aid aisle for gloves and scissors. I'd also like some dishcloths, and shoelaces, if you have them."

"Y-yes, of course," Don said. His gaze flashed over to Aidy and slid away. He tried to shoo some interested bystanders away. One woman's strident voice rose over the crowd.

"How the hell am I supposed to get my buffalo butter?" she snapped.

I rolled my eyes. The selfishness of some people was unbelievable. Aidy's jaw clamped tight and her eyes began to bug.

"Keep her breathing, Lillian," I said. "It looks like we're in business here."

Lillian side-eyed me but continued her melodious one-sided conversation with Aidy as I worked to remove her socks and shoes. Her toenails were painted a cute hot pink that caused me to think of gumballs.

I nodded. "These weren't painted last night," I said, trying to divert Aidy's focus from what appeared to be an intense contraction.

She panted. "That's because I did it today when I got home."

I glanced back down at her rock hard abdomen. That was the third contraction I'd counted—all in less than five minutes.

She wasn't going to make it to the hospital.

"If you'd have asked, I would have done it for you," I muttered. I glanced up at Lillian, who was watching our interaction with keen interest.

"I didn't want to bother you," she said.

Instead of telling her she would never be a bother because I wanted to do those things for her, I bit my tongue. Aidy's past made her fiercely independent, and her loser ex made her even more likely to shy away from my good intentions.

One of the employees handed me a plastic baggie containing latex gloves. I thanked the woman as I pulled them out of their packaging and set them aside.

No going back. As my khaleh liked to say, we could only start from right here and do our best to move forward. For me, that meant being the calm, capable physician Aidy needed. I was that man, and I would remain that man for her.

Another contraction hit Aidy hard and she gritted her teeth, her face contorting as the pain lashed through her midsection.

I sucked in a deep breath and prepared to touch—and connect—with Aidy. This shared experience would change our relationship.

I'd never planned to have kids or a family. Not after my front-row seat to the implosion of my own familial unit. I'd been fighting with myself about this since Aidy asked me about coming home to a fussy infant. Much as I cared for Aidy and her baby, I couldn't be involved long term.

Aidy laid back, panting. She stared up at the ceiling—or maybe the green sign that read Milk. She muttered to herself.

I dipped my hands in the steaming hot water one of the employees placed near my hip, wincing at the temperature. I soaped my hands with some yellow bar, going up my forearms.

"It's lemon verbena," the middle-aged woman who'd handed it to me said. "It's a lovely fragrance and antibacterial, anti-viral."

I nodded, gritting my teeth before I plunged my hands back

into the hot water. The scent didn't matter as much as killing the germs to ensure I didn't transfer an infection, but I appreciated her reasoning…sort of. I hissed out a breath as I pulled my red hands from the water, watching the steam rise from them. Once they were dried, I put on the gloves.

"What are you having, dear?" Lillian asked Aidy. She brushed Aidy's hair back from her hot, sweaty face, and I felt a pang of what I was missing. I'd planned to be by her head, holding her hand, letting her squeeze the shit out of my fingers. I would have been an amazing coach.

I wondered if the woman was trying to keep Aidy's mind off the situation.

"A girl," Aidy gritted out. Her voice was almost guttural, telling me she was in serious distress. I wanted to get her to the hospital. I wanted her to have drugs and those ice chips she'd talked about.

"I'm naming her after my-my…" Aidy gasped, grunted and made this guttural, growling noise in her throat. "Oh my… She's coming out right now."

Chapter Thirty
Aidy

"What are you doing?" I gasped, my hands shoving at his hands as he gripped the waistband of my leggings.

"Taking off your pants," he said with a frown. He pulled free of my flailing hands.

"Do you seriously have to take off my pants?"

He raised an eyebrow. "Yes. That is a prerequisite for bringing this little munchkin into the world."

"No," I panted.

He frowned. "I need to…you know…catch her."

"No. Babies are *not* born in the refrigerated section of Whole Grocers. At the very least I need a wading pool, some Bach, and my birth coach," I said, each word clipped because another contraction hit me then. I managed to breathe through it with Lillian's help.

"I'm your birth coach," he pointed out.

"You were my backup," I snapped. "I want Bridget. Or Emmy."

"Unfortunately, neither of them are here right now."

"Go get one of them. Now."

Ryder's lips flipped up and he smiled, his eyes lit with humor, and his focus solely on me. I gasped, and this time it wasn't from a contraction. It was *that look*. More it was the way *that look* made me feel.

I never expected to look into the eyes of my soul mate while I was on the floor of the Whole Grocers' refrigerated section as I gave birth to another man's baby, but that was the story of my life. Everything took a left turn after I told Jeff about the baby.

"I'd do it in a heartbeat if I could. Anything to make you happy, Aidy," Ryder murmured.

The sincerity in his eyes was my undoing. I bit my cheek until it bled to keep from telling him I loved him. I looked forward to his sleepy smile each morning, and his crazy bed head where half his hair struck up and the other side was mashed to his skull. I loved how he insisted on cleaning up the kitchen because he knew I hated that job. I loved how he asked about my day and listened to my ideas.

I loved that he'd dropped his plans for tonight to accompany me to the store and ended up delivering my daughter. There was no one—*no one* I trusted with her wellbeing as much as I did him, not even Dr. Yao. Ryder knew how important she was to me. Just as I knew he was emanating a cool facade that didn't reach his stormy eyes.

"Right now, you're going to work with Lillian and me. We're a dream team." Ryder winked at Lillian, who chuckled softly. When I glared at her, she sobered, her face once again settling into tranquil lines.

"So, Ryder's not the baby's father?" Lillian asked.

Because I was so mortified that Ryder was shucking my pants, the words dripped from my mouth.

"No, Ryder's a much better man than Jeff. He left me a note and some money. He said whatever I wanted to do, it was my choice, but he wasn't interested in kids and not to come back if I decided to keep the baby."

"You didn't tell me that part," Ryder said. His jaw clenched so tight I thought I heard his teeth squeak.

That reaction was why I hadn't told him—told anyone.

"Was he your age?" Lillian asked, her tone delicate.

I snorted. "Nope, he wasn't young and stupid. Well, not *that* young. He's thirty-two. What kind of man can just up and leave his own child?"

I asked this to Lillian, who had begun to rub the back of my neck. Her hands worked their way into the tightest areas, easing some of the strain.

Ryder paused, his breath going rapid and shallow. I shoved my face into the crook of my arm. This day could not get worse.

Another contraction ripped through my lower half. Yes, yes, it could get worse. My baby was shredding my pelvic region.

Lillian pulled my hands from my face and made those weird birthing class faces as she breathed, nodding for me to follow along. As the pain subsided, she scowled while her gentle fingers rubbed my temples.

"I have to say, based on what you just told me, the man is a selfish jerk. You're better off without him."

"She definitely is," Ryder muttered.

I wasn't sure if I was supposed to hear him, so I chose to ignore his statement and kept my gaze on Lillian's sweet, calm brown eyes.

"He freaked out when I told him I was having a girl. You know why? He might have to stop banging his way through…I need to push," I moaned, my head tipping back to stare up at Lillian, who began to rub my jaw.

She smiled at me. "I bet you do. So, why don't you let Dr. Mackay get your pants off and take a look at where this baby is, hmm?"

I blinked up at her. "I guess I don't have a choice."

Lillian grinned. I heard a chuckle from my ankles just before Ryder wiggled my maternity leggings and voluminous preggers panties off my feet.

Chapter Thirty-One
Ryder

"How are you doing, Aidy?" I asked.

She raised her head enough for me to catch her gritted teeth and her red, sweaty cheeks. Her eyes were focused and intense, and I wanted to slide right into those pools.

What this woman did to me. If I hadn't been totally focused on freaking out at the thought of delivering her baby, I'd be freaking out at the thought of how she affected me. Unfortunately, I'd reached my limit of freak out and now had to be calm and collected—that was the only option to get Aidy and her baby through this alive.

So I'd do it.

"Awesome," she mumbled as her gaze drifted over my right shoulder. She was clearly embarrassed.

She *was* doing awesome. Better than most of the women I'd helped during their deliveries. I glanced at Lillian who was keeping Aidy calm, her voice soothing. Her serenity and gentle voice helped reduce my stress levels.

I shifted and my dress slacks stuck to my knees. I hadn't worried about the amniotic fluid when I saw Aidy lying prone in front of the milk. That image was seared into my brain for all eternity. She had no idea how close my heart came to stopping then.

"You're doing really well with your breathing. Keep watching Lillian," I glanced at Lillian to see her nod.

"And you might be having your baby in Whole Grocers, but that'll make for a hell of a story to tell. Think of it as the beginnings of lore."

Aidy's breathy laugh faded into a moan as another contraction rippled over her taut belly. The tiny head crowned. My heart fluttered hard in my chest as other unfamiliar emotions pinged through me. My excitement at being the first to hold Aidy's daughter shocked me.

"You're doing amazingly well, dear," Lillian said.

"The heads out," I said. I turned the baby so she faced up and a new emotion seared through me: fear. Her face, the part I could see, was pale, which wasn't uncommon, but her lips were almost white.

Shit.

Shit. Shit. Shit.

This was much like my nightmares.

Please let me be wrong.

I glanced up at Lillian. "Any idea how long the ambulance will be? We have a nuchal cord situation."

She kept her fingers soothing but her mouth twitched. I hoped my face remained calm because I was not okay.

I bent my head back in time to see her shake her head.

"What's wrong?" Aidy asked, her voice higher in pitch.

"I need you to take a deep breath, and then I need you to push hard, Aidy. Let's get your daughter into the world. On three. One, two, three."

How would I meet her gaze? How could I ever share space with this woman again if I let her daughter die?

No, I wouldn't.

I *couldn't*.

Chapter Thirty-Two
Aidy

Ryder dove under his makeshift tent made up of my bent knees.

"I need another blanket, and do you have fresh, clean water? Where are those shoelaces and scissors?" he called out. I heard a scurry of feet, but I was pretty busy trying not to rip in half.

All the items he requested seemed to appear by magic—attached to the same middle-aged female associate in a green polo shirt and khaki slacks. She scuttled back faster than a crab who'd seen a seagull. I bore down, ignoring everything and everyone and focusing solely on getting my baby out of my body.

I flopped back on Lillian's lap with an exhausted sigh only to rear up and push again. Tears poured out of my eyes as I screamed with the release of the pressure.

"Hang on," Ryder said from my pelvic region. He pulled back, somehow managing to leave the blanket in place over my knees. His hair was tousled, his face set in intense lines. He glanced up at Lillian once again and then down at my splayed legs. She shifted, and I groaned as she moved from my head, removing my head from her plush lap.

"Usually, there's enough cord to unwind, but there isn't in this case, so I'm pinching the cord off."

I felt his hand against my strained pelvis, then heard the snick of scissors.

"Okay, unwrapping the cord. Good."

"What's wrong?" I asked again, my voice rising. My body quivered and shook like it had been through major trauma. I guess that was true. Rising to my elbows took effort—so much effort. I wanted to close my eyes.

"My baby—what's wrong with my baby?" My voice rose, became more strident as fear gripped me even tighter than the contractions.

Neither answered me.

Finally, Lillian looked up, a smile quivering at her lips as her eyes filled with tears. "You did marvelous, Aidy, dear," Lillian said. She beamed as she moved back to my head and wiped my sweaty hair from my even sweatier forehead.

I sat up on my elbows, and I looked down at where Ryder was working between my legs.

"Ryder Mackay, if you know what's good for you…if…if you want cookies ever again, you better answer me *now*."

Chapter Thirty-Three
Ryder

I held the infant I'd freed from the umbilical cord that had been wrapped around her neck and throat—*just* like the situation with Molly. My hands remained steady as I stimulated the baby by rubbing her back.

"Hand me a cloth," I said to Lillian.

She did, and I dried her off. Lilian and I both held our breath, waiting for the signs of pinkening flesh.

"Come on," I muttered low. "*Come on.*"

All this took place in under a minute, but it felt much longer. Lillian's sigh of relief echoed my own as Lilia squawked.

She was alive. Lilia was alive.

My arms felt like jelly, but I tightened my hold a little, protective instincts strong. Without realizing it, I tucked her small weight against my chest, reveling in the closeness, completely unconcerned with the mess.

I glanced up at Lillian, noting her more relaxed posture. She smiled, and the faint shadows that had built in her eyes eased away. Relief flooded me so hard tears welled in my eyes.

I stared down again at the tiny human in my arms.

"Apgar's good. What do you think, Lillian? A seven?"

"Yes, seems right," Lillian said.

Lilia's eyes already had a hint of soft green spiraling out from the softest robin's egg blue center. The baby caught my gaze and held it, her little pink mouth working again. She cried, and I grabbed a new blanket one of the workers—the one who'd told me the soap was lemon verbena—handed me.

"It's organic cotton," she whispered to me, her gaze also soft and fixed on the newborn.

"Thanks," I said. I took the blanket and wrapped it around the baby's now-dry back. I met Aidy's wet, worried eyes, who'd never taken them from me even as people fussed around her. Her eyelids sagged with fatigue, but her face eased with relief as Lillian spoke into her ear. A joyous smile split my face.

"You did it, Aidy. You birthed a baby. She's perfect," I said, my voice cracking. So fucking perfect.

Lillian had moved back to Aidy's side, massaging her stomach to help release the placenta and prevent bleeding. With a sigh, I placed the infant on Aidy's chest with more care than I would a Ming Dynasty vase.

"Skin to skin contact is good for you both," I said. "How's it going, Lillian?"

Aidy's face contorted, letting me know the placenta was coming. I made quick work of it, wrapping it in one of the soiled blankets under Aidy's hips.

Once that was done, I shucked my gloves and cleaned my hands, squirting them with the available sanitizer as an extra precaution. I glanced at the infant, who stared back at me with shocked eyes. The baby blinked, and I noted the wet clump of dark lashes near her cheek. She was a beautiful baby—all soft and pink with almost no swelling and minimal cone-headedness.

I slid in closer, helped Aidy upright enough so that I could wrap my arms around them both. I leaned back against the refrigerated shelf, contentment washing over me. The longer I studied her, the slower my heart rate and breathing became. I smiled again, unable to stop myself. We'd brought this tiny girl into the world—Aidy and I.

I shifted her a little, trying to get a better look at the baby's color and I tested her reflexes, relaxing a little as I caught Lilia's gaze; she looked back, her eyes rounded in her perfect little face. Her skin was pink and her lips red. Her eyes were clear as we studied each other. My heart tripped as I held the baby's gaze, realizing I was the very first person she'd seen. Not well—infant's eyes weren't yet fully formed, but I felt she studied me even as I studied her.

"You're already stunning," I murmured to her as I wiped her cheek with the edge of the blanket. "Stunning and sweet."

Her Apgar score had gone up, thankfully, which meant that even with the cord issue, Lilia would be fine.

I smiled down as she held my gaze, her eyes dazed but filled with wonder. She blinked and her small mouth opened in a yawn. Before I managed to process the emotions swirling through me, I heard some raised voices and then EMTs swarmed around us.

"I've got another blanket for her," one of the EMTs said as she took the infant from Aidy's arms, wrapping her in a second layer of thin cotton.

"You okay?" I asked Aidy.

"I think so. Lilia?"

"She will be. I'll make sure of it," I said. Aidy closed her eyes and rested her head against my chest.

What I wouldn't give to have these women be mine.

I shook off the thought, instead dealing with practical issues.

"I'll call your brothers," I said. "They'll want to know they have a brand-new niece to spoil."

"Later," she said.

I managed to rise to my feet, wincing at the pins and needles sensation burning through them as the EMTs transferred Aidy to the gurney. They popped her up to full height, and I frowned as she shivered under the blankets. No doubt that was her body's reaction to the hormones and the stress of the delivery, but I'd asked Dr. Yao to be sure.

I stepped up to one of the paramedics because he held the clipboard. Keeping my voice hushed, I explained the delivery and the umbilical cord issues though I noted her high Apgar. The EMT bent his head over his paperwork, writing furiously.

"We'll get her checked out ASAP," he promised.

"Her OB/GYN wanted her admitted to Butler," I said.

My eyes darted back down to Aidy, whose lids were lower than half-mast. Some wisps of hair stuck to her forehead and her skin was pale from overexertion.

I felt shaky from the last thirty minutes. Lilia could have died—just as Molly had. And it would have been *my* fault. The need to run, to distance myself from what could have been roared through me, but my feet seemed planted to the wood-planked floor.

Chapter Thirty-Four
Aidy

I tried to keep up with the shifting in my location and situation over the next few hours, but they slid passed in a blur. The ambulance arrived at the hospital. Nurses swarmed my baby who was examined before being whisked off for a bath and...whatever else they did to new babies. I didn't understand the acronyms thrown out. And with each passing moment, my agitation increased because all I could suss out was that because Lilia was premature, the medical staff worried about her body temperature being too low.

"Is she okay?" I asked over and over. Where was Ryder? I needed him to explain the details to me, but he'd gone with Lilia.

Dr. Yao arrived, claiming she was surprised by how well I'd handled my labor.

"Let's get this tear fixed," Dr. Yao said.

Tear? Oh my...*nope*, I didn't even want to know what could tear let alone what *had* torn.

"You're the talk of the unit," Dr. Yao continued with a hint of a smile as she moved toward some wrapped instruments. "Well, you and Dr. Mackay."

I blinked, dazed, as Dr. Yao patted my raised knee.

"I don't think I've ever heard of a birth in a Whole Grocers before," she said.

"Not like I planned that," I said.

"I can't imagine you did. But if you had to deliver outside of the hospital, you picked quite the hero." She winked and my cheeks flamed.

I winced at the shot into my ravaged nether regions, but I was too tired to do more than lay against the pillows. Once Dr. Yao finished up with my issues down there, she patted my knee again. "All set. Why don't you relax now."

"I want to see my daughter."

Dr. Yao brought her to me. "Have you picked out a name?"

I stared down at her, amazed by her tiny, perfect cheeks, and rosebud mouth.

"Yes. I'd already decided on Lilia." I sighed, wondering if it were a coincidence that the kind woman who had helped me at Whole Grocers was also named Lillian. I shook my head.

Nope. That had been a sign. My mother trying to tell me she was with me when I needed her. Ryder also deserved both recognition and thanks for helping me through one of the most difficult and amazing moments of my life. I'd have to thank him somehow.

"Lilia…Parissa Wright." I smiled, thinking of Ryder's sister, Molly.

"Pretty," Dr. Yao said with a smile.

"I think so."

"I'll let you ladies get some rest. I'll be back in the morning to check on you."

"Thanks." I pressed a kiss to Lilia's tiny forehead just between her thin baby eyebrows. My lips fit perfectly, and she puffed a soft sigh against my chin. My heart squeezed with love and hope.

"I'm so glad you're here, Lilia. My little Lily. A beautiful gift in the midst of all this craziness. I'm your mom. And I promise, I won't fail you."

We could do this. I'd figure out motherhood and give Lilia the best life—one so good she'd never miss her birth father. She had me, her uncles, and Ryder.

At least I hoped so. I kept waiting for the door to the room to open, for him to walk in and kiss me.

Chapter Thirty-Five
Ryder

I had to walk home and shower because of my soiled clothing and also because I was too strung out from the adrenaline to consider driving. I dressed in an old T-shirt and jeans, throwing on my tennis shoes. Didn't bother to comb my hair because the need to see Aidy, to ensure baby Lilia's health, nipped at my nerves. I used my key to take Rosie outside for a potty break and even managed to be strong enough to ignore her sad eyes when I locked her back in Aidy's apartment.

I arrived at the hospital, having driven faster than I should have, trepidation eating at me as I headed toward Aidy's room. Though it was after visitation hours, the nurses knew me and no one stopped me. I entered the room quietly, my eyes drawn toward Aidy. Her even breathing told me she was asleep, so I moved toward the bassinet, squirting my hands with the sanitizer on the way—some habits were ingrained.

Lilia's eyes were open, and she wiggled in her loosened blanket, making tiny huffing sounds. Most importantly, she was here, with Aidy, not in the neonatal ICU, which meant my concerns about the air sacs and a million other worries were just that— projected fears.

I scooped her up before I even considered what I was doing. Lilia hiccupped and blinked up at me. I settled into the rocking chair, her eyes never leaving mine.

Whatever connection I thought I'd imagined earlier slammed into me again, causing my heart to swell.

"Hello, Lilia. Aren't you sweet?"

I settled her tighter to my chest and went to the computer in the room. With each note about her temperature readings and changed diaper—already a bowel movement—excellent!—I found myself slowly relaxing. The proof was here, on the monitor, but more so in my arms. Lilia was alert and healthy.

I settled into the rocking chair as I brushed my finger against her downy cheek. She was a beautiful child. Perfect. As I made another pass with my finger on her cheek, she snagged it in her tiny fist. Those soft huffs turned to something like a coo as she met my gaze.

Maybe it was the quiet of the room. Maybe it was the late hour or Aidy lying nearby, but I felt it—my chest ached and tears pressed against my eyes.

I knew what I was: the son of a man who had given me up rather than spend another day in my presence. I was the pain-in-the-ass my aunt inherited, because out of duty to her sister, she couldn't let me stay in foster homes. I was the man who'd spent years trying to atone for my anger and fights that had caused countless hours of strife and heartache for Zara and, later, Tarek.

But, as I sat there, rocking Lilia, I felt like I was more than those pieces.

Maybe I could be more. To Lilia. To Aidy.

The rocking motion relaxed us both, and I drew out my time with her. I told myself I was allowing Aidy to rest, but the reality was I wanted these moments with the infant.

"I had a little sister," I whispered.

Lilia blinked up at me. I smiled but it felt sad.

"Her name was Molly," I said. "She was nine years younger than me, and I loved her so much even though I never had the chance to hold her."

I cleared my throat and peeked up. Aidy still slept, her back to us. It felt, in that moment, that Lilia and I were the only two people awake in the whole unit.

"When I learned she'd died," I said, "I felt like my whole world fell apart."

I'd been wrong. That happened later when my father abandoned me.

I pressed a kiss between Lilia's brows.

"Thank you for being a fighter. I was so scared."

I cleared my throat, but the tears pressed hard against my eyes, making my nose burn. "I was so damn scared I was going to lose you both."

I rocked her back and forth, back and forth, allowing the emotion to wash over me. Slowly, it ebbed, and I breathed easier.

"I love you," I said, keeping my gaze locked on hers. "And it's kind of freaking me out."

I glanced over at Aidy. Her breathing remained even, deep.

"Would you consider making me a deal?" I murmured to Lilia. "What if I try really, really hard to stay in the present? I mean, you did it for me—you survived. That was a big, big deal, and you're right; I should have realized that not every baby dies just because my sister did. But it's hard, you know? It's hard to get past that. Get past what came next. My mom dying sucked, but I was in shock, I think. My dad ditching me… I hate thinking about that. So, we won't. Right? We'll never mention it again."

Rocking was magical—I felt calmer the longer I did so. Even the hospital seemed quiet. Calm. I'd never considered the hospital a relaxing place before.

"Back to my bargain. What if I focus on loving you today? Do you think we could do that? Take it a day at a time?"

That was the same deal I'd made Aidy weeks ago. So far, so good with her.

Lilia made a soft sweet noise and then yawned. That was followed by a loud burst of gas from her rear end.

"Not quite the way I would have chosen to seal our deal," I said with a chuckle. But I rose and changed her diaper, then I rewrapped her swaddle and handed her to sleepy-eyed Aidy, who'd turned over at Lilia's first indignant squawk.

Aidy's smile lit up some of the darkest places in my chest—ones I hadn't realized were starved for light.

Yeah. We could make this work. Being with Aidy and Lilia was everything I never anticipated. More than I deserved. And I'd do anything to keep these ladies happy and safe. Everything my father didn't do for me.

Chapter Thirty-Six
Aidy

Sleep never returned after Ryder's talk with Lilia. He'd sat with me through the night, changing the baby so that I could rest in the bed. I appreciated his kindness, but I knew he needed rest.

"You're going to be exhausted," I said.

He grinned, and it was a little lopsided but full of happiness. "Don't care."

"But you have to see patients."

"You're my first patient of the day. I'll see you and then grab a shower before I have to be at the clinic."

"What about Rosie?" I asked.

"I'll have Knox stop by to let her out and take her to doggy daycare."

I gave up arguing because, by then, it was after four. Ryder didn't think I knew that he continued to check Lilia to ensure she was breathing well and her other vitals, and I chose not to tell him I was worried, too. How could I not be after his heart-to-heart with my daughter?

I fixated on the fact that he loved her.

Her, not me. If he loved me, he would have told her, right?

It bothered me that Ryder knew more about how to care for my child than I did. I mean, I wanted him involved. Of course I did.

Ryder received a call from the clinic. He pressed a kiss to my forehead, telling me he'd be back later to check in on us, and he'd rushed out before my breakfast arrived.

I didn't want him to leave.

I woke from a nap when Bridget's pretty blonde head poked into the room. Her wide smile caused my own to erupt.

"Hi," I mumbled.

"Hi, sweetie. I'm sorry I woke you."

I struggled to sit up. "Have you seen my bab—Lilia?" I needed to get used to calling her by her name.

Bridget peeked over the side of the bassinet. Her face softened as she smiled.

"She's so beautiful, Aidy. Look at that tiny nose! And her sweet mouth—her lips are so red!" Bridget met my gaze, hers solemn. "May you have been blessed with a sleeper."

Worry coiled in my gut. "Why would you say that?"

Bridget shook her head. "Nothing. I'm sure everything will be fine." She pasted on a bright smile and settled on the edge of my bed. "How are you feeling?"

"Okay, I guess. I mean, I had to get stitches."

Bridget winced.

"Did she say anything about how bad they were?" she asked.

"Not too bad. Whatever that means."

Bridget smiled. "You'll heal quickly, then. Good. Do you need anything?"

"I don't know. Maybe a shower."

Bridget nodded. "Absolutely. The nurses said that Ryder dropped off your bag last night."

My belly curled with warmth. I hadn't known that. "He

stayed with me."

Bridget's smile turned softer. "Good man. Now, let's get you cleaned up."

Dr. Yao stopped in around lunchtime to check on me and announced me healthy. "Your pediatrician should stop by later to look her over."

I frowned. "Do you know when?"

She made a note. "Nope, but we'll make sure it happens whether it's Dr. Mackay or someone else."

I nodded, shifting in the bed, uncomfortable with the idea of someone else looking after Lilia. I didn't want another doctor touching her.

I desperately wanted to be a great mom. One Ryder would be proud of. And right now, I was so tired my thoughts seemed turned upside down. When he offered a couple of suggestions during a failed breastfeeding attempt, I struggled not to snap at him. I was supposed to know how to do this part—that's what moms did. They fed their babies. Changed them, fed them, sang to them.

Lilia started to fuss, clearly hungry.

She latched on but released soon after, crying harder. Frustration caused tears to leak down my cheeks.

"We can give her a bottle if you need to sleep," Sandy, my new day nurse, said after she checked Lilia's temperature again.

When Sandy handed me the baby, I straightened her tiny hat and gritted my teeth, once again offering my nipple.

"No. I need to do this. Please. I need to take care of my daughter."

Sandy nodded. "Don't worry. This is a learning experience for both of you, and you have colostrum, which is super thick, so the baby has to work harder to get it. Let me show you how to manually express the colostrum until you both get better at getting the baby to latch on."

"Thanks, I'd like that," I said. I resettled the baby in my arms and took a steadying breath—and forced myself to relax, just as Ryder told me.

My kind grocery store midwife, Lillian, stepped into the room with bags of gifts for both Lilia and me soon after Sandy left.

"Don't you look a picture," she said.

I glanced up, tears of frustration and discomfort starting to leak down my face, but I smiled as she walked closer.

"Hi!" I reached out my hand. "Thank you so much for helping me."

Lillian smiled as she settled the bags and squirted her hands with sanitizer. "That was my pleasure."

"I don't think I could have done it without you," I said.

Lillian laughed. "You'd be surprised what you can do, but I was more than happy to help. Making sure this little one arrived safe and sound was the highlight of my evening. Even if my wife was less than pleased about my lateness to her romantic dinner." Lillian winked.

"Oh, I'm sorry—"

"I'm not," Lillian cut me off. "And neither was she once I explained. But why are you crying?"

"I can't get Lilia to stay latched on. Sandy showed me how to manually express the colostrum, so we know she's getting some.

But latching…what am I doing wrong?"

"Lilia—oh, that's pretty." At my continued sad expression, she touched my shoulder. "Let's see if we can make this a better experience for both of you."

She showed me how to position the baby so she'd be best able to swallow my milk, and I sighed with relief at the change in pressure.

"She's probably just getting colostrum right now. It takes a couple of days for the milk to come in but let her nurse in that position because it stimulates your glands and should ramp up production."

"Thank you," I murmured. I sniffled and then sighed. I'd thought pregnancy hormones were difficult to manage, but in the past twenty-four hours the need to cry kept sneaking up on me, catching me unaware.

"I don't know why I'm upset. I'm sure everything will be fine."

Lillian pressed her hands to her knees and rose. She grabbed a couple of tissues from the box and handed them to me. "I'll let you rest. Do you know when you're going to be released?"

"Soon. I, um, I need to get a car seat for her before I can leave."

"The nurses can help you with that. I'll need your address so that I can have the stuff from the Whole Grocers delivered to you."

I wrote it down for her and she wrapped both the baby and me in a warm hug. "Thank you for gifting this sweet girl with such a special name."

"It's for you," I said. I scrunched my nose. "And my mom."

Lillian's smile grew. "I'm honored to be in such lovely company." She pulled back with a smile as she cupped my chin, just like my mother used to. "And be sure to call me if you need help with the nursing."

I struggled not to sniffle. "I will."

Lillian said her goodbyes and slipped out while a nurse stepped in to get the baby's vitals. Then, she came to me and checked me over. Another woman came in, bringing me the paperwork for Lilia's birth certificate.

I filled it out and handed her the packet. Lilia stirred, squawking, and I changed her before trying to feed her again.

I must have slid back into slumber because the next thing I heard was the door swooshing open and Emmaline tiptoeing into the room.

She waved at me but beelined to the ruffled set of pants Lillian brought.

"These are fabulous," she said with a smile. "Not that I could pull off this look—they'd make my ass look huge. Hey, you took a shower. Looking good, Aidy."

She winked.

"It's amazing what soap can do," I said.

"No, you're seriously one hot mama. I'd do you if I leaned that way."

I giggled. "Thanks for that." I pursed my lips. "If we both did, I never would have ended up with Jeff."

Emmaline wagged her finger. "Which means I wouldn't have this sweet baby in my life. So, if Jeff is what it took to get here, then I guess he was worth something."

"Doubtful."

We broke into giggles, but I stopped as I considered what she said. I might be angry with Jeff—I felt betrayed on many levels—but he'd given me Lilia, and she was precious. So I guess I did have to thank him for that. My mouth twisted in disappointment.

"I wonder if he's going to want visitation rights."

Emmaline snorted. Ryder knocked on the door and poked his head in. Just seeing him again made my heart swell.

"Thank you for bringing my bag," I said, checking him out in his lab coat.

He came over, hesitated for a moment, then pressed a kiss to my forehead.

"How are you feeling?"

"Like I had a baby."

"You changed out of the hospital gown." His Adam's apple dipped. "You look nice."

Emmaline raised her eyebrows at this awkward exchange, and I tried to ignore her. "Thanks. The nurse said you needed to check Lilia."

"I do." He continued to stare at me for another moment before he turned to the bassinet. He plucked his stethoscope from around his neck and fitted the ends in his ears.

Emmaline settled her hip next to mine, her eyes never straying from Ryder's back.

"How much longer are you here?" she asked.

"Dr. Yao planned to check in again this evening, and hopefully I'll be released then. I'm healthy, so—"

Ryder draped his stethoscope around his neck and tilted his head toward me. "I'm finished. She's doing really well, Aidy."

He smiled, the warm one that caused his eyes to glow and made everything in me melt. This was *my* Ryder.

"Except that she needs a diaper change."

"On it," Emmaline said.

"You need to bring her into the clinic in the next couple of days. I wrote down the appointment time for you."

He handed me a card. "Thank you."

"I'm always happy to spend time with you."

I tucked my hair back and focused on my friend. Emmaline handed me the clean baby.

"I…ah…was worried."

"What about?" he asked.

"That you were angry with me. For going into labor at Whole Grocers."

He was beside the bed, his palm against my forehead before I finished. "No. *Never* think that—never. Bringing Lilia into the world was an absolute privilege."

I studied him, trying to understand what was going on with him.

"Okay," I said, my voice soft.

"Knox is bringing us something to eat," Emmaline said. "Do you want to stay, Ryder?"

"If that won't be a problem, sure."

Emmaline smiled. "It won't."

"Good," he said. "I'm hungry."

"We figured."

Knox arrived, annoyance stamped on his brow.

"What's wrong?"

He smiled but it was strained. "Nothing. Nico's on his way

up, too. He needed to deal with a little problem."

"Is it something with work?" I asked. "I'll—"

"Rest," Knox said, kissing my brow. "You'll rest and take care of your beautiful baby. Your puppy's with her sitter for the next couple of days, and Em's going to help us make sure your projects run smoothly."

I wanted to argue, but I needed to trust my brothers. Nico arrived, his face a mask of annoyance. Once he saw me, he leaned in and pressed a kiss to my cheek.

"How are you, slugger?" he asked.

My smile bloomed. "I did it, Nico. She's beautiful."

He studied me for another long moment before he walked over to Knox, who held Lilia.

"She looks just like you," he said, smiling. "Man, she's your exact image."

"Really?"

"You made a mini-me," he said with a laugh. "Let me hold her, Knox. I haven't held a baby since Aidy. It's like coming full circle."

"She's definitely got Aidy's eyes," Ryder murmured.

We ate and laughed at Knox's jokes. Nico offered me the fussing infant, and I had a much more successful feeding session with Emmaline sitting next to me, thanks to Lillian's advice. I kept trying to listen to the guys' conversation, where they stood at the other end of the room, but each time I focused on a snippet of conversation, Emmaline asked me a question.

"Why are you trying to distract me?" I asked as I burped the baby.

"What do you mean?" Emmaline asked.

"Why do the guys look so concerned? What's going on, Emmaline? What are you hiding from me?"

"Jeff called the office this morning," Emmaline said with a sigh. "He's looking for you."

"Oh. I didn't know he was in town again." I bit my lip, wondering if I'd handled that situation correctly.

"He's not. Yet," Emmaline said.

"What's that look for?" Knox asked, walking toward me.

I hesitated and gazed down at Lilia's face as it softened into slumber. "I met with a lawyer. We drew up paperwork that has Jeff releasing all parental rights." I raised my gaze to hers, noting Nico and Ryder had come closer to listen. "I guess he got those."

"And he's not happy," Nico said. He ran his hands through his hair. "He's called the office a few times. I told him you don't want to see him."

"But that might not last long," Ryder said.

I couldn't interpret his look.

"Why?" I asked.

"He's Lilia's *father*," Ryder said. "You listed him on the birth certificate, didn't you?"

I nodded as fear began to coalesce in the pit of my belly. "Shouldn't I have? I mean, he *is* her father…"

"He must want to exercise those rights," Nico said.

Chapter Thirty-Seven
Ryder

The first thing I heard when I stepped out of her shower the next evening was the exhausted, slightly hoarse cry of a newborn. The second was Aidy's soft, off-key voice singing a lullaby. Not going to lie—her halting attempt at "Shenandoah" was the best thing I'd heard all day. I pressed my hand to the wall and closed my eyes, soaking up the sound of Aidy singing. Lilia's cry lessened and then turned into soft hiccoughs.

I'd brought Aidy and Lilia home after a short stand-off with Knox and Nico. Part of me had wanted to kick out Aidy's brothers and pull her into my arms while she held Lilia. The need to ensure Jeff never touched the baby or gave Aidy another reason to cry grew with each passing heartbeat. The problem was those emotions stirred up a slew of memories of my father.

"I love you, Ryder. Nothing will ever change that." He'd said it with such conviction. But that was before—before Molly and my mother died.

What if something happened to Lilia now? Would Aidy resent me? I was, after all, her pediatrician. It would be my fault if she sickened. Just as it would have been my fault if I hadn't been able to remove the umbilical cord in time.

Cold sweat burst across my skin as I remembered Lilia's blue lips. That had been close. *Too close.*

"You're okay, Lily bean. Huh, I guess I just gave you your first nickname. My mother called me Aide-pie. That's where Aidy comes from. No one ever uses my full name: Aidalynn. That's my real name. Aidalynn James Wright. My middle name is like yours, see? It was the name of the EMT that delivered me in the driveway. Mom had something called precipitous labor with me, which I guess is what I had with you.

"My mom—your grandma named me that because she was so happy to get a little girl and happy to be through with her labor so quickly. That's what she always told me. I miss her."

Aidy sniffled, and I pressed my forehead to the wood door. I felt hollow. Though, why I couldn't say. We'd never gotten around to making each other promises either. That was on me—I'd told her we should take our relationship a day at a time. But somewhere in there, physical pleasure was no longer enough. I missed the smell of her hair, her soft breath against my neck and cheek, and the warm, rounded curve of her belly pressed into my side.

I jammed my hands into my pockets and forced myself to step back.

She held Lilia, swaddled tightly in a purple-checked blanket, in her arms. Her hair sat atop her head in a bun that had long tendrils escaping around her face and drifting across her neck. Christ, she was beautiful. And it was effortless because her clothes were loose for comfort. A spit-up stain marred her right shoulder, and she didn't have on any makeup. But her skin was smooth, her cheeks lightly flushed.

There was a knock on her door, and she opened it.

"Are you Ms. Wright?"

When she nodded, he said, "I'm John and that's Matt. We have another load of stuff to bring up. I guess people heard about you having your baby at the store, and they bought some stuff," the bigger of the two said. His voice was gentle and respectful, as if he, too, saw Aidy as a modern Madonna.

She nodded, her eyes wide, a little guarded when she met my gaze across the expanse of her living room.

I moved forward, wanting to be there for her if she needed me. One day at a time. I'd promised myself that—promised the baby. "I'll order some dinner from that place you like around the corner. I wasn't sure if you had anything prepped or if you'd made plans."

Her lashes lifted and she met my eyes, and my breath caught at the gratitude there.

"I'm so glad. Every time I try to do something, Lilia wakes and we start the changing and feeding process over again."

I smiled. "That's what babies do—sleep poorly, poop, and eat often."

She laughed. "Thanks for thinking of dinner, really. That was nice of you."

"Sure thing. You know if you need me to pick you up anything, I'm happy to."

She shook her head. "I can have it delivered." Her eyes took in her place, almost as if she'd never seen it before. "Once I figure out what I need."

"You'll figure it out. You were such a rock star during labor; everything from here on in will be a cakewalk." I laid my hand on her shoulder. I liked the feel of her shirt, warmed from her skin, under my palm.

"You say that to all the new moms," she quipped.

The knock on her door signaled the next load of goodies.

I opened the door and motioned the guys in. They both nodded at me. The guy with Matt labeled on his shirt handed Aidy a thick pile of envelopes held together with a rubber band.

"We managed to get it all on this load," John said. "That way we didn't have to bug you again or wake the baby."

"Thanks, guys," she said with a smile. "That was really thoughtful."

Both John and Matt preened as they began to unload the towering stack of baby-related paraphernalia. It was a good thing the living/dining room in these places was spacious, because the boxes and bags took up most of the floor space. I whistled under my breath at the quantity of stuff. I hoped those weren't all size one diapers, because Aidy was going to find her daughter outgrew clothes and diaper sizes faster than she could blink.

I just bet they were. I narrowed my eyes at John as he continued to gaze at Aidy's face. I walked over and ushered them out, shutting the door firmly behind them.

"Are you planning to stay after dinner?" Aidy asked biting her lip. She licked her lips, eyes darting around. "Lilia will cry—"

"I know. Let me stay here, let me help you."

"And you won't get much sleep."

"I know."

She met my gaze. "You don't have to do this, Ryder."

I stepped forward until I could cup her cheek. "I may not have to, but I want to."

If she only knew how much.

Chapter Thirty-Eight
Aidy

Ryder left me in the morning with a soft kiss and a promise to pick up Rosie.

Worry ate at me as I struggled to manage breakfast one-handed, which meant I made a mess. Frustrated, I gave up and took Lilia to her nursery. My milk finally came in and she gurgled and grunted, smacking her lips. She'd been hungry. I'd failed to meet that need.

The day passed in a multitude of diaper changes and feedings. Ryder showed up that night, Rosie on her leash, and my love for him swelled. I wanted nothing more than to tell him how much he meant to me. I bit back the words.

One day at a time.

That's what he wanted, and I'd give him that.

The next morning, Ryder made sure I showered and then helped me get Lilia into her car seat. We drove separately to the clinic because he'd stay, and I'd come back to my condo. He kissed me before I walked out of the exam room, lugging Lilia's seat, my head spinning from the literature he'd handed me.

"Don't worry, Aidy. I'll help you," he said.

But…for how long? He'd told me he didn't want a family. And this…this was jumping in the deep end of family-land. How could I ask him to stay with me?

How would I be able to cope if he left?

The day proved challenging. Lilia fussed more as the day progressed.

Ryder said she had colic and he wrapped her more tightly in her swaddling, making a shh-ing noise that seemed to calm us both.

The days and nights melded. If Ryder hadn't had to go to work, I'm not sure I would have realized where one ended and the other began.

And all the time, I worried, waiting for Ryder to tell me this—Lilia and I—were more than he wanted to handle.

One day, maybe a week into motherhood, Jeff texted to let me know he'd been called to another fire but planned to visit soon. And he wasn't going to sign any papers yet.

Worry turned into panic and I couldn't rest. Lilia didn't seem to have any sense of time, which meant my sleep schedule went haywire. I hadn't slept in so long I didn't even remember what it felt like. My eyes were gritty, my head fuzzy, and Lilia...she cried. Like, *a lot*. The only time she wasn't crying was when my boob was shoved into her mouth or she fell asleep.

Should I tell Ryder?

Yes, that was the responsible thing to do. So I called him. He didn't answer so I left a hesitant message.

"Um, it's me—Aidy. I hope you're having a good day. Is Rosie being good? So, um, Jeff is planning to visit. I don't know when. I thought...I thought you should know."

I waited for him to call back, but he didn't. Eventually, Lilia needed another change, then she ate again, and the cycle repeated.

"You miss my belly, huh?" I asked.

I missed her in my belly, too. Everything had been so much easier then.

"Let me get some water and then we can rock a bit, okay?"

I shuffled out of the nursery, wondering why I still bothered to go in there—Lilia's hatred of the space seemed to grow. She preferred the living room, which was where I'd dragged the rocking chair. The room's balance was off, but I could look out of the picture window that overlooked the city below, making me feel a tiny bit connected to the reality of the world outside of my apartment.

I glanced around the place, appalled by the clutter that had formed. A light knock sounded at the door, jarring Lilia. She flinched and let out an ear-splitting scream.

I wanted to sob with her. Instead, I zombie-walked to the door, hoping against hope Bridget had decided to come over and work some veteran mama-magic on my infant.

My shoulders slumped when I saw Nico at the door through the peephole.

He held up a bag that had the label of one of my favorite restaurants.

"I brought you something to eat."

I chewed on my chapped lip. I wanted to eat, but I didn't want him to see me this disheveled. I looked halfway to dead and smelled worse.

Lilia's cries grew more insistent.

"I can hear her," Nico said. "I know you're at the door. Open it so I can bring in the food. I'll even rock her for a bit so you can use both hands."

My brother was a ruthless negotiator. I had the door open before my brain caught up. His gaze slid over me in a long, penetrating look. He shook his head as he eased into the space.

"Have you slept?"

"Not much."

His lips tugged down before he turned away and set the bag on the cluttered countertop. I blinked back tears. This wasn't how I wanted him to see me. I'd told him I could handle raising a child alone. Obviously, I'd lied to both of us.

He walked over to my oversized cup emblazoned with the hospital logo. He picked it up, shaking it.

"I'm glad Ryder called me. How many of these have you drunk today?"

Ryder called him? I ran my tongue over my teeth, wondering when I'd last brushed them.

"Um...three? Maybe four. I can't remember."

Lilia's cries reached a fever pitch, and I winced as I shuffled back to the rocker, too tired to care about the state of my life and my embarrassment that my brother was seeing how incompetent I was at caring for my child and home.

Lilia needed to eat, so she'd eat. The rest of the world needed to wait.

I unbuttoned my top and Lilia's cries turned to grunts as she rooted at my breast. I winced as she latched on to my sore nipple, but I managed to cover us in a privacy drape I'd thought to keep on the arm of the chair before my head fell back against the top cushion. The moments while Lilia nursed were the closest I had to peace, and I cherished them.

A straw bumped my lip, causing me to jump. I opened my eyes to find the cup at my lips. I opened them and sucked greedily at the cold water. Nico held it until I finally turned my head, reminding me of my daughter.

He went back to the kitchen, refilled the empty container and brought it back to sit next to my chair. Lilia's suckling eased, and I lifted her to my opposite shoulder. I patted her back in that soft but firm motion Ryder showed me. After a large, loud belch, I shifted Lilia to my other breast and rearranged my clothing.

I touched her cheek with my index finger, shocked by how downy her skin was. Her eyelids fluttered and I smiled, loving the feel of her small body tucked in close to my midsection.

"Where are your plates?" he asked.

"Second cabinet to the left."

He pulled two down and then asked about silverware. I directed him, wondering why he was here.

He plated something that smelled of garlic and lemons.

"Mom looked worse than you those first few weeks. I remember her being so tired—she said you never slept."

I blinked back tears.

"I'm sorry for bringing up those memories, Nico—"

"I'm not," he interrupted. "I'm not sorry to share those memories with you at all. In fact, they make me feel…whole."

"Tell me about work."

Nico caught me up on our current projects. "We have a new project in Newport. I took them to see the Smithsons' cantilevered deck and they want something similar. Definitely the ceramic wood but probably on a stable deck. It's going to look fantastic."

I smiled because I liked that design and was glad our client did, too.

Nico edged further into the living room. "When she finishes nursing, I'll hold her while you eat and shower."

"Really?"

He chuckled. "You don't have to sound so excited."

"But I am. That's like…winning the lottery or something."

"Or something."

Lilia stopped suckling, her mouth now slack. I fixed my clothes and offered Nico the baby. He insisted I eat before I showered, and I was too hungry to argue. A delicious meal and a long, hot shower did wonders.

"Thank you," I said.

He smiled again, and more tears pricked my eyes. *This* was the brother I remembered.

"I missed you," I whispered.

He wrapped his free arm around me. "I missed me, too. Thanks for helping me find my way home."

He pressed a kiss to my temple. Then, he cleared his throat.

My eyes sagged shut.

I woke in my bed with Lilia in the bassinet next to it, the lights low, fussing. I glanced at the clock. Ten p.m. Three solid hours—that was the most sleep I'd gotten in days.

I checked my phone and noted the messages from Ryder.

Mind if I come over?

I bit my lip. I wanted him to hold me, but if I said that, I'd seem desperate.

Lilia's sleep schedule is a mess. You won't get much—if any—if you join me.

Don't care. I want to be with you.

I smiled. My brother was here, talking to me, caring for me. Ryder wanted me.

Then I'd love for you to come over.

He crossed the hall, and I opened the door. Rosie trotted in behind him and made for her bed as Ryder pulled Lilia and me into his embrace.

I never wanted him to let us go.

Chapter Thirty-Nine
Aidy

Jeff called me two weeks later to let me know he was back state-side and wanted to meet at a coffee shop. I rolled my eyes at Jeff's obvious cluelessness when it came to leaving the house with a month-old infant.

Of course, getting Lilia ready for the trip probably took longer than whatever he had to say to me. Not that I wanted him in my space—I didn't. The coffee shop was a much better option.

Still, my heart pounded at the thought of seeing my ex…how would he respond to Lilia? Everyone fell in love with her. What if he wanted to be part of her life? Could I keep them apart? Should I want to? What about Ryder? I worried my lip, concerned. Ryder didn't like Jeff—didn't trust him. I didn't either, but he was my responsibility. Plus, Ryder was at work already.

After two diaper changes, the second of which required outfit changes for both the baby and me, I wasn't sure I could manage leaving my condo.

Most tasks took up more energy than I thought they should. I kept telling myself once I was sleeping through the night, I'd no longer burn in the fog of listlessness. But so far, I didn't seem to be improving.

I sent Ryder a text to let him know where I was going before I finished gathering the extra clothes, burp cloths, diapers, wipes, and toys Lilia might need. I felt my phone vibrate with a text, but my arms were full with the car seat and my keys—at least that's what I told myself when my heart stuttered and the tears returned.

I walked into the shop five minutes early. I picked a table near the back and settled onto the padded bench. I placed Lilia's seat next to mine. Then I pulled out my phone, which had buzzed a few more times while I was driving. Ryder had sent me multiple messages.

Do you want me to join you?

What does he want?

I'm worried.

I blinked at the messages, tension riding my shoulders hard. I bit my lip, unsure of how to answer.

I don't know, I typed into the text box. *Yes, please come if you can.*

"Hey, Aidy."

I yelped, dropping my phone. I stood, bumping the table and causing Lilia to wake. Thankfully, she just blinked up at the toys on the bar across her car seat and didn't cry—yet. She would soon. I'd already discovered Lilia didn't like her car seat.

"Jeff," I said with a sigh.

"You look good," he said as his eyes roamed my body, taking in my large breasts and my leggings—regular leggings, not maternity pants. Lilia's constant eating, combined with the challenge of finding time to eat myself, had caused me to drop down within ten pounds of my pre-pregnancy weight. I wasn't sure I liked the reason for the quick reduction.

"Real good," he purred. He blinked, bringing his gaze back up to my face. "I thought you'd be…you know…"

I licked my lip and took him in, too. His hair was buzzed short in a crew cut that barely covered his scalp. His eyes—the ones I used to sigh over because they were such a soft, dreamy brown—blinked at me under sooty lashes. I studied him, trying to see his features in Lilia. With a stab of satisfaction, I realized Nico was correct and Lilia was a mini-me.

"You thought I'd be sloppy and exhausted?" I asked. "Well, I am. Lilia's not a great sleeper."

Flustered, he cleared his throat. "Want a coffee?"

I rolled my eyes. "I can't drink caffeine while I'm nursing. But I'll take a mint tea." Maybe it would calm my nerves. I doubted it.

Jeff didn't bother to answer. He just trotted into line. Lilia began to fuss, so I unbuckled her from her seat. She bounced her tiny mouth against my chest, her cries growing louder and her arms and legs wiggling. I sighed, wishing she could have gone longer between feedings. Jeff returned with my tea as I rooted through the diaper bag for my cover. Once I had that, I opened my shirt and unfastened my bra. Jeff's gaze darted around, his face scarlet.

"Do you have to do that now? I mean, everyone knows you're…you know…"

"Feeding *my* daughter?" I asked. "I imagine they do. But I've covered my boob."

"But it's…"

"Natural," I snapped. "And best for her."

He held up his hand. "Fine. Sure. Look, I don't want to fight with you. I just wanted to meet the kid."

I raised an eyebrow. "Her name is Lilia. Lilia *Wright*." Not Schneider.

He shifted in his seat. "I saw the birth certificate. What's up with the middle name?"

"Parissa. It means fairly-like." I paused. "I named her after the people who helped deliver her." I'd never tell Jeff I'd chosen Parissa because of its association with Ryder. Jeff would go ballistic, and I didn't want to face his jealousy.

Jeff's mouth twisted as his damnable pride roared to life. "The doctor? Is that where that weird middle name comes from? You *do* have a thing going with him."

My chest ached. "Who I see is none of your business."

"It is when my kid's around him." Jeff's lips curved into an ugly grimace. "I don't like him."

"I don't like you, but I'm still sitting here," I snapped.

This conversation wasn't going the way I'd planned. I sucked in a breath and tried to regain my equilibrium.

He dropped his elbows onto the table and lowered his head. "You're really pissed at me for that note."

I met his gaze. "I'll never forgive you for wanting me to 'take care of the problem.' That's why I gave you the out. Just sign the papers, Jeff."

He raised his head, met my gaze. "She's mine, too."

Much as I wanted to rub my forehead, I refrained. "What do you want to do?"

"I want to get to know her. Learn how to care for her."

"Really? After you left me and *made it clear* you didn't want me to have the baby, I never expected you to get involved."

Jeff leaned in, eyes serious. "I wasn't really planning to until I got the papers."

A misstep on my part, then. He might have ignored Lilia and me if I hadn't pushed the issue. I swallowed, wishing I'd made another choice.

"I'm staying here for the week," he said. "Just down the street. I'll come over, spend the days with you."

I nodded because I didn't know what else to do. I needed to consult my lawyer to determine my options—and how to get Jeff out of our lives. But…was that best for Lilia?

He drained the last of his coffee while I stared down at my untouched tea.

I just wasn't sure. About anything. I wanted to talk to Ryder about the situation.

"You can come by later. At four." Four was the beginning of Lilia's daily meltdowns. Ryder said she appeared to have colic, and we'd tried every single one of his suggestions. So far, she continued to cry until she finally fell into a deeper sleep around eight-thirty. Ryder would bring home dinner and then take her from me so I could eat with both hands.

I wasn't sure how I would have managed without him. I didn't want to try.

Jeff smiled. "Sounds great."

He picked up the baby carrier as soon as I buckled Lilia into it, and it took everything in me not to snatch it away.

He asked if he could go with us now, but I demurred, not interested in spending the entire day with him. I was exhausted and tense, especially since I wasn't sure how this situation would play out between Jeff and Ryder, let alone between Ryder and me.

I settled into my car and locked the doors. I stared out the front windshield, unseeing for a long moment. Then, I pulled out my phone and dialed Bridget's number.

"Do you have a few minutes?" I asked.

"Sure. What's up?"

I downloaded the story in as few words as possible. "I know this isn't like your situation with Ben, but is there anything I can do? I don't want Jeff involved."

"And you have a newborn and you don't even have your feet under you. That's a lot to handle, Aidy. Not going to lie. I'd be really stressed in your situation."

I pressed my hand to my cheek and it fluttered downward. "I am. And I don't know how to fix any of it," I whispered.

Bridget was quiet for so long I worried the connection had been severed. "Maybe the best course of action is to let it play out."

Tears filled my eyes. "But what if Ryder leaves me? He hasn't said he plans to stick around and now things are so much more complicated."

Bridget blew out a breath. "I really don't know. My best suggestion is to let him know you care for him and want him involved."

"But what if he decides we're too much work?"

She sighed. "Then I guess you know he isn't the right man for you."

Chapter Forty
Ryder

I'd already planned to stop at my favorite coffee shop and grab a couple of their chocolate, white chocolate chip cookies as a surprise for Aidy when her text came in. I scowled, unhappy with the idea of Jeff showing up and liking even less the idea of Aidy ignoring me while she met with him.

Would Jeff usurp my evenings with Lilia and Aidy?

If he decided to man up and be an actual father to her, would Lilia even remember me, the man who'd delivered her and held her first?

Doubtful. What hurt more was that I wanted to be the man Lilia sought out to soothe her hurts and ask her questions. Not Jeff. *Me*.

I stepped out of my car and strode toward the shop's door. Icy dread built in my guts as Jeff appeared at Aidy's side, holding the baby carrier. I stood rooted to my spot between my vehicle and the minivan to my right, closer to Aidy. I slid back a foot or two, not wanting her to see me.

Jeff handed Aidy the car seat, not bothering to insert it himself. I gnashed my teeth as Aidy maneuvered into her sedan and clicked in the infant seat. She exited the car and refocused on Jeff.

"You have the address?"

"Yeah. I guess I'll see you there."

"At four," she said. "Not before. I mean it."

Aidy settled into her car. Jeff closed her door. He rocked back on his heels and stared after them, a bemused expression on his face. Then, he walked over to a large SUV.

A cold sweat broke out over my skin. I didn't want Jeff anywhere near my girls.

I headed back to my car, no longer interested in cookies or even caffeine, my stomach in knots as I realized I might just lose them both.

Much as I wanted to call the clinic's business manager and tell her I'd need a longer lunch and to please move my patients over to Simon or Sean's schedules, that wasn't the responsible decision— nor was it fair to the rest of the staff.

Even though I wanted to run away. I wanted to simply disappear and pretend the situation never happened.

Like my father. That's *just* what my father did.

I leaned my head back against my car's seat and closed my eyes. "Fuck."

So I drove back to the clinic, dread pooling in my belly. I went through the routine of reading my next patient's chart, all the while thinking about Aidy and Lilia and how Jeff had returned to take my place.

I managed to make it through the afternoon, somehow. I even managed to collect Rosie and drive home. Lilia's cries met me at the elevator, but I continued to my door. I opened it and stepped inside my place, only to realize I couldn't stand being there. Not with Jeff across the hall.

I sent Aidy a text to let her know I was around—if she wanted to see me. When she didn't reply immediately, I took a shower.

Jeff's here. He plans to stay the week.

I replied, *In your condo?*

Fuck, no, I wasn't cool with that.

But what choice did I have?

She didn't respond, probably because she knew I wouldn't like the answer. I gritted my teeth, determined to let the situation play out.

By nine, I still hadn't heard from Aidy. Lilia's cries had turned hoarse. I wanted nothing more than to go over there and help her.

But Aidy didn't contact me.

So I drank a third beer as I watched TV in my bedroom, Rosie's head on my lap as I pet her silky ears.

Sleep didn't come easily.

By five, I was tired of staring at the ceiling, freaking out about what had happened, so I threw on my clothes and walked across the hall. I pressed my ear to the door and listened.

Nothing.

Should I knock?

No.

I turned back to my place and entered, pausing when I heard the elevator ping. I caught a glimpse of Jeff, hair slicked back and bag with the local bagel logo on its side. He knocked on the door.

Aidy opened her door. Her hair was piled in an untidy knot on top of her head. Even from a distance, I could see her exhaustion.

"Why are you here?" she snapped.

"I thought you said the kid got up early."

"We were *sleeping*, Jeff. That doesn't happen often."

She glanced toward my door, but I'd closed it almost completely so I could peek out the peephole. Her shoulders folded in as she held open the door.

"You're here so come in. But wait for me to call you from now on."

"No can-do, Aids. If you'd just let me spend the…"

His words were cut off as she shut the door. I sagged against mine, hands fisted.

She hadn't let him spend the night. He was pushing hard to get what he wanted—namely Aidy and Lilia.

Would he try to talk her into moving back to Houston?

I knew Jeff's type, and I knew he would. I hated that idea. So much so, I struggled to focus on any of my patients that day.

Each time I thought of Jeff trying to sweet talk Aidy into doing things his way, I wanted to rush over to her place and pound him. But this was a decision Aidy had to make. Dammit, I didn't know how to navigate this situation.

I was the one who helped her through these last months. We were close. We were…we'd never defined what we were, and the lack of conversation fueled my unease.

I wasn't giving up on Aidy and Lilia, but I had to figure out how I could fight for my girls. Because this pain in my chest told me that I couldn't simply walk away.

Chapter Forty-One
Aidy

Lilia freaked out more the second day Jeff was around. I worried that was because she could sense my stress, but the truth was, she hadn't slept enough the day before. Each time I tried to set her down, she woke with a startle and began to cry. Jeff picked her up, but she'd screamed the entire time. Breakfast was torture, as was my attempt to bathe her, hoping the water would soothe Lilia enough to relax her into sleep. She continued to cry, now hoarse, which made my head pound.

"Maybe a ride in the car would help her calm down," Jeff suggested.

I was so tired, and my head hurt so much that I couldn't come up with a better plan. We took Lilia to my car and I let him drive. I was so exhausted that the minute Lilia hushed, my eyes slammed closed.

I woke to Lilia's cries. Jeff was in the back seat, cursing as he attempted to change her diaper. Her little arms and legs flailed and her back arched.

"Jeff," I said, getting out of the car. "You're scaring her."

"What do you mean?" he asked.

Thankfully, Lilia was too young to roll because he'd backed away from her so quickly that she was half in and half out of her diaper, lying on the car's seat.

"I mean, you have a low, angry tone filled with growly frustration. That's scaring her."

He speared his fingers through his hair. "Then, by all means, you do it."

I bit my tongue, unwilling to fight with him, especially now. Instead, I finished changing her and then settled into the seat to nurse her. I breathed a sigh, thankful for the partial privacy of the backseat. Jeff's constant presence made nursing—everything— more challenging.

"Your phone beeped while you were sleeping. There's a notification."

I leaned forward and took my phone out of the cup holder where I'd set it earlier. I had the text from Ryder I hadn't answered last night—I'd fallen asleep.

And…I cursed. We had an appointment with him in twenty minutes.

Could this day get any worse?

I texted him to let him know that Jeff wasn't staying with me and that I'd fallen asleep.

I then let him know that Jeff was planning to attend Lilia's well checkup.

He didn't respond.

"Can you stop at a store or gas station?" I asked.

"Why?" Jeff's lips tightened.

"Because I'm thirsty, and I didn't bring my water."

"Jesus. You have your entire apartment in the back seat but you didn't bring a bottle of water?"

"No. I forgot. Lilia was crying, remember?"

"That's all she ever does," Jeff grumbled.

I closed my eyes, praying for the patience that just wasn't there.

"She's a baby. They cry." A lot. At least in Lilia's case.

"I can't promise we'll have time to stop for a drink since you're still nursing."

"Jeff," I said with a sigh. "She's a month old. She eats so often because she's growing, and I need water to make more milk."

He grumbled some more but stayed in the front seat, probably messaging some woman he planned to hook up with as soon as he returned to Houston.

"Is this what you want, Jeff? I mean, really?"

He lifted his head and met my gaze in the mirror. His eyes were stormy. "I don't know, Aidy. It's a lot harder than I thought it would be."

"Do you love her? Would you do *anything* for her? Will she come first in your life?" I gestured toward his phone. "Before the women? Before partying? Because Lilia needs to. She needs that stability."

He remained silent even after I'd burped her and buckled us both in. I settled into the back seat, giving him space. And hoping that he'd make the best decision for Lilia—and me.

Chapter Forty-Two
Ryder

I stared down at the screen, reading Aidy's texts again. I gnashed my teeth as frustration oozed from my every pore. Jeff planned to attend today's visit. The ass showed no signs of backing down. He might not, ever.

He'd be in Aidy's and Lilia's life, which left me unsure how to proceed.

Sean was with a patient; otherwise I might have asked him to swap with me. Instead, I forced myself to enter the exam room.

"So, we're here for the one-month check-up," I said. I'd tried to brace myself for seeing the three of them together, but my breath whooshed from my lungs. They looked good together. No, they looked *right*.

Jeff was the big, all-American guy that other men looked up to. With my dark coloring, I'd been picked on enough to know that blond hair would have served me much better—just like Mackay was a better last name for Jamaica Plain schools than Hadid, which was part of why I'd refused to have my aunt adopt me.

That, and I'd expected my father to return for me.

Aidy placed Lilia on the exam table. I looked down at the plump-legged cherub and couldn't help but grin. She waved her arms, making small huffing noises. I bent over her, and she smiled.

"Oh," Aidy said, her voice faint.

"What?" Jeff asked.

Lilia kept looking at me, gaze steady as it had been when I'd first held her.

"What?" Jeff asked again.

Lilia smiled again.

"Oh, that's so sweet," Aidy whispered.

"Early, too," I said. "Most babies don't smile for a few more weeks."

"Well, that's a good sign, right?" Aidy asked.

"I'm sure she'll be as smart as her mother."

We shared a look, but Jeff cleared his throat, glaring at me. He moved in closer and laid his hand on Aidy's waist. I turned away, tuning them out, focusing on my patient. I spoke to Lilia softly, smiling back at each of her toothless grins.

"She's doing really well," I said to Aidy, who hovered over the baby. "You can pick her up but don't get her dressed yet. She's due for her immunizations."

Jeff moved and now lounged in one of the plastic chairs, seemingly without a care. Though I did catch his narrowed-eye gaze directed at me.

Aidy seemed tense.

"But she's crying."

"More than she did before? Outside her four to eight time frame?" I asked.

Aidy nodded. "I'm worried something's wrong. She's too young for teeth, and she wants to nurse constantly."

I made a note in the chart.

"We can do a test for GERD—gastro-esophageal reflux disorder," I said. "You'd have to bring her in for an ultrasound."

"Is that bad? Is she hurting?" Aidy asked.

The anxiety that laced her words made me want to take her hand. Instead, I retreated to my seat and began typing on my computer.

"It's like heartburn, so it doesn't feel good."

"Okay."

"And you wouldn't be able to feed her beforehand," I said. "Her stomach would need to be empty."

"So you want to make her cry more?" Jeff said. He muttered something that sounded like sadistic bastard.

I bristled but returned my gaze to Aidy. She seemed wrung out.

"Whatever you think is best," she said.

I tried to smile at her, but I feared I'd failed. "We'll see you next week." I rose, needing to get away from Aidy.

"Jeff, would you give me a minute with Dr. Mackay?" Aidy asked.

My shoulders tensed. I didn't want to be alone with Aidy. Not right now. Not while I was reeling from seeing them together. I needed time to process.

"Why?"

"Because I need to discuss a personal issue about nursing, and I'm not comfortable doing that while you're in here. Plus, when the nurse gives Lilia her shots, she's going to cry."

Aidy kept her eyes trained on me, not bothering to look at her ex. Much as I wanted to find that reassuring, I didn't.

As soon as he strode out of the room, she said, "You're mad at me."

I shook my head. "I'm angry with myself. I lived in a fantasy world with you. One that was never going to last…" I paused at her flinch.

"Why wouldn't it?" she asked, her tone low.

"Because Jeff's involved."

"So you'd break off what we have because of *Jeff*?"

"I think it would be best if you found another pediatrician," I said. "I'll write down a few names."

Her eyes filled with tears. "You don't want to see us anymore?"

I shoved my thumbs into my pockets. "Aidy, I—I can't do this," I said. My voice cracked and I sealed my lips.

"This is your workplace, so I won't do anything that makes you uncomfortable." Aidy looked back at her daughter, who was cuddled to her chest. "But you need to know—what you just said hurt me. That cut me to the quick, Ryder."

I dipped my head toward the hallway, my own anger and fear seeping into my words. "You let him right back into your life, your apartment."

"I did no such thing."

"But he's here to be part of Lilia's life?"

"Maybe…" She worried her lower lip. "I don't know. It's complicated."

"Then, I don't fit into that picture," I said. "I'll take care of Rosie for you this weekend."

She blinked at me, trying to shift gears no doubt by my non sequitur.

"You have a lot going on and don't need to worry about the puppy." I needed the dog's quiet sweetness more right now, and, selfishly, I refused to give that up.

Before Aidy could speak again, I rushed on, "Much as I want to be part of your life, Lilia has a father—one who has to love her more than I could."

Aidy's lip quivered. "Why would you say that? After all we've shared."

I swallowed hard, and my breath hitched but I refused to look away from Aidy's eyes. "You know I never planned to have a family."

I opened the door and walked out.

Simon asked me a few times throughout the afternoon if I were okay, and I replied with a curt response. But, as our workday wound down, and I faced the horrible realization I had to be in the flat across the hall from Aidy, I asked Simon to join me for a beer. He agreed, and I spilled my concerns before we managed to even order a drink.

When the waiter came back he ordered and then turned to face me.

"You fucked up," Simon said.

"What? How is this my fault?"

"You let that arsehole weasel in on your girls."

"But that's just it, Simon. They aren't mine, are they?"

"And you think they're bloody well *his*?"

My hands fisted. "No."

He laid his forearms on the table and leaned closer to me. His gaze was steady. "If you didn't tell Aidy that, then you fucked up."

I shoved my fingers into my hair. I waited, hoping he'd say

more about Aidy and Lilia.

The British wanker didn't, and the gleam in his eye told me he knew exactly what he was doing.

"So, are you going to explain to me why you ditched a lovely woman and one of the three most adorable baby girls on the planet?"

"The other two being yours?" I asked, tone dry.

His smile grew so wide, I worried his face would split. "Too right."

"How is Bridget?"

"Gorgeous. Perfect," Simon said as he nodded to the waiter. He thanked him for the pint and turned back to me, his eyes intense. "I don't get it, Ryder. What's the problem?"

I shifted in my chair. He leaned back in his, looking like a man well-pleased with his world.

"Me," I snapped. Raising my gaze and stiffening my spine. "*I'm* the problem. Jeff's Lilia's father, *not* me."

Simon raised an eyebrow. "By that logic, I'm not a father to Brendan."

I slid my fingers in my hair and tugged. "You get the difference. Ben's dead. You're not."

"An oversimplification but true."

"So you see the problem," I said.

"Nope."

My frustration boiled over. "I'm not like you, okay? I don't have two parents that were so overly protective of my life that they flew to Providence to make sure I wasn't making a muck of my life. I spent nearly nine weeks in foster care before the state managed to find my aunt."

Simon's frown deepened. "So, your aunt mistreated you?"

"No." I frowned. "My aunt flew back from Haiti—"

"Why was she in Haiti?" Simon asked.

"She was part of the Doctors Without Borders program."

"So, she flew in, picked you up, and?"

I shrugged. "Got a job at a hospital in Boston."

Simon sipped his beer, staring down into the amber liquid. Finally, he met my gaze. "As you so kindly pointed out, Brendan isn't my son by birth, but he *is* mine by love. I enjoy spending time with him. Hell, I make a point to carve out time *because* of the pleasure I get when I interact with him."

This time, I was the one who stared down into my beer, searching for answers.

"Can you cover for me at the clinic tomorrow?" I asked.

Simon shrugged. "Not sure. But if you can't make it in, we'll figure something out."

"I need to talk to my aunt."

Simon slid out of the booth and patted me on the shoulder. "Sounds smart. And for what it's worth, I think Jeff and Bridget's former husband Ben are cut from the same selfish cloth. Thanks for the beer." He headed toward the exit, ignoring the few women who showed interest in him.

I pushed my unfinished beer away and pulled out my phone. I called my aunt.

"Hi, *Khaleh*. Are you home?" I asked.

She laughed. "Just about finished with my shift, but I'll be home in an hour. What's up?"

"I wanted to talk to you and Uncle Tarek. In person. If you're up for it."

"I always love seeing you, Ryder. You know that."

The warmth in her voice settled over me like a warm blanket. "I'm beginning to realize that. And I miss you. So, I thought I'd drop in. Want me to bring dinner?"

"Instead of eating a Zara special PB&J, you mean?" She chuckled. "No, no. Tarek has been taking cooking classes. I won't say it's five-star cuisine, but retirement never tasted so good."

"See you soon."

Her smile reached through the phone and wrapped me even tighter in that blanket. "I look forward to seeing you."

Chapter Forty-Three
Aidy

This is what drowning feels like.

I couldn't seem to get a full breath. My head swam and my chest ached. Lilia fretted and fussed, clearly unhappy from her shots. Jeff dropped us back at my condo, and I rocked Lilia for a long time after she finished nursing, unable to find the interest of getting up. Of making any effort.

Ryder didn't want us. The ironic thing was Jeff didn't either— he never had. But Ryder…I'd expected more from him.

Tears burned in my eyes. I didn't bother to turn my head when Jeff came in. He settled a large glass of water in my hand.

"Drink."

I did because I knew I should. I let him bully me into a meal because I knew that was important, too.

Jeff asked to stay the night, and I didn't fight with him on that either—why should I? There wasn't anything left for me to fight for. Morning came after another long, interrupted night; I noted with satisfaction that exhaustion had settled over Jeff's face.

He made breakfast, burning the eggs to the point we had to air out the space. I kept my phone close, hoping for a message from Ryder. He never contacted me.

The day passed in a blur of feedings and diaper changes. Jeff left long enough to grab a shower and clean clothes. He turned up with another meal and I picked at it, not overly interested in it.

"Let me hold her so you can shower," he said.

"Why?"

"Because she's my daughter and you…you leaked through your shirt."

I glanced down, noting the dried stain over my left breast. I shrugged. "It'll just happen again," I said.

"But at least you won't smell," he said, wrinkling his nose.

"Lilia comes first."

"Not so much that you have to be a zombie." He ran his hands through his hair. "Look, I get that something went down between you and the doctor. I even get that I…maybe made that situation raw. Whatever. But I know that Lilia needs you healthy. I don't have the ability to feed her, and I don't have the stamina you've pulled out for these all-hours feedings. So, do us both a favor and shower, brush your teeth, comb your hair and take a nap."

"I'll wait until Emmaline and Knox show up tonight, but thank you."

He met my gaze. His lips curled into a sardonic smirk. "You think I'd take her from you?" he asked, his tone soft. "So you called in backup to make sure I don't disappear."

I met his gaze. "You've broken every promise you ever made me," I said. "You broke my heart, too. And, now, you're partially responsible for destroying the best relationship I've ever had. All because you hate to lose. So, yes, I'm worried you'd take *my* baby from me."

The tears I'd fought since Ryder walked out on me yesterday poured down my cheeks. I wasn't sure what, exactly, I was crying about or for in that moment. Maybe for my naive self who'd actually seen Jeff as a man I'd want to spend my life with. Or maybe for the fact that when he grew bored again, I'd be alone and *still* heartbroken. Or maybe for the fact that Ryder had pushed past his fear of delivering my daughter and saved her only for me to lose him to his fears of what a perfect family looked like—and why he'd never fit into that scenario.

I could have told Ryder that he was crazy. But even I had to agree that Jeff looked the part of a dad. Unfortunately, his inner self didn't match the exterior, and if I'd realized that sooner, I…I couldn't go there because then I wouldn't have Lilia. I wouldn't have met Ryder and he wouldn't have loved me as a man should all these months.

Even if Ryder were willing to throw us away, I now knew what I'd missed out on before—with Jeff and in my previous relationships.

Jeff slouched down onto the couch, not meeting my eyes.

"I'm not a bad guy, Aids. You seem to think that, but I'm here, aren't I?"

"What have you done here that wasn't for you? You pushed yourself into our day, into our life. You refused to follow my simplest of requests. You complain about Lilia's schedule and your lack of sleep and how bored you are. No, I don't think you've changed. I think your sweetheart of a sister pushed you into coming."

At his flinch, I sighed. I hadn't wanted to be right about that.

"I appreciate your attempts to help this week, but we both know this isn't the real you." I waited until he met my gaze. "The real you is going to burst forth sooner or later. And he's going to hurt Lilia and he's going to try to hurt me."

"You have a shit opinion of me," he muttered.

"Is it wrong?" I asked.

"I think it's wrong that you're crying over some other guy while I'm here," he snapped.

I swallowed and wiped my nose on my sleeve. I was already disgusting anyway, in my leaked-through shirt and unwashed body.

"Here's the deal: I'm going to stay in Providence. It's my home. My career is here, and I've made something of myself—I've taken on a puppy and a baby, all within a few months, and while they're both challenging, I'm managing." I closed my eyes. "No, Rosie and Lilia are and will continue to thrive. Because of me."

I thumped my chest, uncaring that my fist came away wet from the fresh milk dripping through my bra. I was a mess, but I'd managed to get through, as Bridget said, a lot of stress. I had no choice but to continue to do so.

I straightened my spine.

"I met the love of my life—and I might have lost him, too. But you...you're still Jeff. You're still going to leave me for weeks at a time, maybe more. And you're not willing to be faithful. You aren't what I want. You never will be."

Chapter Forty-Four
Ryder

I pulled up in front of my aunt and uncle's house in Jamaica Plain. I looked back at Rosie, who I'd picked up from doggy daycare, as I did every day. The puppy sat in the back seat on the blanket I kept there for her. She wagged her tail.

I blinked, shocked and freaked out that I didn't remember much of the drive. I sat in my car, my hands clammy and my head all over the place.

I grabbed Rosie's leash as she bounded out of the car and strode up to their door. I rang the bell. Zara opened it and her gaze softened with concern as she took me in. Without words, she pulled me in for a hug, and I settled into her embrace, needing her warmth and the faint hint of exotic spices that always clung to her.

Finally, she led me to the couch. Tarek came over and shook my hand. His lined face broke into a smile as I pulled him closer, into a hug.

"I'm glad you're here, even if you look much like when you wrecked your first car."

I shook my head, a small smile flitting across my lips. "I caused you both so much pain."

"You were a teenager," Tarek said, settling into the nearest armchair.

"I was an angry punk who didn't like rules."

"You acted out because you didn't know where to put the pain of your father leaving you," Zara said. Her eyes were soft, full of understanding I wasn't sure I deserved.

"I…" I bowed my head.

"Dinner will be ready soon," Tarek said. "I'll put the dog in the back yard."

"Don't go," I said, raising my head. "This…this is for both of you."

I picked up Rosie, petting her to give myself a moment to collect my thoughts. She nuzzled her head closer. I had it bad for Aidy's dog, too.

"Jeff's back. He's Aidy's ex-fiancé, Lilia's father."

My fisted hands dropped to my thighs. Zara scooted closer to me and ran a soothing hand down my back.

"What will be is meant to be," Zara said, though her countenance showed concern.

"I love her, Aunt Zara."

Understanding broke across her face. "So you're willing to let her go. Back to this Jeff who clearly hurt her and disappeared for months." Zara shook her head, anger flooding her eyes. "I thought you are more of a man than that, Ryder."

I gawped. "That was…"

"Exactly what you needed to hear," Tarek said. "She said the same to me when I worried about marrying her and becoming a father to you."

Dazed, I shook my head. Tarek had doubts about me? Well, shit. That just made this whole situation muddier.

"You were the best thing that came into my life—you and Zara."

"We tried to be," he said. His lip curled a little. "But I worried because I know you loved your father, as any good son would."

"He wasn't a good father," I said. I looked down at my clenched fists. "What if I'm like *him*?"

Zara gripped my cheeks in her surgeon's hands, the hold nearly as fierce as her eyes. "You are *not* your father, Ryder. Tarek has been your father for more years than Damon. I stepped into my sister's role filled with grief but a light heart because I never expected to have a child—but then I had you."

I fidgeted, feeling like the naughty boy who'd eaten a bag of Oreos before dinner—mainly to see what Aunt Zara would do. If she would leave like my mother.

And in that moment, I realized she'd never left. She'd been sad, frustrated, angry, disappointed, but she'd always communicated what she was feeling and why I deserved the consequences of my actions. And, then, she'd cup my face like she had moments ago and tell me she loved me.

I got it, *finally*. She was trying to force those words, that understanding into my head. But I'd been too stubborn—no, too *scared*—to hear her. To accept her love. Hers and Tarek's.

I glanced over at my uncle, sitting so still in his armchair, his dress slacks and button-down perfectly starched. "Tarek taught me to play lacrosse. You took me to those medical camps at Harvard and BU so I could further my passion. You and Tarek took me back to Persia so I could learn more about our family." I licked my lips, my heart hammering too fast as Zara and Tarek's actions crystallized.

Rosie pressed in closer to my side, and I slid my fingers into her thick fur. She made a noise that I interpreted to be comforting, and my heart swelled with gratitude.

"You taught me Farsi. Tarek sat with me in the principal's office when I got in another fight, and you and he always found me another school."

Her smile curled those soft lips. "You understand now. I'll *never* leave you. You are the child of my heart."

I squeezed her hands, then I pulled her in for a hug. "You will, one day. And I'm going to miss you so much."

"Oh, *azizam*. I'll miss you more. You are the light of my life, Ryder Yusuf Mackay."

"You put up with a lot of shit from me."

She chuckled. "We did our best. But we are not perfect. And it took you until you were thirty-one years old to actually admit Damon hurt you."

I closed my eyes. "He devastated me. Foster care was rough. I wasn't prepared—for any of it."

Once again she wrapped me into her embrace. I rested my head against her shoulder and looped my arms around her back. And I held her, and she held me, and we cried for the hell I'd gone through then and had never fully released.

"I would have come sooner. I would *never* have left you. I would have fought Damon for custody, I would have—"

I shushed her. "You loved me even when I didn't feel like I deserved it. Especially then. Thank you. And thank you, Tarek."

I smiled at the graying gentleman who hovered now at the side of the couch, clearly out of his depth, but determined to stand by his family.

Zara sniffled as she pulled back, hand fluttering in front of her eyes. "You've made me so happy. Except you're not happy at all, which makes me sad. I feel like I'm in emotional overload."

"Welcome to my world," I muttered.

I sat quietly for a moment. She dabbed at her eyes with a handkerchief Tarek handed her.

I lifted my gaze to the quiet man with his white goatee and deep laugh and worry lines intermingled across his cheeks and forehead.

"Tarek, you were a good father to me," I said.

"My pleasure, Ryder," he said. The warmth in his eyes matched the affection in the arms he wrapped around us both as he settled on the other side of Zara.

I winked at Zara. "Thank you for marrying him."

She laughed. "*That* was truly my pleasure."

We continued to hug one another until Tarek stifled a curse. "Dinner!"

We all laughed.

I kissed the side of Zara's head before I helped her to her feet. I stared out the front window.

"Can I stay here this weekend, with you?"

"Of course. We'd love your company."

Zara and I walked into the kitchen, where Tarek pulled something out of the oven.

We ate and then settled into the living room where Tarek put on his Sinatra CDs.

I sipped the arak *razzouk*, an anise-flavored liqueur, that Tarek preferred. He said it reminded him of his father, who liked to sit on their small balcony in Beirut and sip it while he smoked cigars.

The night was peaceful, calm. But I missed Aidy. I wished even for Lilia's cries, but more to cuddle her warm, tiny body. I closed my eyes and brought up her gummy grin, the wide bright eyes that lit up when she saw me.

Could I give that up?

I woke with a stiff neck that matched my stiff legs. I pushed back the down-filled comforter from my shoulder and sat up, wincing. I'd fallen asleep on the couch. Granted, I'd been helping Aidy with Lilia's nighttime awakenings until the last couple of days, but there was no reason for me to be that tired.

The strained tendons in my neck made my head pound, but at the same time, my mind sharpened, my thoughts clearer than they'd been in months.

"Oh, good. You're awake," Zara said. "Tarek will bring us coffee."

I shrugged off the comforter and began to fold it as Tarek brought in a large, silver tray with a silver coffee pot and three small, porcelain espresso cups. I raised mine and sipped, closing my eyes as the decadent warmth slid down my throat.

"I delivered Lilia." I stared down into my glass. "She was blue. The umbilical cord..."

Aunt Zara gasped, fingers to her lips, eyes wide. Tarek laid his hand on my shoulder.

I blew out a breath. "It was like Molly, but worse. Because I had to save her, and I wasn't sure I could."

Tears spilled over my lashes. I was a blubbering fucking mess. So many emotions had poured out of me and it seemed I had more left in me.

"She almost died, *Khaleh*, and then Aidy would have, too. And that means I'd be my father."

Zara lifted my face, hers filled with concern. "Shhh, my darling." She spoke in Farsi, her tone soothing. "Shhh. You used all those years of medical training and remained calm. You saved Aidy's daughter. You saved Aidy. You gave them both the chance for a long life. I'm so proud of you. Of the man you've become."

"She is well? Lilia?" Tarek asked.

"Yes, she's beautiful. Perfect. Well, not perfect. She's colicky, maybe has GERD, though I wasn't sure—you know it's not that common. And she hates tummy time. And she wants to nurse pretty much constantly from five until eight." My heart swelled with love. I fumbled for my pocket, pulled out my phone and showed them the latest photos I had—from the night before Jeff showed up. I touched the screen, which showed Lilia's plump cheek.

"I left her." That's what stuck in my head. "I saw Aidy with Jeff and they looked like the perfect family."

Zara raised her eyebrows. "You sure about that?"

Desperate as I was to trust her, I had to say the words that my ten-year-old self had always believed: "What if…" I took in a breath. This fear stemmed from my other one—from being the one to leave her. But I knew now I didn't want to leave Aidy. Or Lilia. I needed them. Still, I didn't know how to face this possibility. "What if Aidy leaves me, too? Like my father did. Then, then I'll have nothing."

She raised her other hand to hold my face between both of hers. "Oh, Ryder. I know that's how it feels. And I can't take away that hurt. But you're forgetting something important: Samirah adored you and never planned to leave you."

"But she did. And Aidy's with Jeff."

"Is she?"

"I told you, he's here—"

"But is she *with* him?"

My shoulders slumped. "I don't know. I kind of...well, I just left so she couldn't tell me." Hurt me. "I didn't want it to be like my father all over again."

There it was. The ugly truth I still struggled to understand: my father abandoned me when I needed him the most.

A growl erupted from Tarek's mouth. "Damon is a weak man who failed not just you but his wife and daughter."

Tarek pressed his lips together for a long minute. "You know how Zara sent you to therapy?"

I nodded.

"Well, Zara and I went, too, once we decided to marry."

"I was so angry with Damon," Zara said. "So very angry he left you like he did. I don't have good answers."

"And I went because I was so thankful for you, the son I always wanted. I feared I'd never be able to give you up should Damon come to his senses and return." I met Tarek's fathomless gaze.

"He never did," I said. "Come for me."

Tarek's bushy brows pulled down and he darted a glance at Zara. She nodded.

"He came," Tarek said.

"What? When?"

"Just after you turned fourteen. He'd decided he wanted to take you to Ireland. County Clare where his great-grandparents were born."

I opened my mouth but nothing came out.

"He planned to have you work at some pub he was thinking of managing. As the busboy."

Zara sat forward and gripped my hands. "We wanted more for you. So we told him he should come back when he was settled. That we'd figure out a fair custody agreement."

Her face grimaced.

"I offered him money to not come back," Tarek said. His voice was soft but his eyes steely.

"What?" Zara gasped.

"I told him I'd transfer every penny I could liquidate. Five hundred sixty-four thousand dollars. Every bit of my savings and retirement accounts."

Zara pressed her fingers to her lips. "I never knew."

Tarek's gaze slashed to hers, then came back to me. "He agreed."

Those words hit my stomach hard, reverberated outward, sending a massive shockwave over my system. My father traded me for cash.

"He never got the money," Tarek said, correctly reading my expression. "He never came back for it."

I stared down at my knees, absorbing the story. Absorbing what Tarek had planned to do to keep his family intact. The hurt eased a little as I stared into Tarek's dark eyes. Something fierce—something that looked like pride and love—shone from their depths.

Love *for me*. Pride in the man Tarek raised. Tarek—not Damon.

"I understand if you're angry with me. Zara is." Tarek's face remained implacable. Quiet, stoic Tarek, who'd seemed happy to let Zara drive their marriage, drive my upbringing.

"Why?" I asked.

"I had to decide what you were worth to me. What I was willing to give up for you."

Tarek's gaze slid over my face before he tucked his chin to his chest. "You were—you are—worth everything."

Chapter Forty-Five
Aidy

The rest of the weekend past in a haze, much like the previous few weeks. Lilia still cried during her tummy sessions, but she'd also mastered lifting her head and following the soft plush toys. This was Jeff's favorite time with her. He liked to bounce and toss the toys and Lilia seemed to enjoy tracking the plush bunny and rubber giraffe.

We took her to the test for GERD on Monday, and Sean called me back the next morning, assuring me that while Lilia showed reflux, just as Ryder predicted, medication would help.

Jeff picked up the medicine, and, after the first dose, Lilia calmed…a little. She was still fussy, but the cries were less stringent and her need to nurse constantly diminished.

I huddled on the side of the couch, wishing I could simply melt into it. I wanted Rosie's reassuring weight against my thigh. I mourned that Ryder was keeping his promise to take care of her. That was something else we'd have to work out—he loved Rosie as much as I did, and the dog reciprocated that emotion just as deeply.

How did my life get so damn complicated?

I missed Ryder's warmth pressed to my back. I missed his arm cinching against my ribs. I missed his breath tickling the hair on my neck. I missed his scratchy midnight voice and his crazy bed head. I missed him sitting next to me in the quiet of the night with just the night light glow offering relief on his features as he waited for Lilia to finish nursing.

I missed his advice and knowledge.

I missed him.

And instead, I had Jeff throwing a freaking stuffed bunny and making car-chase noises. I didn't want *this* to be my life.

I'd called Emmaline in tears the night after Ryder broke it off, laying out the whole story. Since then Knox, Emmaline, and Nico stopped by each day. The tension with Jeff was palpable. Typically, I would have tried to cut through the stress, but now... now, I just didn't care. Even Nico's voluminous hug couldn't touch the coldest places inside me.

I'd had love. I'd known, when I looked into Ryder's determined face as I lay panting on Whole Grocer's floor that he was my soul mate.

And because I hadn't told him how I felt, because I'd been scared to admit those feelings, I'd lost him.

Only Lilia's needs kept me going.

Tuesday slid into Wednesday. Jeff planned to return to Houston that afternoon. I couldn't even gather the energy to care about that—though I would like my couch back. I was tired of tripping over Jeff's blankets and his duffel bag.

He'd brought the bag with him Saturday, and I hadn't argued. What was the point?

Jeff settled on the couch next to me, Lilia snuggled against his chest. He'd just changed her diaper—the snaps on her sleeper were off by one. I pressed my lips together, trying not to express my flash of annoyance.

He shoved a glass of water in my hand, and, out of habit, I drained it. He took it and handed me the baby.

"I had a bad childhood," Jeff said. He shuddered as if shaking off a memory. He met my eyes. "It's why I was so sure I didn't want kids—why I wanted you to…"

He trailed off and I stiffened, pulling Lilia's tiny body tighter to my chest. "I'm sorry that happened to you." I thought of Ryder—he'd had a terrible childhood but managed to connect with Lilia from the start. "It's okay, Jeff. We don't need your help or financial support."

He nodded though his eyes turned sad. "You're right. You don't need me. You've built yourself a hell of a life. I didn't think you had it in you. I really thought you'd come back—or at least want me to take care of you, like I did in Houston."

"I'm not that naive girl anymore. I believed those lies once."

"You did. And I'm not sorry."

I tilted my head, trying to get a better read on him. He appeared both calm and nervous—like he'd get before a big fire.

"She's your daughter," he said. "I can already see some of that quiet spirit of yours in her."

I laid Lilia in her swing, tensing a bit until I was sure she'd stay sleeping. I faced him fully. "What's this about, really?"

He settled on the edge of the couch cushion, his face solemn. "You were right. My sister pushed me to come here, to be involved."

He cleared his throat. "I care about Lilia, and you. I always will."

I waited for him to get to his point.

"You're good with her—talking and singing, patient. I'm out of my depth. I have no idea how to connect with her."

"Those bunny flips were inspired," I deadpanned.

He grinned, his cheeks flaming. "Not really. I was just doing aeronautical…" He cleared his throat. "Look, this isn't for me. Not the day-to-day. When I hold her, I'm worried I'll break her, and she senses that." He rubbed his palm over the short hairs on the back of his neck.

"She'll get bigger, Jeff. Grow into her personality."

"I know. And I want her to know me, and for me to know her. I've spent this time here, well the last few months, thinking. I treated you badly, and I'm sorry," he said, meeting my gaze. There was a wealth of pain and other emotions in them.

"I freaked out when you told me you were pregnant. That's on me. And I was angry that you blew up my lifestyle. I like being able to come and go."

I bit my lip to keep from saying *in other women.* Though, I wasn't going to forget his cheating.

"I was wrong to kick you out," he said. "To try and tell you what to do about your pregnancy. I really fucked up a lot of things, but I plan to work on that. Be a role model for Lilia. Someone you can respect."

Again, I didn't see Jeff trading in his hookups for tea parties, but I remained quiet because he'd given me more honesty today than I'd ever had from him.

"But I do want you to know I see how much you love her." Jeff reached over and patted my knee. For the first time since he stormed out, leaving that note, I didn't stiffen. He met my gaze and something softer passed between us. One day, maybe, I'd be able to forgive him.

Maybe.

"I'm glad she has you," he said.

"I'm glad I have her," I said.

He nodded.

"Can we figure something out? I mean, I understand you'll need it legal and we can go through the lawyers. But I promise I won't get in the way of you and…Ryder."

I clutched my palms together tightly even as I dropped my gaze to my lap. I wasn't ready to discuss Ryder—especially with Jeff.

"She smiled at him," Jeff said. He sighed, but still I couldn't look at him. Tears burned against my eyelids.

"She knew him by sight, by voice. She connected with him. *Way* more than me. That's why I got pissy."

He was quiet for a long moment.

"Lilia loves him."

There wasn't even jealousy in his tone, which surprised me.

"Doesn't matter," I said, the hollowness sucking at me. I hated feeling like this, but I had no idea how to move on.

Jeff dropped his gaze. "I think it does. And if I hadn't shown up, he'd be the one here, with you. And both of you would be happier." He gestured to Lilia and me.

"But he left. And I don't—"

Jeff placed his fingers over my lips, stifling my words. I stared at him, unsure of how to react.

"I wish I'd realized how special you were. When you were mine."

I pulled back and met his gaze. "We never would have worked. You were right about that."

He gave me a sad smile. "I know. That's why I was with other women. Because you were going to leave, and I needed to be okay with that."

"That makes no…" But it did make sense. I'd chosen Jeff because I knew on some level he didn't really want to be with me forever. I'd made him wait to have sex until he asked me to move in with him. It had been a half-hearted request but the passion in his eyes had been real. We'd danced around our emotions, our fears, never actually addressing them.

I gritted my teeth. I'd learned nothing from my time with Jeff. In fact, I'd actively sabotaged our relationship—just as I had the few before Jeff.

If I'd told Ryder how I felt, about my fears, would he have cut me out, cut me off so easily? I wasn't sure.

Frustration and grief settled in my chest. I might never get the chance to tell him how I felt. How it scared me but also made me believe in a future.

"I'm not cut out for love," Jeff said.

I snapped back into the present, my mind still spinning from my revelations.

"And you…" He smiled. "After losing your parents, after how I treated you, you still have this capacity for it. I think you make more of it, somehow. That's hard to do." He looked down at Lilia, ran his finger over her cheek, then met my gaze.

"You gave me something more precious than I deserved. But that doesn't mean I'm not going to try to deserve her. Or make it up to you."

"Jeff," I said on a long sigh. "I don't want you to feel beholden. I don't want anything from you."

Not to hate him, not to blame him. Something eased inside me at the realization I just wanted to let him and what he did to me go.

"Which is exactly what makes me want to give it to you. You gotta admit, Aids, I'm a stubborn cuss."

He pressed a kiss to my cheek.

"I'll be in touch."

"Okay," I said.

He gathered his bag and snagged his keys from my bowl by the door. Then, he walked out of my condo. I stood and went over, locking the bolt. Then I stared around the empty space, wishing I'd managed a different ending with the right guy.

Chapter Forty-Six
Ryder

Going to work the following Monday settled some of my nervous energy, but I was still drained. I'd spent the weekend and both Monday and Tuesday nights with my aunt and uncle because I'd needed time to learn what Tarek knew about Damon and hash out my feelings about my past.

Zara's anger melted when she realized I wasn't upset with Tarek for keeping Damon from me.

I understood. I'd wanted to do the same for Lilia. And, yes, for Aidy. Keeping them safe from Jeff was part of what I couldn't reconcile, though. He was Lilia's birth father. He deserved the opportunity to be with her.

"But does he?" Zara had asked, her dark eyes bright when I shared this concern with her.

"What?"

"Does he deserve that chance? If I'd pushed the issue sooner with Damon instead of heading off to Haiti for the year, you never would have ended up in that foster home. I did that to lessen my grief and frustration, so I bear some of the blame for your hurt." She pressed her lips together. "That time changed you. Hurt you."

"I was small, skinny, and I cried. The other kids saw me as weak and set about proving it."

She closed her eyes, grief and anger etched in her face. "And you would want that for Lilia?"

"No." The word came out forceful.

"Then, I don't understand, Ryder. What, exactly, are you fighting?"

Those words continued to rattle through my head every day since. What was I fighting?

I stared at my tablet's screen that afternoon as the answer bubbled up. I was fighting myself. No, I was fighting the fear of possibilities. I'd stepped back, away from Aidy and Lilia in an effort to protect myself—so I wouldn't have to feel as I had in that foster home, where my heart had been crushed long before my bones or body.

Before I left Providence on Friday, I'd let Aidy know I was taking care of Rosie. She'd responded with a thank you but nothing more. At least she trusted me with her dog.

But I wanted her to trust me with her heart and her future.

Simon tapped on my door.

"You headed home?" he asked.

"Yeah."

"Are you going to talk to Aidy?"

"Yeah."

He hesitated. "She called Bridget after Jeff showed up. She's not...doing well."

I rose, a rush of adrenaline pumping through me. "What do you mean?"

"Be kind to her, Ryder. Whatever you do, she's dealing with a lot."

I nodded. He hesitated before he strode down the hall. I grabbed my keys and phone and charged after him.

I needed to see Aidy, to evaluate the situation myself. Fear tussled with anticipation in my belly as Rosie and I drove home.

The hall was quiet, which was unusual for this time of evening. Maybe Jeff had been able to work out Lilia's needs, maybe he was more adept at handling the situation than I was.

No. I might not be perfect, but I loved Aidy. I loved Lilia. I couldn't control Jeff's actions, and I didn't need to—because I could choose to make my own.

I knocked on her door, palms damp. She opened it, phone pressed to her ear. She wore a rumpled asymmetrical sweatshirt and leggings. Her hair half-tumbled from her ponytail and her eyes darkened with emotion. Before I realized what I was doing, I leaned in and pressed my lips to hers.

Love.

That was what I'd been missing. I hadn't known what to look for because it was quiet, calm. It was *home*.

"What…Ryder. I'm going to have to call you back, Emmaline."

"Is she okay?" I asked.

Aidy shook her head. "No. She and Knox aren't…" She touched her hair before she faltered, her hand falling to her side. "That's between them, but no, she's not good. What are you doing?"

"I…" Words failed me as I searched her gaze. "I needed to see you."

Her brows pinched. "But, you said…"

"May I come in? Please?"

She studied me, apprehension stamped on her features. I held my breath. She opened the door wider. I stepped in, clasping her hand in mine, fighting the urge to wrap her in my arms. Rosie tugged at the leash, and I let it go. The puppy darted inside, moaning as she flopped into her bed.

"Rosie," Aidy said with a sigh of relief. She knelt beside the puppy, stroking her soft fur.

"I think Tarek overdid the treats. And the walks. He loved having her there," I said.

Aidy and I shared a smile but hers slid away quickly.

"How are you feeling?" I asked.

She blinked up at me. Her lip trembled. I pulled her to her feet and settled her on the couch, sitting next to her.

"Overwhelmed. Exhausted. Unsure of how to take the next step and wanting more control."

I nodded. "I can help you with some of that, if you'll let me."

Her eyes searched mine. "Why would you? I mean, you told me you didn't want a family."

"Which was a lie." I sighed. "I've wanted a family since I was a kid, Aidy. I was scared if I tried with you, you'd leave me."

She tilted her head. "Like your dad."

"Yes. And my mother. Molly and my mom dying messed me up. I know that. But knowing and overriding my subconscious fears of being abandoned again or, just as bad, repeating the cycle and abandoning someone I claimed to care about…I got caught in that, especially once Jeff showed up. I kept thinking that loving you, loving Lilia could only lead to you leaving me, which has been harder."

"I don't want you to hurt, Ryder."

She closed her eyes and leaned back against the cushion, which gave me time to take in the shadows under her eyes. Even her mouth dropped with exhaustion.

"This past week has been hell," she said.

"Because of Jeff?"

She shook her head. "Ironically, no. He's not a half-bad caretaker."

I gritted my teeth.

"But he also wasn't the man I wanted here, with me. I...I missed you." She sucked in a breath, her face tense as she turned her head to meet my gaze.

Shit. She was going to kick me out. Aidy had her own scars, her own fears about loss that ran just as deep as my own.

"I love you, Ryder."

My breath whooshed from me and every muscle sagged.

"I love you, too. So damn much it made me crazy."

I tucked a loose strand of her hair back behind her ear. As much as I wanted to kiss her again, to hold her, she deserved to understand.

"I became a doctor so that I could control outcomes. If I had medicine and technology, then no other baby would have to die, no other family would be ripped apart like mine was. But with you, at Whole Grocer, I had none of my tools—my weapons. I just had my hands. Lilia...she could have died."

Aidy closed her hands over mine. "She didn't."

"I know. And Lilia's healthy. I can't tell you how much of a relief that was."

Aidy raised her eyebrows. "A catharsis?"

"Yes."

She nodded. "I had one of those, too."

"Tell me."

She leaned her head back and stared up at the ceiling. "I chose Jeff, knowing, deep down, we'd never work out." She glanced at me from the corner of her eye. "For a lot of the same reasons you pushed Lilia and me away. It was easier knowing for certain that I'd be left, so that I could make it on my terms." She bit her lip. "Even if those terms hurt."

She inhaled and met my gaze once more. "But I don't want to run anymore, Ryder. I want to be solid for Lilia. I want her to know she'll always have my love, my support."

"I want that, too."

"Are you sure? Because I can't keep going around on this cycle. I love you. What we've shared…these have been the best months of my life, but you leaving? That broke me."

I closed my eyes, hating hearing her words, hating the truth in them.

She glanced down, gasped and started laughing and crying together. "I'm leaking through my fucking bra. Again."

Unable to stand another moment, I pressed a soft kiss to her lips. She quit sobbing and blinked up at me.

"This—you—is natural. You're a new mother. You're dealing with more conflict than most people, and you're still willing to give me a chance. You, Aidalynn, are a strong, capable woman who's used to managing her life."

I cupped her cheeks, bringing her flush against me because I needed to feel her.

"I know you can do it alone. But I don't want you to. I want to be with you, during all the crazy, uncontrollable moments. Please. Let me, sweet girl, let me in."

She leaned in even more, her chest brushing mine. "Okay."

Elation surged through me. "I worried you'd say no."

She cupped my cheeks. "Just promise me that if you get scared, if you're hurting, you stay and talk to me. *Promise.*"

"Yes. I promise."

"Okay," Aidy said. "And for the record, I don't know what Jeff will do. This whole situation is challenging." Her shoulders slumped. "I never wanted to be in a scenario where I had to split time with my child but I even less want to live with Jeff, so we're making do with the hand we've been dealt."

"My father didn't do that," I said, my words falling in slow, neat precision from my mouth. "I hadn't realized until now." I shook my head. "He had to deal with incredible grief. I can't imagine what that was like. But he didn't handle it—he shut down. He hurt me."

Aidy's eyes narrowed into slits of blue fire. "He scarred you emotionally. That's *not* good parenting."

I pressed a kiss to her temple, a soft smile forming as I felt her vibrate under my skin.

"Are you laughing at me?" she demanded.

"No. I'm enjoying how fierce you are when you feel like one of your own has been slighted."

Her expression stayed tense. "That was more than a slight."

Her face changed, softening. "I get that there's a little boy in you who's always going to ask what he did to make his father leave him, but I want you to hear me: you didn't do anything wrong. I need to make you understand so that one day I can make Lilia understand. She didn't do anything wrong. Jeff's demons are his own, and the way he treats his daughter, and me, are not because of anything we did. They're all on him."

I clasped her hand in mine. "I'm getting that. Really, I am. Nearly losing you definitely put everything in crystal-clear focus. I love you. I love Lilia. I won't ever abandon her because I know what that feels like and because she deserves a father who is present."

Aidy wrapped her hand around my wrist. "You've always been her father, you know. From that first night at dinner, when she danced for you in utero. She chose you, and you've taken such good care of both of us."

I pulled Aidy into my arms, us both swaying a little in that natural rhythm that developed with an infant. The motion was comforting.

Her fear reminded me of my own, but it was more than that. I hadn't seen what was so obvious now: I had the choice to let my past define and cripple my life. I almost had.

Instead, with Zara's help, I'd stared straight into those fears and managed to push them back. That didn't mean they'd stay buried, but they weren't supposed to. I needed to air them, talk about my feelings surrounding them—actually confront those fears.

And I would, with both myself and with Aidy. She made me strong enough to do so on the days I wanted to cower back.

Because with her love, I was whole.

Finally.

She wrapped her arms around me, hugging me tightly. "I may need counseling or something."

"I'll help you. Hell, I'll go with you."

"Why?"

"Because I love you. And I want you well. And, fuck, telling you that makes me hot." My cheeks burned but I met her gaze. I'd promised her honesty and I planned on delivering.

Her smile widened, turning sultry. "You've only had sex with me while I was hugely pregnant. You might find out I'm bad at it."

I placed a kiss on the crown of her head. "Not going to happen, sweetheart. When you touch me…" I trembled at the memories of us together. "Fuck. Definitely not a problem."

She worried her lower lip.

"I'm not interested in another kid right away. You can't look at me like some kind of baby-making machine."

I lifted my hands until my palms held her breasts. "These are gorgeous, and I love how large they are, so no promises there." I pressed a kiss to her neck. "Practicing baby-making with you is going to be my favorite pastime."

"Ryder," she said.

"Yeah, I heard you. No more babies right now. I get it, Aidy. You need to adjust. Hell, I do, too. Six months ago, I was a single guy casually dating a career woman. Now, I'm a live-in daddy to the sweetest little munchkin with a sexy-as-fuck girl-friend who's already planning her first home purchase based on school ratings."

When she bit her lip, I smiled. Gotcha. I *knew* she wanted to move into a house. One she'd either build or remodel.

I kissed her softly.

"We've leveled up," she said. "Both of us."

Epilogue | Three years later
Ryder

There was something amazing about shower sex. The heat, the steam. The slippery feel of Aidy's body against mine. I slid my rigid cock against her folds, trying to contain my groan of pleasure at the slick heat.

"Again?" she asked, glancing back at me over her shoulder. Her hair was wet, plastered to her head and water dripped from her eyelashes and dribbled down her cheeks.

"What can I say? I'm insatiable."

"No kidding," she said. "Are you going to try and tell me you're still making up for those few weeks after Lilia was born?" She pushed back against me, letting me know that she didn't want me to stop. Not that I could—or would.

"Would you believe me if I said yes?"

She moaned as I skimmed my fingers over her breasts, tweaking her pebbled nipples. "I would."

"Good. Because it's true. I only want you. I only think of you. I'm never going to stop wanting you." I kissed her neck, leaving my tongue over her wet skin.

"I dream about you being inside me."

"I wish you wouldn't go on business trips anymore," I said.

"It's my career, Ryder."

I canted my hips and plunged into her warm, welcoming body.

My hands covered her breasts, molding the soft tissue to my palms, and I kissed her neck. "But then I can't do this to you."

She moaned.

"I love that you love your career. You're so damn good at it, but, damn, I *miss* you."

I looked out through the steamed glass and saw our silhouette in the mirror. That turned me on even more. Aidy had outdone herself with our bathroom—the whole house. We'd moved into the same neighborhood as her brother Knox, not too far from the water, close enough for Lilia to walk to school once she started. Our place was an airy Cape Cod positioned on a large lot at the bottom of a cul-de-sac. As soon as I pulled up, I felt the ping, telling me it was perfect for raising kids, for *us*. Except we had too many bedrooms.

And I really wanted to fill some of them up.

I trailed my fingers down her belly and gripped her hips. My thrusts became more and more demanding as she took me, squeezed me, made me insane with the need to orgasm again.

"Ryder," she gasped, her back bowing as she shivered with pleasure.

Aidy coming apart was a sight I'd never tire of seeing. Her lips parted and her cheeks softened, then slackened. Her head fell back on my shoulder, baring the long line of her throat to my lips. All this beauty as her body milked my cock.

I thrust twice more and joined her in ecstasy.

"Happy anniversary," she whispered.

"This is how we should celebrate each of our anniversaries. Forget paper or silver. I want to fuck you hoarse."

I felt her cheek curve with a smile as she leaned back against me. "You got it."

Once I was sure her legs would bear her weight, I removed my hands from her waist and went to work washing her hair. She hummed as my fingernails scraped her scalp. Her eyes closed. I conditioned her hair and then soaped her body in long, languid caresses. She returned the favor, spending special attention to my stomach and between my legs. Not that I was complaining. I liked her hands there, ensuring my…well-being.

"I could do that again," she murmured as she stepped out from the spray. She had an impish look in her eye as she looked back over her wet shoulder at me, a small smile curving her lips.

"Twice in the shower wasn't enough for you, woman?"

She grabbed a towel and handed it back to me. She grabbed another and wrapped it around herself, ignoring her dripping hair for the moment.

"Oh, twice in the shower was a good start, but I meant another baby."

I gaped at her. How had she known?

For the past few months, my desire for another infant to snuggle had grown in tandem with Lilia's transition from a sweet, plump-faced toddler who gave messy kisses to a loud, sometimes demanding preschooler who only wore tutus, Spiderman shirts, and rain boots and read books to "herself" in the book nook I'd built into a small linen closet off our living room. I liked to sit and read with her—when she let me. We were currently working our way through *Paddington*, and I enjoyed each of our pre-bed sessions.

The clinic allowed me to work four days so that I had plenty of time with Lilia, whereas Aidy telecommuted at least once a week—that's what happened when you were a partner in the most in-demand firm in New England. The Mac's design won several awards and brought in a slew of interest from other boutique hotels and restaurants. She was currently working on a new Naval History Museum renovation that blew me away. As if that weren't enough, Aidy was a guest lecturer in RISD's capstone environmental design course. To say we were busy was an understatement, but we balanced, and we managed to eat dinner together most nights—all those she was in town. Because that's what families did.

Aidy made that happen for me—she knew I still struggled with my fears she'd leave me. By enforcing our dinner-time rule, she was showing me that Lilia and I were her priority. I loved her more for that than I could ever tell her.

"Another baby, huh?" I asked. "Will I get to deliver this one, too?"

"First you have to make one," she taunted.

I tossed aside my towel and ran at her. She squealed and darted into the bedroom. I caught her before she could run into our walk-in closet and ripped the towel from her body.

I sent a silent thank-you that Lilia was with Jeff for the weekend. It was the first time he'd felt comfortable spending multiple days alone with her—he normally visited her here for a weekend that included short outings and Lilia sleeping in her own bed. But he'd chosen to rent a place in Jamaica Plain for four days, which gave Aidy and me time to celebrate our anniversary with a stay-cation, especially since Lilia insisted on taking Rosie, her best friend, with her.

Aidy had worried, as had I. But we'd talked to Lilia when she woke earlier and she was excited to go to the aquarium, and Jeff promised to text us photos. The guy was still a douche, but he was working on his humanity.

"Oh, we're making a baby," I said with enthusiasm. "Right now."

She laughed as she bounced on the bed, wet hair fanned out around her. Love overwhelmed me as I knelt next to her, cupping her face.

"I love you, Mrs. Mackay."

Her face softened, her eyes doing that dreamy thing that told me how happy she was.

"I love you, too, Dr. Mackay. But I really don't want to have another baby in Whole Grocers."

I hovered over her, my cock throbbing at the idea of getting to take her again—of seeing her belly round out with my child. Of seeing another baby suckle at her luscious tits.

"We'll do a home delivery," I said. "We can call Lillian. I'm sure she'll be happy to assist."

She smiled even brighter. "Sounds like a solid plan."

Want to keep up with all of the new releases in Vi Keeland and Penelope Ward's Cocky Hero Club world? Make sure you sign up for the official Cocky Hero Club newsletter for all the latest on our upcoming books:
https://www.subscribepage.com/CockyHeroClub

Check out other books in the Cocky Hero Club series:
http://www.cockyheroclub.com

ACKNOWLEDGMENTS

Thank you, Deborah Nemeth, for helping me take this manuscript from a decent premise to a novel I'm proud to have written.

Thanks to Kathleen Page and Charity Chimni for their time and amazing proofreading skills. You ladies are the best nitpickers and I'm so thankful to have you on my team!

And, as always, to Chris. You help me in so many ways—like this rockin' cover! Thank you for all that you do for me professionally, but more, for putting up with my crazy all these years.

To my awesome PR team at The Next Step PR, you ladies rock! Working with you is pure joy.

And to my readers. Well, clearly, without you, none of this would be possible. The fact that you trust me with your time is the greatest compliment. Thank you so, so much.

ABOUT THE AUTHOR

USA Today bestseller Alexa Padgett's books have garnered accolades from prestigious organizations, including *Kirkus Reviews*, National Indie Excellence Awards, and *Publishers Weekly*.

Alexa spent a good part of her youth traveling. From Budapest to Belize, Calgary to Coober Pedy, she soaked in the myriad smells, sounds, and feels of these gorgeous places, wishing she could live in them all–at least for a while. And she does in her books.

She lives in New Mexico with her husband, children, and Great Pyrenees pup, Ash. When not writing, schlepping, or volunteering, she can be found in her tiny kitchen, channeling her inner Barefoot Contessa.